T0274493

Disney

Hercules

BEMUSED

Dedicated to the memory of Brenda Mitchell, who instilled a love of Greek mythology in thousands of students over the years, including this one.

Printed in the United States of America
First Hardcover Edition, January 2025
10 9 8 7 6 5 4 3 2 1
FAC-004510-24298

Library of Congress Control Number: 2024933407
ISBN 978-1-368-09870-0

Designed by Catalina Castro
Visit disneybooks.com

Logo Applies to Text Stock Only

Disney

HERCULES

BEMUSED

Farrah Rochon

Disney PRESS
Los Angeles • New York

DRAMATIS PERSONAE

THE MUSES

Calliope (Cal-LIE-oh-pee) .... *Muse of Epic Poetry*
Clio (CLEE-oh) .... *Muse of History*
Melpomene (Mel-PAH-muh-nee) .... *Muse of Tragedy*
Terpsichore (Terp-SIC-or-ree) .... *Muse of Dance*
Thalia (THAL-ee-uh) .... *Muse of Comedy*

GODS OF THE TITANOMACHY

Mnemosyne (Nem-AH-suh-nee) .... *Goddess of Memory*
Ouranos .... *Her Father*
Gaea .... *Her Mother*
Cronus .... *Her Brother*
Rhea .... *Cronus's Wife*
Themis and Phoebe .... *Mnemosyne's Sisters*
Prometheus and Epimetheus .... *Mnemosyne's Nephews*

VILLAGERS OF KRYMMENOS

Sivas Anastasios .... *An Olive Farmer*
Cressida Anastasios .... *His Sister*
Mr. Samaras .... *The Saddlemaker*

THE UNDERWORLD

Hades..*God of the Underworld*
Pain and Panic...*His Minions*

GODS OF OLYMPUS

Zeus.......................................*Ruler of Olympus and Hera's Husband*
Hera..*Goddess of Women and Zeus's Wife*
Apollo..*God of Music, Dance, and the Sun*
Hermes...*Herald of the Gods*
Athena..*Goddess of Wisdom and Warfare*
Amphitrite.........................*Goddess of the Sea and Poseidon's Wife*
Poseidon.........................*God of the Sea and Amphitrite's Husband*
Demeter..*Goddess of the Harvest*
Aphrodite...*Goddess of Love and Beauty*
Hephaestus..*God of the Forge*
Dionysus...*God of Wine and Festivity*
Artemis...*Goddess of the Hunt*
Ares..*God of War*

OTHERS

Circe...*An Enchantress*
Queen...*Her Pet Lion*
Ibid..*Athena's Owl*

Prologue

MNEMOSYNE

Mnemosyne stood on the edge of the craggy cliff, listening to the whistle of the brisk wind blowing through the barren tree branches below. The blanket of thick gray storm clouds that had shrouded the valley for the past few days had finally lifted. She took in a huge lungful of the clean mountain air. It was invigorating. And comforting.

And she was far enough away from the oppressive demands of Mount Olympus that she could finally feel a sense of calm. She had not experienced true peace in so long that even she, the Goddess of Memory, could barely recall what it felt like.

Her fear had lessened with every moment that passed after she'd fled from Mount Olympus, the place where she'd spent so many onerous years. Now, she had a new destiny to fulfill. Had the time finally come?

A loud crack, followed by a harsh, high-pitched squawk, sent Mnemosyne scrambling for cover. She looked up just in time to see a bird swooping overhead, its wings extending out several feet on each side.

An eagle.

Mnemosyne's breath caught in her throat. Eagles signified courage, a sign that one was ready to embark on a journey.

But *was* she ready? Was this the right time?

She'd told herself she would know when the time came, that moment when the world was ready to receive the beautiful creatures that were still only ideas in her head and sketches in her journal.

Her girls.

Ironically, if it had not been for her determination to make a deal with Zeus, the supreme leader of the gods of Olympus, and the one who'd held her very existence in his mighty hands, Mnemosyne would have never dreamed up the idea for her girls. But that was all the credit she was willing to give to Zeus. They would be *her* girls. She was the one who would be responsible for their lives once they finally came to be. She intended to weave a connection into the very fabric of their souls, a thread that would keep them bonded both to her and to one another.

Had the time to create them arrived?

Suddenly, a sense of tranquility washed over her.

"It has," Mnemosyne whispered.

Fear. Anticipation. Joy. Curiosity.

They all swirled around in her stomach, a delightfully chaotic dance of emotions that refused to dissipate now that she was ready to turn her idea into real-life beings. Mnemosyne retreated into her tiny cottage, the third she had lived in since escaping Olympus months ago, and retrieved her journal. The pages were filled with drawings and cleverly coded ciphers describing each of her creations.

She settled her back against the thick trunk of the tree next to her cottage and stared out at the small clearing in front of her.

"And who shall be the first?" Mnemosyne mused.

A smile curved up the corner of her mouth. The answer to that question had been clear from the moment she first conceived of the idea for her girls.

"Calliope," she spoke into the wind.

Her first daughter would be the composed, unflappable leader of the pack; the sister the other girls turned to for guidance. Mnemosyne would give her the gift of storytelling. The thought of another being sharing her love of the written word filled Mnemosyne's heart with unspeakable joy.

She closed her eyes and whispered Calliope's name over and over and over, like a heartfelt, desperate mantra.

Moments later, she heard a soft suckling sound coming from just over her shoulder. She scrambled up from the ground and ran toward it.

Mnemosyne's breath rushed out in a choked gasp at the sight of the stunningly beautiful brown-skinned baby nestled cozily upon a bed of leaves, her thumb stuck between her lips.

"It's you. You're here," she whispered.

She had done it. She had brought one of the magnificent creations she had designed to life. Her hands trembled as she reached down and picked up the baby. Mnemosyne untied her cape from around her own neck and swaddled the girl in the soft fabric.

"Oh, my dear Calliope," she cooed.

There was no turning back now.

Not that she ever would. One look at her daughter and Mnemosyne knew her life would never be complete without all five of her girls. She was suddenly desperate to meet them all.

But she must be patient. She recalled the story Athena shared regarding the uproar that had ensued after the flower merchant in Thebes birthed three identical children on the same day. She was accused of being a witch. If Mnemosyne were to create all her girls at once, it would bring unwanted scrutiny.

"I must fit in with these mortals if I want me and my girls to remain safe," Mnemosyne murmured.

She would wait. Each of her girls would come into this world in due time.

The baby looked up at her with large, luminous eyes.

"You will do amazing things, my dear Calli. I cannot wait to see you live up to your full potential." Mnemosyne nuzzled her plump cheeks. "Keeping you safe is now my sole purpose in life. I will never allow harm to come to you or to the sisters you will soon have. I promise you."

PROLOGUE

Four years later . . .

"Mother, Clio is pestering me again."

Mnemosyne turned at the sound of Calli's annoyed voice. Her three- and four-year-old sat in the middle of the common room, examining the leaves they had picked while out for their daily walk.

"I only asked if she knew that the olive leaf can be eaten just like the fruit from the tree," Clio said, twirling a sprig of slim leaves between her fingers. "Not many people know that."

Mnemosyne had designed Clio to be inquisitive, and her second daughter did not disappoint. No notion went uncontested when Clio was around. Mnemosyne was careful not to dampen her daughter's thirst for knowledge. It was her best asset. Clio would one day teach the world how to appreciate the history of what had come to pass and how to value all that now surrounded them.

It was for that same reason that Mnemosyne did not suppress her daughters' extraordinary intellect, despite several of the villagers remarking on the peculiar girls who spoke with the vocabulary of children twice their age. She first feared the unwanted attention Clio's and Calli's advanced aptitude would bring, but then decided the scrutiny would be worth it. Her children were exceptional because she had created them that way. The rest of the world would just have to deal with it.

"There, you see," Mnemosyne said to Calli. "Your sister was not pestering you; she was only trying to inform you." She turned to Clio. "But maybe you can put the leaves aside for now and help me with the baby."

She brought her youngest, Melpomene, to where the girls sat, and settled her in the cloth-lined basket she used to carry her around.

"Do you like my leaves, Mel?" Clio asked, holding the cluster up to the baby's face.

Melpomene immediately broke out into a bloodcurdling scream. Calli and Clio both covered their ears with their palms.

"It is just leaves," Mnemosyne said, scooping the baby into her arms. "Nothing for you to be alarmed about."

Rocking from side to side, Mnemosyne began to hum the song she and the god Apollo used to sing together to welcome the dawn of a new day. She stopped short, surprised the tune had even come to her. She did her best to put all thoughts of her days on Olympus behind her, but the song was a pleasant reminder that not all her time with the gods had been miserable. She had made great friends, friends she had grown to love and that she missed dearly.

"Melpomene, my beautiful melody," Mnemosyne whispered, nuzzling the plump rolls of her baby's neck. The strong feelings this one evoked would never be denied. "You may be prone to dramatics, but that's what makes you so special, isn't it?"

As she continued to hum, allowing the sweet melody to tickle her ears, Mnemosyne found herself torn. The music brought joy for all she had experienced back on Olympus, while at the same time bringing sadness that she would likely never have those experiences again.

But she couldn't rekindle the friendships she'd shared with a few of the gods without alerting the wrong people to her daughters' existence. Nothing was more important to her than her girls.

After changing the soggy linens wrapped around Mel's bottom, Mnemosyne gathered her daughters so they could go to the river to launder more of them.

"Come, girls," Mnemosyne called.

She led the way out of the mud-brick home they had moved into just before she had created Mel, but as she walked outside, a strange feeling came over her. Mnemosyne held Calli back with a hand.

"What is wrong, Mo—"

"Shhh," Mnemosyne said to Clio. She heard a flutter and looked toward the trees.

Was that . . . ?

She could not be certain, but she thought she saw the winged ankles of Hermes, Zeus's messenger. If there was anyone Zeus would send to find her, it would be Hermes.

She had hoped the ruler of the gods would have forgotten about her by now, but she should have known better.

"Back in the house," Mnemosyne whispered to her girls, her heart thudding within her chest. "Let us go. Hurry."

It pained her to leave this comfortable home she'd found. Her plan had been to remain here until she brought forth her remaining daughters, but that was not to be.

"Come, girls," Mnemosyne said. "It is time for another adventure."

Five years later . . .

Mnemosyne paused, her hand that held the ink-filled reed hovering above the papyrus. She tilted her head to the side, listening for the sound again.

There it was. Was that laughter or was one of the girls throwing a tantrum?

She had tried to give them their space, knowing what they were up to that day and not wanting to ruin the surprise. Every year, her daughters treated her to a performance for her birthday. The tradition began just after she'd created her youngest, Thalia. Calli had assembled her other three younger sisters, and together they had performed a song Calli had written herself, based on the story of the Moirae, the three Goddesses of Fate. Thalia had joined in the festivities as soon as she was old enough, and the girls always picked from one of the stories Mnemosyne regaled them with at bedtime.

There was that squeal again.

PROLOGUE

Mnemosyne set down the reed and her journal and went into the common room. This cottage was bigger than any of the previous ones they had lived in. She vowed this would be their forever home, a place where her girls could finally find some stability. Elassona was far enough from Olympus that she finally felt safe. There would be no need to move again.

Mnemosyne found her five daughters lined up in a row from oldest to youngest: Calliope, Clio, Melpomene, Terpsichore, and Thalia.

As usual, Terpsichore, whom the girls called Ree, could not keep still. She twisted back and forth, moving her arms as if they were blowing in the wind. Mnemosyne's fierce little dancer had learned to perform before she learned to walk and had gracefully glided through life ever since. Terpsichore's energy and enthusiasm annoyed her sisters, but where was the fun in creating a family that always got along?

At least, Mnemosyne had once felt that way. But as her daughters grew older and their individual personalities began to blossom, she wondered if she should have taken a bit more care with their temperaments.

"What are you girls up to?" Mnemosyne asked.

"It's a surprise!" Melpomene cheered.

"Shhh," Clio told her. "You'll spoil it."

"No, I won't!" Mel cried. "Mother, tell her I will not spoil your birthday surprise!"

Mnemosyne had to bite her bottom lip to prevent herself from laughing.

"No, you will not," she answered. "I will be completely surprised, no matter what. But I do hope that I get at least one song from my girls. The five of you are never more powerful than when you lift your voices together."

Mel clapped excitedly. "There *is* a song!"

"Wait!" Thalia stuck her pudgy fingers out at her. "We are not ready." She looked to Calli. "We are not ready, are we?"

"We *are* ready," Calli said. With a poise normally displayed by people twice her age, Calliope took several steps forward and in a strong voice said, "It is your birthday, Mother. To mark this glorious occasion, we, your daughters, would like to present to you a musical extravaganza."

Mnemosyne silently recited the words along with her. Calli had opened every birthday performance in the same way for the past five years.

She clapped excitedly, pretending to be surprised. "How lovely. And what story will you present today?"

Calli nodded toward Ree, who nodded in return before completing a full twirl and leaping in the air.

"Sit back and relax, dear Mother, as we entertain you," Ree said.

She pointed to Mel, who took two steps forward and with bubbly anticipation continued, "With a story that is certain to thrill you."

Thalia barreled forward. "With blood and bore."

"It's blood and *gore*," Ree chastised in a loud whisper.

Mnemosyne's head snapped back. *Blood and gore?*

"But in the end, we'll have you wanting more!" Clio said.

Calli took center stage once again. "Watch as we present how the mighty Zeus defeated the horrible Titans."

Mnemosyne went completely still as a knot formed in her stomach. "Where . . . where did you hear this? I never told you this story."

"I read it in a book!" Clio said. She ran to the table where she kept the stack of books she'd borrowed from their village's small library and held up a thick tome that would have made any other eight-year-old recoil. "See?"

"Now, no more interrupting, Mother," Ree said. She executed another perfect twirl. "It is time for the musical extravaganza to begin."

Mnemosyne forced a smile, knowing it must look strained. She'd regaled her daughters with many tales of the gods over the years, but there were some stories she would rather stay buried forever.

She considered wiping their memories clean of anything dealing with the Titans but then thought better of it. As far as her daughters knew, the horrible Titans were myths like all the other stories she'd shared with them.

She planned to keep it that way.

At Calli's command, the girls burst into song, telling the story of a time in Mnemosyne's life that she had tried so very hard to forget.

I

CALLI

Ten years later . . .

The melodious cadence of the waves crashing against the rocky shoreline of Krymmenos was hypnotizing. Calliope closed her eyes and allowed the sound to settle into her psyche, calming her frayed nerves and clearing her mind. She'd slipped away from the home she shared with her mother and four sisters, craving a few moments of peace before the consequential day that lay ahead.

Perched upon her favorite hagstone, Calli untied the leather closure on her satchel and retrieved her journal. Her skin began to tingle with a familiar excitement. She had started writing this epic tale over a year before, but she always felt the same rush of joy whenever she prepared to work. She had been inspired by the many tales her mother used to share with her and her sisters at bedtime—stirring sagas about mythical figures from far-off lands. When she grew old enough to read on her own, she'd gravitated to the gripping stories composed by the great writers of their time, like Alcaeus and Aeschylus.

But unlike those lauded bards who told of brawny warriors, Calli had decided it was time for another kind of hero to take center stage. Her story featured Andreia, a courageous mother who had taken it upon herself to defend her people from the wrath of Typhon, the father of all monsters.

Calli grinned as she read over what she had previously transcribed. In some ways, her protagonist reminded her of her own mother, kind and compassionate. But in other ways, they were total opposites. Andreia never displayed the unexplained fear Calli sometimes saw in her mother's eyes. Her fearless warrior would never disrupt her family's lives time and time again, moving them from town to town without ever explaining why. And while her mother claimed that Krymmenos would be their permanent home, history would not allow Calli to take this promise to heart. She had claimed the same about Petra and Leivithra.

Their inability to ever settle down no longer bothered Calli, because she was preparing to make her own move soon. She would move to Thebes, where she would have all the time in the world to work on her epic tale.

The brave Andreia had just tackled her most harrowing obstacle thus far on her quest to save humankind from the treacherous Typhon. Calli must now give her an even more dire deed to complete, one that would test her inner strength.

As she set the tip of her reed to the papyrus, she heard a loud call.

"Calli! Are you out here?"

Her shoulders sagged in defeat. A few minutes to herself. Was that too much to ask?

"Calliope, please! I need you!"

Apparently, it *was* too much to ask.

Calli returned the journal to her satchel and twisted around on the rock just in time to see her sister Melpomene approaching. The brisk wind blowing off the sea caused Mel's thick, flowing locks to whip around her.

"What is it, Mel?" Calli asked.

"Oh, my gods, there you are!" Mel slapped a hand to her chest and sucked in several deep breaths, as if she had just escaped the clutches of the nine-headed Hydra. Of course, her sister would have the same reaction if she were to encounter a tiny field mouse. When it came to Mel it was either serene calm or full-on hysteria; there was no in between.

"Was there something you needed?" Calli asked.

"Yes!" cried Mel. "I can't find my lyre! I put it down for one second, and it simply vanished. How am I supposed to perform today without my lyre? Do you think someone stole it? I'll bet it was that shady fellow who sells bait down at the docks."

"Mel!" Calli exclaimed. "Calm down."

She climbed from her seat atop the rock and captured her sister by the shoulders. Mel's hair whipped around again, this time slapping Calli in the face.

She gathered the thick strands, twisted them into a voluminous braid, and settled the braid over Mel's shoulder.

"That's better," Calli said. "Now, about your lyre. Take a moment to calm your nerves and then think about where you were when you last held it."

Mel closed her eyes and sucked in another of those deep, cleansing breaths. She slowly nodded.

"Mother had just asked me to remove the linens from the lines outside," she said.

"And . . . ?" Calli prompted.

"And . . ." Mel's eyes popped open. "The linen basket! I set the lyre at the bottom of the empty linen basket! I'll bet I tossed the clean linens on top of it without realizing what I had done."

Calli managed to hold in her weary sigh. "That seems like the most logical answer."

She could tell something still troubled Mel. The corners of her mouth were taut.

"Melpomene, what is it?"

Mel's shoulders slumped. "It's just . . . I know Ree has been working hard for this day, but I fear Mother will not approve."

Calli shared Mel's apprehension, but she did not want to show it. Terpsichore had been secretly teaching dance to a couple of the village children for the past six months without their mother's knowledge. Sensing that their mother would not approve—Mnemosyne had only just begun to allow them to visit the village square without her supervision—Calli had first objected to Ree's plans to rent the old pottery shop and turn it into a dance studio. But ultimately, Calli understood her sister's yearning to pursue her ambitions, and she didn't want her mother's misgivings to get in the way of Ree's dream. After all, she harbored dreams of her own and would hate to have them quashed before she ever got the chance to realize them.

So Calli had supported Ree's plan for her studio, and she had since marveled at her sister's dedication to raising money for the rent. She'd helped till the beds of daffodils and peonies for the flowermonger and delivered bread for the baker. She had earned the right to open her studio.

Now, Ree ran the studio in secret from their mother, even as Mnemosyne continued to impress upon them the dangers they faced as a household of women.

Calli understood her worry. Sort of. But they were not the only family composed solely of women in this village. The widow Papadakis shared a home with her two daughters, yet she wasn't nearly as smothering as Mnemosyne. They all felt their mother's overprotectiveness was a bit excessive, but Mnemosyne had been this way for as long as Calli could remember. It was part of her nature.

Calli was more concerned about emotional harm than physical harm being inflicted upon her sister. Some of Krymmenos's residents had treated her family as outsiders for so long that Calli considered their gradual acceptance to be nothing more than pretense. She would never forget how the baker had refused to sell them bread when they first moved here, and how the same potter who welcomed Ree's assistance now had closed his shop door when they'd tried to buy jars for their wines and oil a year before, and all because their family had not originated from this area.

It did not matter to Calli that the shopkeepers had eventually warmed to her mother and sisters; she would never completely trust them.

Ree had finally decided that she was done with hiding the studio from their mother. After the sisters discussed it, they'd determined that they could host their mother's annual birthday performance at the studio's upcoming showcase day and make the big reveal.

The day had arrived, and though Calli wasn't so sure they had made the best choice, she kept her concern to herself. Mel was already overly worried; Calli didn't want to add to her sister's anxiety.

"All will be just fine," Calli told her. "Why don't you go look for your lyre and I'll meet you back at the house."

Mel nodded, gathering the flapping hem of her robe and taking off.

"Mel," Calli called. She waited for her sister to face her before continuing. "You may want to think twice before accusing longtime villagers of theft. If you had done so in the public square, it is very likely the people of Krymmenos would have sided with the bait merchant. He has been a resident of this village his entire life, whereas we are still seen as strangers by most, even though we've lived here for two years now."

To Calli's recollection, it was the longest they had remained in one place.

Mel nodded, her trembling chin an indication of the tears that were undoubtedly on the way if Calli did not take action.

She reached for her sister's hands. "It's okay, Mel. I just want you to be mindful of what you say. It has taken our family a long time to win over the people of this village; we don't want to needlessly get on anyone's bad side."

"You're right. I won't do it again." Mel wrapped her arms around Calli. "Thanks, Calli. I can always count on you to steer me in the right direction. What would our family do without you?"

She kissed Calli's cheek, then spun around and took off down the shoreline, toward their humble seaside home. As she watched her sister's retreating form, a disquieting feeling settled in the pit of Calli's stomach.

What *would* her family do without her?

That very question swirled around in her head like the sand currently swirling at her feet. She had convinced herself that her family would do just fine without her. Mel would have eventually found her lyre, even if Calli hadn't been there to direct her to retrace her steps. Melpomene tended to blow things out of proportion, but Calli saw her emotional and empathetic nature as an asset.

She would do just fine, whether Calli remained in Krymmenos or took off for the big city.

The same could be said for Clio. Just a year younger than Calli, Clio was an absolute genius! Her intelligence was sometimes mistaken for pretentiousness—okay, so her sister *was* pretentious at times—but her levelheaded approach to life would serve her well. And Clio's seriousness would rub off on the never-serious Thalia soon enough, wouldn't it?

Not that there was anything wrong with Thalia's jovial, carefree disposition. Calli admired her youngest sister's ability to see the joy in every circumstance. Who knew, maybe Thalia would thrive even more if Calli were to leave. She constantly complained about how her older sisters—namely Calli and Clio—were downers.

And Terpsichore. Ree had her dance studio; she was well on her way to making her mark on the world. They would all make their mark.

Calli and her sisters possessed musical talent that was unmatched in all of Krymmenos. They had never had the chance to showcase it outside their home, so she knew that when they finally did, the people here would be as blown away by their singing as their mother was whenever they performed for her.

The family didn't need Calli to remain here, conducting their day-to-day life like a discordant yet surprisingly harmonious orchestra. It was time she set out and made her own mark.

Instead of reassurance, she felt a growing discomfort.

"Calliope? Calli, are you out there?"

Calli's eyes fell shut. Maybe she should find another secret hideaway.

"I'm right here, Ree."

Her second-youngest sister, Terpsichore, rounded the collection of rocks.

"Oh, Calli, the worst thing has happened!"

Calli's stomach dropped. "What is the matter, Ree?"

"Cressida has injured her foot, and Nephele is afraid to perform on her own! What am I to do? How am I to show the villagers what their children can learn if they join my dance studio when my only two students cannot perform?"

"Ree, calm down," Calli said.

This was a bit of a conundrum, but Calli purposefully hid her worry. She did not want to further agitate her sister.

Though Ree normally wasn't nearly as excitable as Mel, she had been a fit of nerves in these last few days leading up to the performance. Calli understood; there was much riding on the event. Every year for their mother's birthday, they tried to top the performance from the previous year. But given how their mother had delighted in Thalia's portrayal of Prometheus, the God of Fire and a known trickster, last year's performance would be tough to beat.

However, entertaining their mother was secondary to attracting new students to Ree's dance studio. That was what today's showcase was all about. Her sister had worked hard, and she deserved to find success for her budding venture.

"We are still performing a routine that you choreographed," Calli reminded her. "Which means you *are* presenting to the people what their children can learn if they attend your dance studio, right?"

Ree pulled in a shaky breath and nodded. "I guess you're right."

"Aren't I always," Calli said in a teasing voice. She bumped Ree with her hip. "Come on. I was just making my way back to the house."

"Do you know your part?" Ree asked. "Because I'm convinced Thalia does not know hers. She clowns around too much, even with the important stuff. You should talk to her, Calli. Remind her that not everything is a joke."

"I will," Calli said. She wrapped an arm around her sister's shoulders. "Don't worry about Thalia, or Cressida and Nephele, or anything else regarding the performance. It is all going to work out wonderfully, Ree."

Although Calli still wasn't convinced the residents of Krymmenos deserved to be entertained by the same people they'd shunned for nearly a year. Her sisters seemed to have gotten over how they were treated when they had first moved to this village, but she hadn't.

"You really think so?" Ree asked, her wide eyes filled with a mixture of hope and apprehension.

"I promise," Calli said.

Surely this was a promise she could keep, right?

By the time they made it to the wooden fence that surrounded their humble yet comfortable seaside home, Calli had convinced Ree that she would have every young child in Krymmenos lining up to join her studio. With luck, her sister would remain calm until the start of the performance. Calli wouldn't have to worry about her once Ree took to the stage, because when her sister started to dance, everything else in the world faded away.

As for her remaining three sisters, Calli knew she would have to dip into her reserve of patience if she wanted to make it through the rest of the day without snapping.

She entered the house and was both surprised and relieved to discover that chaos had not erupted in her absence. Clio flitted past on her long legs, humming the melody of the closing act of today's performance. Mel stopped her on her way to the room she shared with Thalia, holding up her lyre.

"Found it." Mel beamed. "It was in the linen basket, just as I suspected." She pointed to Calli. "I draped your peplos over your bed. You should get dressed while Mother is still out of the house. We don't have much time."

"I'm going," Calli said. "I only need a few minutes."

The last thing Calli wanted to do was add to Ree's anxiety by running late for today's performance. She quickly disrobed and donned the clean peplos Mel had left on the bed for her. For more than a season, Clio had spent the last part of each day meticulously embroidering the hem of their matching robes with a curlicue design, done in a beautiful golden thread. Her sister's talent continued to amaze Calli.

She used a pendant to secure the flap of her shawl to her shoulder, then sat before the small looking glass to ready her face. She rubbed her finger into the mixture of crushed rose petals and beeswax and colored her lips, then dipped the end of an eagle feather into the pot of olive oil and charcoal and drew it delicately along her lower eyelid.

Calli caught movement out of the corner of her eye and turned to the door.

"There you are," her youngest sister, Thalia, greeted in a deep, overly dramatic voice.

She was already in character. Lovely.

Calli rolled her eyes and went back to her task. "Save it for the performance."

"Oh, Calliope, darling, I have no need to save anything. I have plenty to spare." Thalia propped a hand on her hip and shimmied. Then she continued her foray into the room.

Thalia ran her fingers along the edge of Calli's robe and, in a husky voice, said, "You look ravishing in your peplos. Wherever did you find such a fine garment? Down by the seashore?"

Calli released an exasperated sigh. "Are you quite finished?"

"Why so testy, sister?" Thalia asked, her voice back to normal. "Learn to take a joke."

She stomped out of the room.

This was an ongoing sentiment among her sisters. When it came to levity, she and Thalia were opposites. Calli no longer bothered to remind them that she didn't have the time to joke, not when she was constantly putting out her younger sisters' proverbial fires.

But that was her role in her family, and she took her job seriously. Her mother tried as best she could, but sometimes she'd wander off by herself for hours and stare into nothingness, completely unaware of everything happening around her. During these sitting spells—a term Mel had coined for those long stretches of time—Calli was there to step in.

Calli knew what her sisters needed, and she did her best to offer what their mother was sometimes incapable of providing.

But if she left to pursue her own dreams, who would be there to step into her sandals? Clio was the most pragmatic choice, with her even temper and sharp mind, but it wasn't fair for Calli to thrust her burden onto her sister just because she wanted to move to Thebes to write epic poetry.

And yet, if she was forced to remain in this little seaside village for another season, she would lose her mind.

And what if you go to Thebes and cannot make it as a storyteller?

Calli set the eagle feather on the table and stared at herself in the looking glass, her chest suddenly tight with unease. She had never questioned her abilities before. She had memories of herself as a young child, spinning sweeping epic tales. For as long as she could remember, her true heart's desire had been to entertain people with her gift.

Yet now, she could not help wondering if these doubts had been lingering in her mind all along. Was it a lack of confidence that kept her rooted in Krymmenos? Had she been using her family's reliance on her as an excuse this entire time?

Calli studied the face staring back at her.

There were a number of words she used to describe herself: *loyal, reliable, strong-willed.* But there was one that she never thought she would use: *coward.*

II

REE

Using a torn piece of linen she'd brought from home, Ree dusted off the stone benches that lined the walls of her tiny but adequate dance studio. She recalled the day she had walked past the pottery shop and discovered it would soon be available to rent. Only the night before, she had dreamed about opening her own dance school. She'd taken all that as a sign that it was time to finally pursue her dream.

The building offered more than enough space for the mere two students she currently taught, but she wanted to gain even more students. That was one of the reasons for today's performance: to show the people of this village the beauty of dance and convince them to trade their goods or hard-earned drachmas for lessons for their children. If all went according to her plans, she would have a dozen or more students soon.

That was, if she could convince her mother that this modest little dance studio would not lead to the end of all humankind.

Ree had kept her studio to a small scale for the past six months because she hadn't wanted her mother to find out about it. For reasons never shared with her daughters, their mother had forbidden them from showcasing their talents outside of their home. They could perform for her and for one another, but no one else. Ree had always thought the rule unusual, but until recently, she had never questioned it.

Now that she was older, not only did she question it, but she planned to defy it. Her dancing was a huge part of who she was, and it was unfair of her mother to want to keep it hidden from the rest of the world.

"It will be fine," she whispered to herself.

Ree spotted a speck of dirt she'd missed and quickly swept it away. It wasn't as if she expected the crowd to wear their most regal finery to the performance, but to have patrons walking away with dust on their clothes would not be good for business.

After ensuring that she'd cleaned all the benches, she stood in the middle of the studio and turned in a slow circle. With both Cressida and Nephele unable to perform, Ree could not rest until she was sure everything else was perfect for today.

She could hear Calliope's voice in her head, warning her that striving for perfection was only setting herself up for failure, but Ree didn't care. It *must* be perfect. Her entire reason for living hinged on today's outcome.

She released an exceedingly dramatic sigh.

"Now you're being as dramatic as Mel," she chided herself.

Her life might not depend on the crowd's reaction to the extravaganza of music and dance she and her sisters planned to entertain them with today, but her happiness did. Dancing was her life. And sharing her gift with the children of Krymmenos would be her every wish come true.

Well, maybe not her *every* wish.

Do not think about him. Not right now.

She still had too much to do. She could not allow herself to get carried away with thoughts of a certain mild-mannered, gorgeous olive farmer who just so happened to be the older brother of one of her students.

Would he be here today, despite his sister's no longer taking part in the showcase?

Ree's heart twirled with delight while, at the same time, panic rushed through her limbs. Sivas Anastasios tended to bring those contrasting feelings out of her every time he was near.

Sivas had started bringing his younger sister, Cressida, to her dance lesson before he continued to his job at the olive grove in the northern region of the village. At first, their father came to retrieve Cressida at the conclusion of class, but after a while, Sivas would leave work to do that, too.

In recent weeks, he had invented the most nonsensical reasons for returning to the studio in the middle of their lessons—he'd wanted to bring Cressida a shawl in case she became cold, or he'd picked a ripe apple and wanted to make sure his sister could enjoy it at peak freshness. Then, instead of returning to the olive grove, he would shrug and say he could stay until the end of the lesson.

But Ree noticed that Sivas rarely watched his sister during her class. He often watched *her.*

Her face heated just thinking about how she would glance his way and catch him watching her with his kind eyes. He would smile softly, shyly. But he would not look away.

More recently, Ree had learned that Sivas also loved playing music. On his most recent visit, Sivas had arrived with a kithara and had offered to play for Ree and her students since she couldn't handle an instrument while dancing at the same time. Soon, Ree learned that he also played the lute, oud, and aulos.

He'd invited her to come to the village center on Saturday to hear him play, but Ree had yet to find the courage to ask her mother if she could go. Maybe if she convinced Clio or Mel to come with her . . .

But then her sisters would find out about Sivas, and she was not ready to discuss him with any of them yet. The heat returned to her face. Her sisters would never let her hear the end of it if they knew she had fallen for a boy.

Oh, please come today.

"Well, we're here, Twinkle Toes. Where do you want us?"

Ree whipped around at the sound of Thalia's boisterous voice.

She, Clio, and Mel entered the studio, carrying the vases they would use for props and looking glorious in their cream-and-gold peploses.

"Did Calli convince Mother to come to the village center?" Ree asked.

They had contrived a story about a traveling painter showcasing his sketches as a means of convincing their mother to leave the cottage and venture into town.

"Do not worry. Both Calli and Mother will be here," Clio said, resting her hand on Ree's shoulder. "Is there anything you need us to do before the guests began to arrive?"

"If we have any guests," Ree mumbled, unable to stave off the depressing thought.

"Of course we'll have guests. I've been telling everybody, except Mama, of course," Thalia said. "The shoemaker, the winemaker, the barley farmer, *every*body down at the fish market, and the baker. I even told the money changer who sits at the edge of the village. It took a little arm-twisting, but they all said they would be here."

Ree nodded, some of her anxiety lifting. She had no doubt Thalia had sold the performance as the biggest thing to happen in Krymmenos since the albino whale that washed up on the shoreline last year. If their singing and dancing didn't win over the crowd, her younger sister's endearing personality would.

"It sounds as if we're about to host the entire village," Clio said.

Mel stepped up to her, her forehead wrinkling with uncertainty as she fidgeted with the collar of her robe.

"Are you sure about this, Ree?" Mel asked. "Think about how Mother reacted when she learned that Thalia and I wanted to put on that skit in the middle of the market for Founder's Day."

"That's just because she didn't get the humor in the skit," Thalia said. "Everything is going to be just fine."

Ree sucked in a deep breath. "Thalia's right. It'll be fine." She looked to her sisters. "We'd better get ready."

They scrambled to get the props in place, and by the time the guests began filing into the studio, four of Mnemosyne's girls stood in position, ready to start the show. Ree was astounded by the size of the crowd. Thalia had been right; there must have been at least fifty of their fellow villagers here, including Mr. Samaras, the saddlemaker and town gossip. Knowing him, word about her dance studio would spread within hours of their performance. Ree grew even more determined to put on a show the audience would never forget.

Yet they could do nothing until Calli and their mother arrived.

"Where are they?" Ree whispered to Mel through a clenched smile.

"They will be here," Mel whispered back. "I hope."

Ree swung her gaze toward the door but stopped halfway when she spotted a familiar, stunningly handsome face in the crowd.

Sivas!

When had he arrived? And how had she not noticed that he was in her studio until just then? Her body flushed both hot and cold, and her heart began to thump a chaotic rhythm.

He's here! He's here! He's here!

But her mother and Calli were *not* there, and that should be her only concern at the moment. The show could not go on until they were both in this building. Just as Ree was about to break her pose to go in search of them, Calli entered the studio, their mother following behind her.

Her mother halted abruptly as she looked around at the crowd gathered. Her brow wrinkled with curiosity and apprehension.

"What . . . what is the meaning of this?" Ree could hear her mother ask Calli even from where she stood.

Ree looked at her other three sisters, trepidation coiling in her stomach at the alarm in her mother's voice.

"Happy birthday, Mama!" Thalia announced.

Ree scowled at her. That was *not* what they had rehearsed. They were not supposed to acknowledge their mother's birthday until the third song, when Clio would pull a bouquet of bellflowers from one of the vases and present them to her.

Thalia ran to their mother's side and, with Calli's help, guided her to her place of honor, the very center of the stone bench that ran along the left wall. Her sisters then quickly made their way to where the rest of them stood in the center of the room, and Calli motioned for Ree to begin.

A fluttery sensation pranced about in her stomach, but she thought of what her mother always said: She and her sisters were never more powerful than when they lifted their voices together.

With a deep breath, Ree calmed her nerves and began.

"Thank you all for coming to today's showcase. I am Terpsichore, and I am delighted to see such a large crowd. I, along with my sisters, have prepared a musical extravaganza unlike anything the people of Krymmenos have ever seen." She looked back at the girls. "Ready, ladies?"

They collectively struck their practiced poses. "Ready," the four of them answered.

"Let's do it." She snapped her fingers four times, and they began singing the first number, a jaunty tune about a sea nymph who discovers her love for the land.

The crowd's reaction was everything Ree could have hoped for. They cheered as she performed a simple twirl, marveling at the move as if it were something magical.

Ree did her best to maintain a bright smile even as she watched her mother's countenance grow more disturbed with every line they sang. She had expected her to be upset over Ree's breaking her "no public displays" rule, but Mother seemed more fearful than upset. Panicked, even. Ree didn't know what to make of it.

She glanced at Mel to see if she had noticed; Mel always picked up on others' emotions. Ree motioned surreptitiously with her head and raised a questioning brow. Mel answered with a discreet hunch of her shoulders and matching quizzical lift to her brow. Something was not right, but she would have to wait until after their performance before she could root out the cause.

As they brought the opening number to a close, the audience broke out in thunderous applause. Excitement rippled through Ree as she took in their animated expressions. Everyone was enthralled.

Except for her mother, still looking ill at ease.

Clio and Thalia walked to the center of the room to present the dance routine Ree had choreographed for them, both seemingly unaware that anything was amiss. Ree decided to put aside her worry for a moment to enjoy the fruits of her many hours of labor. She danced along with them in her head, mimicking every kick and turn. Clio needed to work on her timing; she was off by half a step.

When her sisters delivered the final spin of their second routine, the crowd erupted into even louder cheers. As usual, Thalia went beyond the appropriate curtsy and bow, encouraging the crowd to cheer louder.

Mnemosyne's eyes grew wide with horror. She put a hand up to her mouth, shaking her head as her gaze darted around the studio.

Calli slid next to Ree and asked under her breath, "What is going on with her?"

"I don't know," Ree answered. "I figured she might be a bit upset about us performing outside the house, but she seems troubled."

Fortunately, the rest of the villagers didn't seem to notice their mother's unease; they appeared to be enjoying themselves immensely.

"And now for the final number!" Thalia gave an exuberant call.

"No! No more!" their mother shouted, standing up. "Stop this at once!"

A collective gasp echoed around the studio.

"Stop?" Thalia asked. She and Clio finally appeared to have caught on to their mother's strangeness, too.

Murmurs flittered through the room as their mother fled from the studio. The moment brought back memories from their first year in Krymmenos, when the villagers had whispered about their family from the moment of their arrival. The gossip and mistrustful glances had subsided only within the last year, after her mother had allowed Ree and her sisters to venture out more freely. Most of the residents of Krymmenos came to realize that they were harmless, charming additions to the village.

Sensing the crowd growing restless, Ree said, "Uh, please give us a brief moment."

"No, you all should continue with the closing number," Calli told them. "I will go after her."

"We *all* should go after her," Mel said, taking a step toward the exit.

"Don't," Calli said, catching her by the shoulder. "The show will not be complete without the closing number. Give this crowd what they deserve."

The four of them nodded in unison at Calli's directive, but the jovial mood of the afternoon had been broken.

Ree turned to the audience and gave them her best smile. "Have no fear, the show will go on!"

The crowd's cheer buoyed her spirits.

She chanced a glance at Sivas, finding his normally smooth forehead wrinkled with worriment. His concern warmed her. Despite their mother's disturbing outburst, the performance had garnered the exact kind of reaction she had hoped for from the rest of the crowd. As she listened to their enthusiastic applause, she had no doubt that word of Krymmenos's new dance studio would spread far and wide.

III

CALLI

Calli left the dance studio, the sound of her sisters singing the closing song she'd written carrying through the air. She would have loved to be there with them; she wanted to see the crowd's reaction to her words, to see if they were as moved by the song's imagery as she had been while composing it. But she knew she would not be able to concentrate on anything until she uncovered what was behind her mother's troubling behavior.

Given her mother's rules, Calli had anticipated a level of crossness, possibly even anger, at their defiance. But the vehemence they had been subjected to was outside the realm of anything she would have ever expected from their mild-mannered mother. Her outburst had shaken Calli to her core.

Their mother had come to anticipate the private concert Calli and her sisters always performed for her birthday, so Calli hadn't needed to do much coaxing to tear her mother away from the beautiful mountain landscape she had been working on. In fact, she'd smiled as brightly as a young child who had just received a plate of sweets as she followed Calli out of the cottage.

But from the moment they entered the studio, Calli could sense that this would not go as she and her sisters had hoped.

Mnemosyne had never explained exactly *why* they were prohibited from performing in public. Maybe if she had, Calli would better understand her reaction. But they were no longer little girls, and their mother could not expect them to continue the way they had, keeping their talents shielded within the confines of their little seaside cottage.

Or could she? Was her gentle, warmhearted mother selfish enough to want to keep her daughters' talents all to herself?

There was only one way to find out.

Calli spotted her shortly after she exited the studio. She was rushing in the direction of their house, fidgeting with her hands and mumbling to herself. Calli caught up to her just at the edges of the village.

"Mother, what is the meaning of this?" Calli asked.

Mnemosyne stopped short and stared at her. "That is *my* question to *you*! What were you girls thinking?"

Calli slapped a hand to her chest. "Us? We were thinking that our mother would enjoy hearing her girls sing to her on her birthday, the way she has for years. We surely did not think you would cause such a scene, and for no good reason."

"No, Calliope, I am not the one who caused a scene today," Mnemosyne said. She closed her eyes and pulled in a shuddering breath. "I'm sorry for my reaction, but you girls have no idea what you have done."

She resumed her pacing.

"We have been living a nice and quiet life in this village," her mother continued. "That is all I have ever wanted, a safe and peaceful existence for me and my girls. But what you did today may have ruined it all."

Calli shook her head as she tried to keep up with her mother, her confusion rising with every word her mother spoke.

"This makes no sense," Calli said. "Today's performance was simply a means of entertaining the villagers. Now, I'm sure you're upset that Ree kept her new dance studio a secret from you, but how can anyone blame her after your reaction?"

Her mother whipped around. "*Ree's* new dance studio?"

Calli inwardly cringed. How could she have been so careless with that information?

"Yes, the building where we performed today is Ree's dance studio," Calli said. "She has been operating it for the past six months."

Mnemosyne gasped. "How could she?"

"Mother, this is a good thing. Ree is an excellent dancer and a wonderful teacher. She wanted to showcase her dance studio so that she could garner more students, and we thought what better way to do so than with such a performance?"

"Terpsichore cannot have a dance studio! It is too dangerous! And what you and your sisters engaged in today was not a performance, it was a spectacle," Mnemosyne said. "If word about it reaches the wrong people, the consequences are . . ." She fisted her hand and brought it to her mouth. "They are too horrible to bear thinking about."

Calli's mind spun with bewilderment. How could Ree's dance studio be dangerous? Her mother was talking nonsense.

Before she could speak again, she heard a commotion behind her, and her sisters came barreling up behind them.

"What's happened?"

"What's going on?"

"Is Mother all right?"

Mnemosyne's worried eyes darted behind them, back toward the studio. "Were you followed?"

"Followed? Who would follow us?" Clio asked.

"We must return home now," Mnemosyne said.

Their mother hurried off, and they had no choice but to follow her back to the cottage. Once there, she ran to close the door behind them, then rested the back of her head against it and closed her eyes tight. The strained frown pulling at her lips spoke of the distress that Calli could tell was rioting within her.

She and her sisters all stared at one another with matching bewildered expressions. After several weighty moments had passed, Mnemosyne opened her eyes, her gaze sweeping across the room.

"The damage has been done," their mother said. "There is but one solution. We must leave."

Five distinct gasps rang out.

"What?" Mel screeched.

"You cannot be serious," Clio said.

"You heard me," their mother bellowed. "We cannot remain in Krymmenos. I have fallen in love with this village as much as you all have, but remaining here after that . . . that performance you put on today is too big a risk." She seared them with a look that brooked no argument. "Pack your things. No more than two bags each, and only what you can carry. We must leave as soon as possible."

Mnemosyne swept out of the room, leaving a trail of stunned silence in her wake. When the sisters reclaimed the ability to speak, it was all at once. They converged on Calli.

"She cannot mean what she says!" Clio said.

"This has to be a joke," Thalia said.

"I won't do it!" Ree yelled so loudly it jolted the others in the room into silence. They all stared with their mouths agape as their sister wailed, screaming at the top of her lungs. "I will not! I will not! I will not!"

Tears streaked Ree's face as she gathered the hem of her peplos in her hands and ran out of the house.

The room remained silent for several more seconds before Thalia said, "I'm taking a nap. When I wake up, I want everything to be back to normal."

She marched out of the room toward the bedroom she shared with Ree and Mel.

Clio still appeared to be shell-shocked by what had just taken place. It was exactly how Calli felt. She could not understand how this day, which had begun with her quiet, serene visit to the beach, could have turned into such a catastrophe.

An uneasy feeling traveled like fingertips along Calli's spine when she spotted Mel standing off to the side. She was quiet—too quiet. Her drawn, solemn expression set off a bevy of alarms within Calli's head.

"Mel?" she called.

Mel snapped to attention. She rushed over to Calli and grabbed both of her hands, squeezing them so hard that Calli winced.

"What is it, Mel?" Calli asked.

"I do not understand what is going on, but something isn't right. I don't know how to describe it, but I feel it." She pointed to her stomach. "Right here. Something unusual is going on with Mother. I can tell that her heart is heavy with sadness. And something else, something that feels like . . ." She paused for a moment, staring just past Calli's shoulder. When she looked back at Calli, her eyes were haunted. "Fear. *True* fear. But why would she feel that way?"

Calli shook her head. "I don't know."

She glanced in the direction her mother had fled, then in the opposite direction, where Ree had dashed off to. She was torn between them, unsure who needed her attention more.

She sought out Ree first, because as unnerving as it was to see her mother in such distress, Calli was even more concerned by her sister's outburst. Ree had been wound tight leading up to the performance, and their mother's pronouncement had been upsetting, but there was something more to her sister's reaction.

She searched the area surrounding the house, peering around the chicken coop and running over to the well. Ree was nowhere to be found.

She started back for the house but stopped as the obvious occurred to her. She took off for the dance studio.

She found her sister kneeling on the floor in the very center of the studio, her head hanging low and her shoulders shaking with silent sobs.

"Oh, Ree," Calli gasped, sweeping inside and wrapping her arms around her sister. "Come now," she murmured against her hair. "There is no need for such a display."

"No need?" Ree asked, her head popping up and barely missing Calli's chin. "How can you say that? Mother just told us we have to leave our home! How did you expect me to react?"

"Well, I did not expect you to storm out of the house and leave your sisters alone to face the same stunning news that you received. Even Mel was able to hold herself together better than you did."

Ree slapped her hand to her chest. "I am not the one you should be questioning right now. What about Mother? Why are you not seeking to find out why she wants to tear us away from all that we know? I cannot leave, Calli, not when Siv—not when I may have several new students."

Calli's eyes narrowed as she studied her sister's face.

She had noticed the subtle looks shared between Ree and the olive farmer's son at the performance. Calli had not thought much of it, but now she wondered if the boy—Sivas, she believed they called him—had something to do with her sister's outrage.

"Well?" Ree asked. "Are you going to talk to mother?"

Calli closed her eyes and pulled in a deep breath. It felt as if one of the hagstones that dotted the shoreline had settled upon her shoulders. But who of the five of them would confront their mother if not her? It was what her sisters expected of her.

"Of course I will talk to Mother," Calli said. "But I am here with you now. I have never witnessed such vehemence from you. Why did you react in such a way?"

Ree bit her lower lip. "I . . . I just . . ."

"Terpsichore?"

"I don't want to leave, Calli. I'm tired of always moving. Isn't that enough?"

They were all tired of moving.

"You know how long it took us to fit in here," Ree continued. "Do you really want to go through that again? Those looks of distrust from the villagers? People whispering behind our backs, wanting to know about the odd unwed woman and her strange daughters but too afraid to ask?"

She didn't need reminding about those early days in Krymmenos.

Calli bumped her with her shoulder. "You have to admit that it was funny when the fishmonger thought Clio was a witch because she knew more about the type of fish he sold than he did."

Ree chuckled. "He demanded she go back into the sea where she had come from."

Calli laughed at the memory, one of the sisters' shared favorites. Thalia sometimes coaxed Clio into reenacting the scene, with herself as the befuddled fishmonger, of course.

"We managed to weather that storm," Calli said. "And now we're able to buy whatever kind of fish we want." She gave her another teasing bump with her shoulder. "Do not worry, Ree. We are not going back to being strangers." She helped Ree stand. "This is our home. I'll help Mother see reason. Expecting us to pack up and leave our home is irrational."

"It is unacceptable," Ree said. "She cannot make us do it."

"Calm down," Calli demanded. She placed her palms on Ree's cheeks and looked into her eyes. "All will be fine. I promise you."

One thing was clearer now to Calli than it had ever been. There was no way she could even entertain the idea of leaving her family to pursue her own dreams in Thebes. Not when they were amid such upheaval.

Possibly not ever.

IV

MNEMOSYNE

Mnemosyne sat on a smooth slab of limestone, cradling her head in her hands. She had come to the one place in this village where she could always find solace and clear her mind: the small temple the villagers had built to honor Amphitrite, the Goddess of the Sea and wife of Poseidon.

But today, the temple only muddled her head more. What would happen if Amphitrite, Poseidon, or any of the other gods caught wind of her clueless daughters' grand performance today?

And whose fault is it that your beautiful creations are clueless to the danger they have put themselves in?

Mnemosyne shook her head. She could resume the internal debate she often had about whether she should have told the girls of their peculiar origins some other time. Right now, she must think!

The gods wouldn't find them. They *couldn't*!

"They don't remember you. You made certain of that," Mnemosyne reminded herself.

She had wiped the memories of herself from all who dwelled on Olympus, but she could not be sure the act was permanent. Her power to erase memories had yet to be put to the test—what if the ability had a hidden weakness, just like the exposed spot on the heel of the great warrior Achilles?

Mnemosyne tried to assure herself that, even if it the memory erasure was somehow reversed, none of the gods would care enough to remember her after all this time. But there was always a possibility. She imagined all the ways news of her girls could reach Mount Olympus. Commerce had increased since they'd settled here, with fishermen and olive growers making regular trips to the surrounding villages and to Thebes. All it would take was a single whisper about the extraordinary display of singing and dancing one of them had seen while in Krymmenos and, just like that, all she had worked so tirelessly to keep hidden could be revealed.

Mnemosyne wrapped her arms around her middle and doubled over, her fear sparking physical pain that threatened to consume her.

Of course, she knew that casual chatter between villagers conducting trade was not her biggest worry. Zeus and the other gods of Olympus had their ways. If the most powerful god in all of Olympus wanted to find her, he had a multitude of methods at his disposal.

Mnemosyne had spent nearly two decades keeping an eye out for his most powerful method: Hermes. The messenger god traveled freely between the mortal and divine worlds, relaying anything of interest to Zeus. She had no way of knowing if Zeus had ever dispatched Hermes on a specific mission to find her, but she knew better than to take any chances.

Mnemosyne peered up at the sky and gauged the movement of the sun. Had enough time passed since the spectacle the girls had put on today for it to have gotten back to any of the gods?

"You are panicking for no reason," she said. She was mostly certain her memory spell had held strong. Even it had not, surely her reneging on the deal with Zeus by running away was water under the bridge by now.

A heavy weight settled in the pit of her stomach.

Zeus was not known for his forgiving nature. The passage of time meant nothing to immortal gods. She could not be too cautious when it came to Zeus and his ilk and the havoc they could wreak on the nice, safe, quiet life she had managed to create for herself and her girls.

She closed her eyes tight and tried to stave off the wave of panic that threatened to overwhelm her.

She had made the choice to leave this village, and that was what she and her girls would do. There was no way around it.

"Mother! There you are!"

Mnemosyne turned at the sound of Calli's relieved cry.

"I have been looking everywhere for you," Calli said. The worry clouding her face brought on a wave of guilt. The last thing Mnemosyne ever wanted to do was cause her daughters harm. That desire was the reason behind every single decision she had made since fleeing Mount Olympus nearly two decades before.

"Why are you here?" Mnemosyne asked. "Why are you not at home packing your things as I ordered?"

Calli stood up taller, her expression unyielding. "Because I am not going."

Clio, Mel, Thalia, and Ree rounded the side of the temple.

"Neither are we," the four said in unison.

Mnemosyne gasped at their collective display of defiance. When creating her girls, she had been deliberate in her choice to instill a staunch sense of tenacity in each of them. She wanted them to know that they did not have to back down from anything or anyone.

But there were some days, like today, when she cursed that decision.

"Girls, please do not question me on this. It is for your own good—you must trust me."

"How is this for our own good?" Ree asked. "What are you not telling us, Mother? We are not little girls anymore. Stop keeping things from us."

Mnemosyne noticed the puffiness around her eyes and realized Ree had been crying. Her guilt intensified tenfold.

She looked at each of her daughters, these brilliant beings she had conjured using everything that was good and sweet and pure in this world. She saw the stress in their eyes and the fear shadowing their faces.

She could not keep them in the dark any longer. Maybe if they understood the history of their creation, she could convince them that leaving this village was the only option.

"It is time I told you all the truth," Mnemosyne said.

She gestured to the limestone bench where she had spent countless hours over these past two years, looking upon the face of Amphitrite.

"You may want to take a seat," she continued. "What I am about to share will not be easy to hear."

V

HADES

Tortured moans and desperate wails floating up from the slow-moving currents of the River Styx were so loud they reached all the way to Hades's throne room. He assumed the unharmonious cacophony was meant to move him, but instead the cries annoyed him. He was in no mood to hear the complaints of those who had found themselves navigating the boundary between the living and the dead.

"Make better choices," Hades called out to the wretched souls.

Speaking of dead, that was how the Underworld felt today. Not that there was ever much going on in his lair at any given time, but come on. What did a guy have to do to get a little fun in the sun?

Oh, yeah. That's right. He was stuck there. No fun. No sun. Nothing but doom and gloom for mean old Hades. At least, that was the way things should be according to his brother.

Hades's hand tightened into a fist just at the thought of Zeus, the self-appointed ruler of both gods and mortals.

Fine, so Zeus hadn't exactly appointed himself as Olympus's ruler. He had won his little title when he'd led the battle against those clumsy Titans. The first-generation gods from Mount Othrys were descended from Ouranos and Gaea, and they had been no match for Zeus. Still, Hades was convinced his brother was made ruler only because the simpletons who occupied this universe were easily swayed by rule-followers with good hair.

He smoothed a hand over the blue flames flickering atop his head. He had the hair for it. The rule-following? Not so much.

And that was why he was stuck in this dull, shadowy realm that was void of all things fun.

"That's okay, Zeus," Hades remarked with a scowl. "When it comes to fun, I make my own."

And he would eventually make his way back into the land of the living, and onto his brother's throne. If only he could come up with a plan that would actually work.

Hades snarled as a montage of his numerous failed attempts to exact revenge on Zeus played through his mind. No matter what he did, something always went awry, leaving him looking and feeling like a fool.

Well, he was done being made to look like a buffoon by his little brother.

He wanted more than revenge; he wanted satisfaction. And he wouldn't be satisfied until Zeus was cast down here to the Underworld. Not to rule it, but to spend eternity languishing in anguish in the River Acheron.

Hades closed his eyes and released a blissful sigh. What he

wouldn't give to see his baby brother staring up at him from underneath the murky surface of the water, those crystal-blue eyes filled with agony and fear. The thought was more delicious than a five-course meal.

If only he could figure out a way to get those other wishy-washy gods living the sweet life on Olympus to realize just how much better their lives *could* be if they tossed Zeus out and installed Hades as their ruler instead. But noooo. No one wanted to rock the boat. There were only a few Hades would dare approach, knowing that most of them would run back and tell Zeus like the little followers they were. And still, whenever his minions attempted to recruit others into a rebellion against Zeus, they were met with resistance. He should have them all tossed down to Tartarus when he finally took over as ruler.

He clenched his fists until his brittle fingers began to throb in pain. But Hades welcomed it. Whenever he felt pain, he reminded himself that Zeus would eventually experience the same—and at his big brother's hand.

"Eventually, little brother," Hades said. "Eventually."

Until that day, he would carry on with his rule of this realm. It wasn't all bad. He spent the majority of his days at leisure, filling in the hours with his own brand of entertainment.

Speaking of . . .

Hades unlatched the birdcage perched on the table next to his throne. He reached inside, pulled out a hummingbird, and examined its pointed beak. Squinting, he lined the tiny bird up with the target on the wall and sent it sailing, its sharp beak hitting just outside of the bull's-eye.

Hades slammed his hands down on the throne's armrest.

"Who moved my target?" he growled, the blue flames surrounding his head flaring red. "Pain! Panic! Get in here!"

Hades flexed his fingers as he waited impatiently for his minions to arrive. A corner of his mouth twisted up in disgust as the two imps came barreling into his lair, fumbling over each other.

"Yes, boss?" the duo asked simultaneously as they stood at attention in front of him.

Hades stared down his nose at them, his expression purposely blank. He took an obscene amount of pleasure in watching their little bodies squirm.

"Uh . . . boss?" Panic said. "You called?"

Hades continued silently staring. Panic shrank under his glare, condensing himself until he was the size of a bug. Their shapeshifting capabilities made them most valuable to Hades. That and their unwavering loyalty.

Who was he kidding? These two weren't loyal to him. They *feared* him. *That* was what kept them in line.

Oh, and he owned their souls. He could not forget the role that played in his minions' allegiance. Now that he thought about it, owning the souls of those who resided here was a perk he wouldn't enjoy on Olympus. But fealty by force wasn't as rewarding as the unwavering obedience Zeus enjoyed from those he ruled over.

"Enough of your nonsense." Hades snapped his fingers, and Panic returned to his regular size. "Now, tell me, has either of you been playing around with my target?"

"No way, boss," Panic said.

"Never!" Pain said.

He pointed at the wall, where the little hummingbird's tiny wings still flapped like mad.

"So why did I miss?" Hades asked in a deceptively smooth voice.

Pain and Panic glanced at each other and then back at Hades. Hunching his shoulders, Pain said, "Um, maybe you're not as good as you—"

"What did you say?" Hades bellowed, blowing them both back by several feet.

"I said you are the greatest to ever live . . . die . . . umm . . ." Pain tipped his head to the side. "What are you, anyway? Dead or alive?"

"Fix the target," Hades gritted through clenched teeth. He was already tired of this conversation.

As the two imbeciles started for the target, Hades heard Panic mumble, "Maybe we should bring in that singing troupe the fishmonger from Chalcis mentioned to sing for the boss."

"Yeah, if they really put everyone who hears them in a good mood, we could use them down here in the Underworld. Especially for you-know-who."

"What was that?" Hades asked.

"Uh, nothing. Nothing at all, boss," Panic said.

But this was not nothing. Not if he'd heard what he thought he'd heard.

"Come back here," Hades ordered. The two scrambled back to his throne. "Now, what did you say about a singing troupe?"

Panic shook his head. "Nothing."

"Tell me," Hades grunted through clenched teeth.

"Uh, well, you see," Panic went on, "me and Pain were spying on that magistrate in Thebes like you asked us to, and we heard about these singers from one of the villages out near the sea. They held a performance today, and it's all people are talking about. Apparently, they are the best singers anyone has ever heard."

Hades's skin tingled with anticipation. Could these singers be who he suspected? If so . . . that could change everything.

"Are they gods or mortals?" he asked.

"Umm . . . I don't know of any gods who live in villages by the sea."

Panic's response showed just how much the imps didn't know about how the two realms operated. There were gods who dwelled among mortals every day, living quiet lives, with the mortals being none the wiser.

There was one goddess in particular, a Titan who had escaped Zeus's wrath during the war. Someone Hades had sought for nearly two decades since her disappearance from Olympus.

Mnemosyne.

After Zeus had captured her, he'd coerced her into revealing that she possessed the ability to control memory. Ah, what Hades wouldn't give to wield that kind of power. He had understood what her remarkable gift was capable of—and how he might be able to use it for his own ends—so, unlike the other gods, he had taken measures to protect himself against Mnemosyne's abilities.

He bounded up from his throne and went in search of the journal he'd kept with him for nearly twenty years. He thumbed through the pages, a smile curving up the corners of his lips. Mnemosyne had been clever, but *he* was the cleverest of them all.

Here it was. He had taken scores of notes where she was concerned, just in case she ever decided to use her gift on the gods on Olympus. That was what he would have done if he had such an ability.

He pored over the journal until he arrived at the pages about the deal she'd made with Zeus. His grip on the book tightened as the words triggered memories of his last encounter with Mnemosyne. Hades had been so sure that he could convince the goddess to join his cause. It was her own Titan brothers, after all, whom Zeus had conquered during the war. And even though Zeus had spared her from a life of misery imprisoned in Tartarus along with her family, she had not had any real freedom while living among the Olympians. She had been little more than Zeus's prisoner.

But like all the others, Mnemosyne had rejected Hades's

proposal. Instead of seeking revenge, Mnemosyne had approached Zeus with an offer, no doubt to secure his good will.

So much for sibling loyalty. Hades knew a thing or two about that.

Hades returned to his notes, where he'd recorded the arrangement the Titan goddess had made with Zeus: she'd planned to create a troupe of singers with talent so exceptional that it could change the mood of all who heard them. This troupe could very well be the same one Pain and Panic had heard about in Thebes.

Of course, he could be wrong. He'd chased leads like this before, but they'd led to nothing. So what were the chances that these singers were the beings Mnemosyne had agreed to create on Zeus's behalf?

He would not rest until he knew for certain. If Mnemosyne had resurfaced, he needed to get his hands on her.

With Mnemosyne's potent abilities under his control, Hades's chances of finally defeating his brother and ruling Olympus would increase exponentially.

"I need you to track down those performers," Hades ordered the imps. "And once you find them—bring the whole group to me."

Vengeance would be his. He could taste it. Zeus would finally be brought to heel, and Hades could not wait to be the one to do it.

VI

CALLI

A prickle of unease skittered down Calli's spine at the gravity in her mother's tone and her constant pacing. She only moved liked that when she was nervous or upset—so, hardly ever. Calli more commonly found her sitting quietly under a tree, working on one of her paintings, writing in her journal, or just staring off into the distance.

"Why don't we return to the house?" Calli suggested.

"No. Calli, please sit," Mnemosyne said. "We do not have much time to waste, and now that I have decided to share this with you girls, it is best we get this over and done."

Thalia patted the spot next to her on the bench. "Come on, Calli. It sounds as if this story is going to be a good one."

How could Thalia not realize that whatever their mother was on the brink of imparting would likely shake the foundation of their lives? But, of course, Thalia always found the upside to whatever life threw her way, even when there was clearly no upside to be had.

Calli looked over at Mel and, ironically, felt a measure of relief at the concerned frown blanketing her sister's face. She trusted

Melpomene's tendency to sense when something was amiss. She had a right to feel as unsettled as she did.

"What I will share with you girls will not be easy to hear," their mother began. "And it is to be kept in the strictest confidence. I had hoped that I would never have to tell you any of this, though I recognize how foolish my thinking was. I did all I could to keep you safe, but apparently, it was not enough."

"Mother, please," Ree said. "Just tell us!"

"I am a Titan," Mnemosyne blurted out.

Calli's head jerked back. "A . . . Titan?"

"But the books I've read say that the Titans are deities that no longer exist," Clio said. "They were defeated by the mighty Zeus." She turned to Ree. "You see, it all started when the god Ouranos put a curse on his own son, Cronus. And then Cronus's wife, Rhea, teamed up with her mother-in-law, Gaea, to trick Cronus! And—"

"Clio." Mnemosyne stopped her. "Please, let me finish. What you read is only partially true. The Olympians, led by Zeus, did defeat the Titans. However, they do still exist."

"But Titans are huge monsters," Clio said. "All the books describe them that way." She motioned to their mother. "You look nothing like that."

"I am a first-generation Titan," Mnemosyne explained. "The gargantuan Titans you've read about belong to the second generation. My siblings and I more closely resemble the gods of Olympus.

Both mortals and other gods often mistook us for one of them, which is a good thing. I never would have been able to blend in to the various places I've lived otherwise."

"If they still exist, then where are they?" Clio asked. Calli knew she liked order and logic, and the news their mother had just imparted did not seem logical. How could she be a goddess?

"Most of the Titans were banished to Tartarus after the war," Mnemosyne answered. "However, a small number of us avoided the fate others in our family suffered. Including me."

"Why were you not banished like the others?" Mel asked.

Their mother began to pace again.

"Well, I made a deal with the victors of the war and negotiated for my freedom." She held up her hands. "But only a *measure* of freedom. Although I was allowed to live freely among the gods of Mount Olympus, numerous watchful eyes were always on me. And I knew if I stepped out of line that a price would be paid."

"What about our father?" Thalia asked, excitement coloring her tone. "Is he in Tartarus with the rest of the Titans? Is there a chance we can meet him?"

"It is not that simple," Mnemosyne answered Thalia. She closed her eyes again, pulling her quivering bottom lip between her teeth. When she opened her eyes, they glistened with fresh tears.

Calli's heart lurched. "Mother, what is it?"

Mnemosyne gripped Calli's hands. After a few tension-filled

moments had passed, she finally spoke in a timid, fearful voice. "You do not have a father."

"Did you two have a falling-out?" Ree asked. "Is that why you never talk about him?"

Their mother shook her head. "No, you do not understand. You have never had a father. He does not exist."

Calli dropped her mother's hands and took a step back. "What . . . what do you mean?"

"I mean exactly what I said. You have no father."

Clio approached their mother with a blunt expression. "That is not only improbable, but also impossible."

"Not when you are a god," Mnemosyne said.

She took both Clio and Calli by the hand and led them back to the bench. She settled in the middle of her daughters, with Mel and Thalia on one side; Clio, Ree, and Calli on the other.

"What Clio read in those books is true. The war was called the Titanomachy, and a Titan god named Cronus started it." She took a deep breath. "Cronus was my brother, and Zeus was his son."

Thalia's eyes went wide. "Zeus is our relative?"

"I would use that term loosely," Mnemosyne said. "Familial relationships are different among the gods. They are much more concerned with alliances forged through loyalty than blood."

"Get to the rest of the story," Calli said.

"Cronus was power hungry and did not want to share the

universe with anyone, including mortals," their mother continued. "Zeus believed mortals had their place and wanted to live in peace with them—while still having control over them, of course. No god would ever fully give up control. Zeus led the other Olympians in the Titanomachy, and they proved victorious.

"I did not take a side in the war, but I knew that would not matter to Zeus. I was a Titan. So before I could be banished to Tartarus, I approached Zeus with an idea."

"You approached *the* Zeus?" Ree asked.

Mnemosyne nodded. "I approached *the* Zeus."

"I don't know if I'm brave enough to even speak to Zeus," Thalia said. "I would fall away in a dead faint if he even looked my way."

"Thalia, please," Calli chastised. "What was your idea, Mother? How did you persuade Zeus to spare you?"

"I appealed to his ego," Mnemosyne answered with a shrug. "I convinced him that his victory over the Titans merited constant praise and, as a way to prove my loyalty, offered to create an entity that would continually remind the people of Olympus what he had done for them."

"What did he say to your offer?" Thalia asked.

"He accepted it, of course," Mnemosyne said. "But then he countered with a proposal that would benefit not only himself but all of Olympus. You see, the great battle had caused much turmoil throughout the lands. Zeus wanted something that would bring healing to the people who had survived the war.

"In my mind, there was nothing more healing to the soul than the written word, and music, and dance, and comedy, and inspiration. So that is what I decided to create." She looked them each in the eye. "I decided to create you. Each of you would bring joy through your own unique talents, while also singing Zeus's praises for saving the world from the Titans."

A bout of silence fell over them as they all took in the words their mother had spoken. After several moments, Clio broke through the quiet.

"There is something I do not understand," she said. "Actually, there is much I do not understand about this, but you said we have no father, and that you created us for Zeus. So does that make Zeus our father?"

Mnemosyne shook her head. "No. Girls, I promise, I will explain all of this to you in earnest once we arrive somewhere safe, but we must leave. Now!"

Calli barely registered the urgency in her mother's voice. The reality of what her mother was saying finally began to sink in. How could any of this be?

"You still have not explained how we came to be, Mother," Calli said. "I have never asked you this question directly, though it has always been my right—the right of all of us—to do so. But I am asking now. Who fathered us?"

"I know this is difficult to comprehend," Mnemosyne said. "Which is why I never told you."

She trailed off and stared at the image of Amphitrite. Calli knew that look. It was one she saw often, when her mother drifted into one of her sitting spells. Well, they did not have time for her to drift off today.

"Mother!" Calli said.

Mnemosyne snapped to attention. "What was I saying?"

"You were not saying anything, which is the problem. You owe it to us to share the identity of our father. Now, you said you made a deal with Zeus to prove your loyalty to the Olympians and that we were part of that deal. How is our father connected to that deal?"

She put a hand to her head. "Girls, I know it is difficult to understand, but consider what I just shared with you. I am a goddess. As a goddess, I can accomplish feats that mortals cannot even fathom. One of those feats was creating the five of you without the assistance of a male partner. You are my creation.

"And, although I originally agreed to create you all for Zeus, I was unsure I could trust him. Maybe I was wrong? Maybe I became too attached to the idea of you, but I felt it was too dangerous to remain in Olympus. So before you were born, I left and started hiding in small mountain towns and villages. It was the only way to keep you all safe."

"What was so dangerous to make you flee?" Calli asked.

"Was there another war?" Thalia asked.

"Did the Titans return?" Clio asked.

"Girls, girls!" Mnemosyne held up her hands. She stood. "I will explain everything to you in due time, but for now we must go."

"Why?" Ree asked, her voice stony. "Krymmenos is our home. We like it here. Why do you want us to leave it?"

"Because, like my former home, it is no longer safe," their mother said.

"What are you not telling us?" Calli asked. "What about Krymmenos is no longer safe? And what did our performance at Ree's studio have to do with it? Why did it leave you so troubled?"

Mnemosyne shook her head. "I do not want to get into any of that. Just trust me."

"Trust you?" Ree asked. "You want us to trust you when you have kept all of this from us our entire lives?"

Calli noticed that Mel was unusually quiet. She would have expected the opposite from her. But instead of engaging in theatrics like her sisters, Mel stared silently at the ground.

"Melpomene, what is it?" Calli asked quietly.

She looked up and whispered, "I have a very bad feeling about this. I do not know why, but I just . . . Something is not right. There is much that Mother is not telling us about this situation."

"I fear you are right," Calli whispered back to Mel.

"What should we do?" her sister asked.

Despite the news their mother had shared about her being a Titan, and the distrust it had stoked, Calli still believed in their mother's love for them and her desire to keep them safe above all else.

If she felt so strongly that they must flee their home, it was what they must do.

Calli captured Mel's hand and stood.

"Okay, Mother. If this is what you feel is best, we will join you," Calli said.

Ree gasped. "No!" she shouted.

"We must, Ree."

"Yes, you must," Mnemosyne said. "We must leave, and soon. Too much time has passed."

"You still have not told us from whom we are fleeing," Clio said. "Is Zeus after us?"

"We will have time to discuss this later," their mother said. "Once we have found a safe place to land." She turned to Ree. "Terpsichore, I know you are upset, but I promise, once you girls are no longer in danger of . . . Once the danger has passed, we can consider returning to Krymmenos. But only if it is safe," she emphasized. "For now, we must go."

"She is right, Ree," Calli said.

The look of betrayal in Ree's eyes sent Calli's guilt soaring, but it could not be helped. She would make it up to her once they were settled.

Wherever they settled.

The rest of her sisters were unusually quiet. The momentousness of what they had to do—and why they had to do it—weighed on them all. Their mother had not shared the full story with them, and she was asking a lot of them to trust her after revealing that she, their own mother, was a goddess. And that they had no father? What did that even mean?

"Let us get back to the house and pack our things," Calli said. "All will be well. As long as we are together, all will be well."

Maybe if she repeated it to herself over and over again, she would come to believe it.

VII

REE

Ree tried to suck air into her lungs, but it felt as if a barrier prevented all but a tiny bit from entering. Her entire world was closing in on her. How had a day that had started with so much promise come to this? She could not go along with what her mother proposed.

As she traveled with her family back to their home, Ree tried to think of a way out of this mess. What if they never returned? Could she survive never seeing Krymmenos again? Never seeing her students improve as dancers? Never seeing Sivas?

Even thinking such a thing was too horrible to bear.

They arrived at the house, and their mother instructed them to pack their things as quickly as possible. Ree followed Clio to the room they shared. Once there, Clio took two burlap sacks from under the bed and handed one to her.

"Hurry," her sister said.

Ree tossed the sack on the floor. "Clio, don't you think we need to discuss this? Are we supposed to just accept Mother's explanation without questioning it?"

"We can question her further once we get to wherever we are going," Clio said.

"But it isn't fair!"

"Terpsichore!" her sister shouted in a voice more strident than any Ree had ever heard her use before. "Did you not hear the fear in Mother's voice or see it in her eyes? She is absolutely terrified. Even if this threat does not turn out to be as grave as she believes it is, we still owe it to her to take it seriously."

"How can you so easily leave everything behind?" she asked Clio.

"Do you think this is easy?" Clio asked. "You know that I have always wanted to explore the world, but I have been comforted in knowing that wherever I *do* travel, I will always have a home to return to. But how can I think of going on any great explorations now if my entire family has left Krymmenos?"

Clio's words brought home the true depths of Ree's selfishness. She was not the only one sacrificing her dreams. All her sisters had them, and they would all be leaving behind something important to them with this rash departure.

Just then, a loud commotion rang out from the front of the house.

Ree and Clio looked at each other and, without another word, raced out of their room. When Ree reached the common area, her heart practically stopped at the sight of two large unfamiliar men standing in front of the door—and holding their mother between them. The man on their mother's right was tall and slim, clad in a turquoise exomis and worn sandals, and the one on her left was stout, wearing a crimson robe.

Calli, Thalia, and Mel arrived, their expressions as alarmed as Ree's. Mel gasped and collapsed onto the floor in a dead faint. Clio ran to her aid, but Ree was rooted where she stood as dozens of questions swirled around in her mind.

Calli stepped forward, lifting her head in the air.

"What is the meaning of this?" Calli asked, with a confidence Ree could only hope she would one day be able to display.

"Do not question us," the stout one replied. "We have it on good authority that this citizen has engaged in wrongdoing."

"He is speaking falsehoods," Mnemosyne said. "I have never—"

The tall man clamped a hand over their mother's mouth.

Thalia stormed up to them. "Get your hands off her!"

"Get back," the stout one warned in an ugly tone. To the one in turquoise, he said, "We'll have to finish the job later. This one is too much to control on my own."

Their mother tried to wrestle out of their hold, but the two men were too strong. They each tightened their grip on her, limiting her movements, and started for the door.

Ree could not stand by and watch this happen.

She ran toward them at the same time Calli did, but they both halted when their mother bit down on the tall man's hand, forcing him to uncover her mouth.

"No, girls!" Mnemosyne called out to them. "Do not come any closer. I don't want you to get hurt."

"Yes, listen to her, girls," the one in turquoise said.

"Mother, we cannot just let them take you!" Thalia said.

"You have no other choice," the other man said. "She's coming with us."

"Calli," their mother called. "There is one thing you consider most precious. I have one of my own. Find it! It will tell you everything you need to know—those you can trust, and those you cannot. The bird that flies at night will be your strongest guide."

The man in crimson hauled her up by the arm. "It's time to go."

Ree, Thalia, and Calli charged toward them, but the one in turquoise reached into his pocket and pulled something out. Before Ree could react, he threw out some sort of black dust that quickly covered all of them. Ree's body froze, her arms suspended in the air.

"Wha . . . what's happening?" Thalia sputtered. "I can't move!"

"And you won't be able to move until we return," the slim one said.

"The boss won't be happy about us leaving them," said the stout one.

The slim one shrugged. "They aren't going anywhere. The boss said the potion should keep them frozen in place all night. We'll come back once the sun goes down. It will be easier to get the five of them out of here without anyone seeing us."

Ree and her sisters watched in horror, unable to do anything as the two men hauled their mother out the door.

"Did he say we'll be stuck like this all night?" Thalia asked.

"Or until they come back for us," Ree said.

She gritted her teeth as she struggled to break free from the invisible bonds rooting her to the spot. Soon, the despair set in, and she let out a sigh. How could a day that held such promise take such an awful turn?

On instinct, she tried to recapture some of the joy she'd felt from earlier, closing her eyes and humming the melody of the first song they had sung at today's performance.

Suddenly, her fingers moved. Then her hands.

She started singing the words and was able to move her arms.

"Sing!" Ree yelled. "Close your eyes and sing the song from our performance this morning."

The other girls joined in, and after a few moments, Calli yelled, "It's working!"

"My leg is moving," Thalia said. "How did you figure this out?"

"I don't know; I just did," Ree said. "Keep singing."

Once her body was released from whatever spell that black dust had put her under, Ree ran to the door and out into the courtyard, but there was no sign of those men or her mother. She returned to the common room to find her sisters free as well and converged on Mel, whose head was currently cradled in Clio's lap.

"They're gone," Ree said.

"But they will be back for us," Clio said.

"Where's . . . where's Mother?" Mel asked, her body still limp.

"They took her!" Thalia yelled. "How could we just stand here and do nothing?"

"That dust clearly froze us," Ree said, rolling her eyes. "Besides, Mother ordered us not to come any closer."

"She was protecting us. As she always does," Calli said. She looked to Clio. "Take care of Mel."

"Where are you going?" Ree asked her.

"Mother left us with a clue. She said it would tell us everything we need to know," Calli answered. "We must find it quickly, before those hooligans return."

"She said to look for the bird that flies at night," Thalia said. "Do you think she meant the nightingale? Or maybe an owl, or a hawk?"

"What about a raven?" Ree asked. "Do they fly at night?"

"We need to figure out which bird and where to find this clue," Clio said.

"Mother told us where to find it," Calli said. "She gave us two hints. We must find her journal."

"Journal?" Clio and Ree asked at the same time.

Calli nodded. "Mother said she had one of the things I hold most precious."

Calli ran into her bedroom and came back with her satchel. She reached into it and pulled out the journal Ree had seen her writing in on occasion. "This has to be what Mother was talking about. She must have a journal. We need to find it."

"Her room," Mel said. With Clio's help, she stood, straightening her peplos. "Look in Mother's room. I'll bet that's where we will find it."

They all took off for their mother's bedroom, a place she typically kept off-limits. Ree had never given it much thought before, but after the revelations that had been dropped on them today, she wondered if her mother had purposely kept them away from her room to guard her secrets.

She swallowed down her disappointment; she would deal with these feelings of betrayal later. Right now, she must focus on the matters at hand: getting out of this house before those men returned, and getting her mother back.

VIII

CALLI

Calli's heart felt as if it were lodged firmly in her throat as she and her sisters frantically rummaged through their mother's things. There were not many places to search; their mother's small room made for close quarters. They found a chest where Mnemosyne kept most of her effects, along with the burlap sacks underneath her bed that held her linens and heavier garments that were used during the colder season.

"Are you sure it is a journal?" Ree asked.

"Mother said she had the same thing that I consider most precious," Calli said. "Other than my sisters, my journal is the thing I hold most dear."

Mel clasped her hands against her chest. "Oh, Calli, that is so sweet of you to say. You are dear to me, too. All of you are."

"Enough with the lovefest," Thalia said, bumping Mel out of the way with her elbow. "Get back to hunting. If it *is* a journal we're looking for, we need to find it as soon as we can so we can leave this town and then get Mother back."

Out of the corner of her eye, Calli caught Clio looking

contemplative. Her sister's haunting eyes were wide and glassy, reminding Calli so much of her mother's recent expression that it stole her breath.

"What is it, Clio?" asked Calli.

"I think Mother has been anticipating something like this happening," said Clio. "And that is why she was adamant that we leave Krymmenos."

Clio's guess held merit. Their mother had seemed distressed, but not as shocked or surprised as Calli would have expected someone to be when faced with two strangers snatching them from their own home.

"There is too much happening all at once," she said as she looked under a wicker basket in the corner of her mother's room.

How could the woman Calli vividly remembered cooking their dinner, tending to their scraped knees and bruised elbows, and showing them how to fix their hair and rouge their cheeks—how could that same woman be a goddess? Didn't goddesses do godlike things?

"We have searched everywhere," Thalia said, her shoulders slumping in defeat. "Isn't there something else that you hold dear? What about a favorite robe?"

"No," Calli said. "It has to be a journal."

"Thalia's right," Mel said. "We have looked in every crevice of this room and there is no journal. There's hardly anything here." She threw her hands up in the air. "Honestly, if Mother is a goddess, she leads a very simple life compared to what I've heard about those of the gods on Olympus. They all live lavishly. I love Krymmenos as much as anyone, but I cannot understand why Mother would give up the life of a goddess to live in this village."

Either their mother loved them so much that she was willing to sacrifice everything for them, including the splendid lifestyle of an Olympian goddess . . . or the threat that sent her running was so great that it made living with the other gods impossible.

"We know there is much more to this story," Ree said. "Mother admitted as much."

"She also said she would explain everything once we got to safety," Calli said. "But we never got to safety. We need to find that journal and get her back. There must be clues; otherwise she wouldn't have bothered to mention it."

But what if . . .

She had assumed her mother would have stashed something like a journal in her room, because that was where Calli kept hers. But maybe her mother had chosen to store her most prized possession somewhere else. Where else did Mother spend most of her time?

"I know where it is," said Calli.

She lifted her peplos above her ankles and raced out of the room, then out of the house, running toward the glen where she so often found her mother staring out into the distance. Calli could hear her sisters in pursuit behind her.

They came upon the massive holm oak—the biggest of all the trees in the glen, with branches that reached out for yards, creating the perfect umbrella for anyone who sought shelter from the sun. Calli had lost count of the number of times she had come upon her mother sitting with her back against the tree's thick gray trunk, her eyes focused on something in the distance.

Another feature of the tree: the hollow cubby halfway up the trunk.

"Do you think she hid it in there?" Thalia asked.

"There's only one way to find out," Calli said. She turned to Clio. "You're the tallest, Clio. Ree and I will will give you a boost."

Clio complied without question, kicking off her slippers and stepping into the cradle Calli and Ree made with their clasped hands.

"Be careful," Mel called. "Oh, this is so dangerous."

"She's climbing a tree, not fighting a lion," Thalia pointed out.

"But she could fall and break her neck!" Mel screeched.

"Thank you for that visual," Clio called.

"Girls, please," Calli said through clenched teeth. Clio was tall and thin, but she was also solid. Calli had to concentrate to keep her arms from giving out.

"Do you see anything?" Ree asked.

"I don't see . . . Wait!" Clio said. She tried to rise on her tiptoes. "I think I see something. Push me up a little more."

"Thalia. Mel. Come help us," Calli called.

The four of them created a set of steps with their arms, giving Clio the leverage she needed to reach farther into the cubby. How had their mother managed to get anything up there? She was at least a head shorter than Clio.

"Do you have it?" Ree asked.

"Is it a journal?" Thalia added.

"I'm not sure, but it's something," Clio said. She reached deeper into the cubby. "I have it!"

Trepidation and excitement danced down Calli's spine as they gently guided Clio down. She held a package wrapped in cowhide and twine.

"You should open it," Clio said, passing the package to Calli. "You're the one Mother gave specific instructions to find it."

Calli accepted the battered leather from her sister, and she sat down with her back against the tree trunk, just as she'd seen her mother do countless times before. She set the package on her lap and pulled at the strings of twine, revealing something wrapped in a linen towel—a journal.

"This is it," Calli breathed.

Her sisters looked down at her with matching expressions of anticipation, fright, and expectation.

"Well," Thalia said. "Read it."

With great care, Calli flipped through the delicate sheets of papyrus, which seemed fit to crumble in her hands at any moment. The pages were faded and frayed at the edges, the writing so light she could barely make it out. She studied what she could see, but like everything else she had encountered today, none of what she read made any sense.

"It's all written in"—Calli cocked her head to the side—"riddles."

"Riddles?" Mel asked.

"Well, maybe not riddles. But it isn't straightforward."

"Let me see it," Thalia said, reaching for the journal.

Calli flattened her hands against the pages. "I think it's best that I handle it."

"Well, at least read it to us," Ree said. "Do you see anything about a bird that flies in the night, like a nightingale or a hawk? Is there anything that would help us figure out who took Mother?"

Calli carefully searched through more pages, peering at the faint writing and drawings.

"She mentions an owl right here," Calli said. She frowned. "But this makes no sense."

"What does it say!" Thalia demanded.

"It says, 'I fashioned my flowers' sense of bravery from the one with the heart of a lion and the wisdom of the owl.' "

"The heart of a lion and wisdom of an owl?" Mel asked.

"That's what it says," Calli said. "There are a number of sketches and riddles that don't seem to make any sense."

"What do some of the other riddles say?" Clio asked. "I'm good at figuring out that kind of thing."

That was true. She should rely on Clio's knack for solving

puzzles. "Take this one, for instance. It says, 'This flower's skill with a pen will help her conquer anything.' And this one says, 'The sound of sweet voices, like those that drift from the ocean near Aeaea, are more powerful than any that speak in anger. Use your voices, little flowers.' "

Thalia snorted. "Flowers can't talk."

"There must be something significant about flowers. She mentions them more than once," Clio pointed out.

"Well, Mother loves to garden," Ree said.

"Where is Aeaea?" Mel asked. "I have never heard of it. Do you think mother once lived there?"

How was she supposed to know? Calli wanted to scream the words, but it wasn't Mel's fault. They were all searching for answers. This day had proven that none of them knew their mother as well as they thought they had.

"I'm not sure," Calli said in a gentle voice. "I'm not sure about any of it."

"Maybe Mother once visited this Aeaea," Ree said. "There's a possibility that someone who lives there knows her. What should we do, Calli? Do you think this is a clue?"

It was difficult to tell what was a clue and what wasn't, but Calli wasn't surprised that her sisters were looking to her to guide them. As the eldest, it was what she did.

She now wondered if this had been by design. Had her mother given her this role because she knew that at some point in time she would need Calli to take the reins? Clio's theory that their mother had been preparing for something like this to happen seemed even more likely.

Calli returned her attention to the journal, one clue her mother *had* left for them. She said it would help. But how?

What was *she* supposed to do?

"There has to be something that I'm missing," Calli said. She pored over the pages, but the vague statements did not give her any more insight into what she should do. "Listen to this one. 'There is a time to be serious, but also a time to laugh'—"

"That's what I always say," Thalia interrupted.

"We know," Terpsichore replied.

"It also says 'My young flower must learn when to do both.'" Calli set the journal on her lap. "This doesn't make any sense. And I do not understand how it helps us! And why was it important enough for Mother to include in this journal?" She looked to her sisters. "We are wasting time."

"Yeah, we gotta figure out what to do," Thalia said.

"Maybe we should go into the village and ask if anyone saw where the men took Mother," Mel suggested. "Someone must have seen *something*, don't you think?"

"Not if they stuck to the shoreline," Clio pointed out.

"Well, we can't just sit around waiting for them to come back tonight. We need to find Mother," Mel said.

"I think we should split up," Clio said. "Two of us go one way, two the other, and Thalia stays in Krymmenos in case Mother comes back."

"Why am *I* the one who gets stuck in this village?" Thalia groused.

"Because you're the youngest," Clio said.

"Wait!" Calli said, cutting off their quarreling. "We should go to Thebes."

"Thebes?" they replied in unison.

"Have you lost your mind?" Ree asked. "Mother would have a conniption. You know she forbade us from ever even discussing Thebes. She said the big city is too dangerous."

Of course Calli knew how her mother felt about Thebes. It was just one of the reasons she had kept her desire to go there to herself. But these were extraordinary times. Their mother's rules should no longer apply.

"We have to go to Thebes," Calli said. "To the temple there. When people need help, they petition at the feet of the gods. I believe that is what we should do."

"Why must we go all the way to Thebes?" Mel asked. "Why don't we return to the temple of Amphitrite and petition her?"

Calli was shaking her head before Mel even finished. "Mother said that she once lived on Olympus. It stands to reason that the Olympian gods would know more about Mother's past than anyone else. Maybe they would even know who is after her. We must go to the temple."

"But we do not have a horse at our disposal, which means the journey to Thebes will take us at least a day, if not longer," Mel said.

"What else do you suggest we do, Mel?" Ree asked. "Do we just leave Mother in the hands of those ruffians who snatched her? Do we just wait around here for them to come back for *us*?"

"Maybe we should," Thalia said. "Then we won't have to search for Mother—they will take us to her."

"We can't be certain of that," Calli said. "There is no guarantee those men will take us to the same place they have taken Mother. They may not take us anywhere at all. They may . . ."

She did not want to finish her statement, but Clio did it for her.

"Dispose of us," Clio said. "We are the only witnesses to their crime of kidnapping Mother."

"That seals it. We're going to Thebes," Calli said. "The best thing we can do is go to the gods and beg for their help. Meanwhile, I'll continue to try to figure out what is written in this journal." Calli pushed away from the tree. "Come on, girls. It's time to get our mother back."

IX

REE

Ree swiped an errant tear from her cheek as she put away the measuring sticks she'd used to teach her students proper alignment. This was not the time for tears. She had to focus on rescuing her mother from those thieves.

Hopefully, she wasn't leaving her studio forever. Since the danger their mother had been trying to outrun had caught up with her anyway, Ree's sisters believed that after they rescued her, she would have a change of heart about leaving their village. Ree wanted to rescue her mother because she wanted her to be safe, but selfishly, she also wanted an explanation.

No, it wasn't selfish. She and her sisters deserved to know.

Back at home, Calli and Clio had entered the house first so they could make sure the two men had not returned. Then they all came up with a plan. They would travel to the acropolis in the heart of Thebes, where the temple to the Olympian gods was located. Once there, they would offer sacrifices to each of the gods. Mel and Thalia had collected locks of their hair, olive oil, incense, and roots from the garden: all proper sacrifices.

Each sister had taken turns keeping watch while they prepared for their journey to Thebes. Ree had quickly packed her essentials, then taken off for the studio to make sure everything was secured.

She was folding a dance tunic when she heard the door open.

An unsure voice called out. “Uh . . . hello?”

Ree whipped around. Her breath caught in her throat at the sight of the man standing halfway in the open door. Some might think of him as just a boy, but not her. Sivas Anastasios was eighteen years old and had all the qualities one could ever want in a companion.

Not that she would ever admit to wanting to be his companion. And not that she knew all his qualities. But what she *did* know, she admired.

“Sivas!” she said, the pitch of her voice embarrassingly high. “Um, what are you doing here?”

“Can I come in?” he asked.

“Of course,” Ree said, stuffing the garment in the studio’s lone closet before walking over to him. “How is Cressida? Is everything all right?”

“Cressida is healing nicely. How are *you*?” Sivas asked. “The performance—which was a great delight, by the way—ended somewhat abruptly. I came to make sure that everything was well with your mother.”

Mel had suggested going into the village to inquire if anyone had seen the men with their mother, but Clio had pointed out that since they had no idea who was behind the kidnapping, it might be unwise. Ree did not suspect that Sivas had anything to do with her mother's abduction, of course, but she couldn't control who else he told.

But what if he could help?

As the owner of one of the largest olive farms in Krymmenos, Sivas's father was well-connected. He could possibly provide something they needed, even if it was just a horse and wagon to make the journey to Thebes quicker and more comfortable.

"We—"

Ree stopped. She could not say anything, not without running it by her sisters first.

"We all had a long talk with my mother after the performance," she said. "She apologized for her outburst."

"Why was she so upset?" Sivas asked, genuinely bewildered. "You and your sisters are beautiful singers. If I'd had my aulos or kithara, I would have joined in with your sister. She was great on the lyre. And your dance was . . . it was brilliant."

Ree's face warmed. "That is very sweet of you to say."

"It is the truth," he said, taking another step into the studio. "Cressida is lucky to have you as her teacher."

"She is one of my better students." She only had two students, but Sivas was gentleman enough not to point that out.

Ree looked toward the open door. Calli would be upset if she did not return to the house soon. "Thank you for your concern about my mother, Sivas, but I need to get home."

"Shall I walk you?" he asked.

"No," Ree said a bit too quickly.

If her sisters saw Sivas walking her home, they would ask questions, and Ree was not ready to admit how she felt about him. What if he did not reciprocate her feelings? What if she only thought she had perceived interest from him? She would carry such embarrassment around forever.

"That is quite all right," she said. "It is but a short walk. However, I do have to get going. I am journeying to Thebes with my sisters," she said, deciding that telling him this half-truth would not be all that bad. "We have family matters to attend to."

Sivas's forehead dipped into a frown. "You and your sisters are going to Thebes alone?"

Ree straightened her spine. "We can take care of ourselves," she said. "Our mother taught us to be strong and independent."

"But Thebes is a big city," Sivas said. "I have only been there a handful of times myself. I dream of playing music there one day, but it is not a place for young women to travel alone."

"I assure you, we will be fine," Ree said, even though her mind was still stuck on his admission that he wished to perform music for the people of Thebes.

"Terpsichore, I . . ." He glanced at the floor, then back up at her. "It would sadden me very much if something were to happen to you."

Ree's heart lurched, and in the pit of her stomach it felt as if a million butterflies had taken flight.

"That is very kind of you to say," she told him. "I know that Cressida has taken well to dance, but there are other studios—"

"This has nothing to do with Cressida," he interrupted. "Well, I am sure Cressida would be sad were you to suffer harm, but my sister is not the reason that I would be sad about it. I—"

"Ree? Ree, where are you?"

Her blood began to pound in her veins at the sound of Calli's frantic voice. Or was it due to the words Sivas had just spoken to her?

"There you are," Calli said as she came into the studio. Her sister stopped short. "Oh. I . . . I thought you were alone."

"Sivas was concerned about Mother," Ree quickly provided. "He witnessed her outburst earlier today." She caught the way Calli's eyes narrowed. "I told him that Mother is well, because she is."

"Yes, she is," Calli said, her mouth pulling into a tight smile.

"I was just finishing up here," Ree said. "I shall be home soon."

"We must be on our way," Calli said.

Sivas took a step forward. "Are you sure about this journey to Thebes?"

Her sister spun around and glared at Ree.

"I told Sivas that we will be fine as we handle this private family matter," she said.

She was right to assume that her sisters would not want anyone to know the reason behind their trip to Thebes, especially Calli. Of all her sisters, Calli had taken the longest to trust the people of Krymmenos, mainly because of how standoffish the villagers had been when they first arrived. Even as the rest of them tried to ingratiate themselves to the town, Calli remained aloof. Ree thought she had finally begun to warm to the villagers following the winter solstice celebration, but maybe she was wrong.

"I would offer to join you for protection," Sivas said, "but I am needed at the olive grove."

"That is very generous of you," Calli said. "But we can fend for ourselves. All seems to be in order here, Ree. Let us return to the house."

Ree's heart sank. She had hoped Calli would allow her a few minutes alone with Sivas, but she should have known better.

"Thank you again for your concern," she told Sivas. "I look forward to seeing you when you bring Cressida to her classes."

Oh, why did she say that? Would he think the only thing that mattered to her was that his little sister was a student? However, she could not very well say that it was *him* she wanted to see—not with Calli standing two feet away and no doubt listening to every word.

"I shall see you upon your return," Sivas said. "Maybe you will come and listen to me perform?"

"I would like that," Ree said.

He smiled and nodded. "Have a safe trip."

And then he was gone.

Ree stared at his retreating form as he exited the same way he had entered the dance studio.

"Terpsichore."

She jumped at the sound of Calli's stern summons. Ree could feel her face heating even more as her sister stared at her with keen, knowing eyes. But, thankfully, Calli did not remark about Sivas or the way she had caught Ree staring at him.

"Let us go," Calli said. "We have a long journey ahead of us."

Yes, they did.

Determined that this would *not* be the last time she saw this room, Ree gave the studio one more look before locking the door.

X

MNEMOSYNE

Mnemosyne covered her ears with her grimy palms, trying to block out the incessant sound of water dripping onto the cold stone floor of her prison. Hades had stashed her in a thick-walled dungeon, empty save for a pallet covered with coarse, dingy linens. She could not bring herself to touch them, let alone cover herself with them.

The wretched God of the Underworld had left the dungeon in a rage after she refused to speak. He had yet to reveal why he'd kidnapped her, but she already knew what Hades wanted: to defeat Zeus and take over as ruler of Olympus.

He'd gotten it into his head that she could help him accomplish his goal—something she would *never* do. She had sensed something sinister in Hades from her very first encounter with him and refused to trust anything he said or did. And she would never subject the gods of Olympus or the mortals under Zeus's rule to a life under Hades.

Mnemosyne would have expected Hades to bring her to his own dominion, but as they were transporting her, one of his henchmen mentioned that she was lucky Hades had *not* ordered her to be brought to the Underworld.

Had he taken her to Olympus? Could that splendid mountain even house this horrid dungeon? She closed her eyes, hoping she could get a sense of the place she once called home, but she had lived on Olympus for such a short time. And although she had become fond of some of its residents, it had never truly felt like home.

She thought back to that tumultuous time when an Olympian first found her, and how the encounter had led to this unpredictable life she now led. The memory suddenly emerged in full force, as though she were living that day again—her goddess abilities proving both a blessing and a curse . . .

Spindly, low-hanging branches whipped across her face, lacerating her skin as she raced through the dense forest, running from the same beings who were supposed to protect her. The scent of war imbued the air—the acrid stench of burning flesh clashing with the aroma of the decaying leaves that crunched beneath her heel.

Mnemosyne stopped for a moment to catch her breath, and to figure out her next move.

Where could she go? Who could she turn to when her own family had turned against her?

Her brothers had promised there would be no more war following the defeat of their father. But she should have known better. Her family was never to be trusted, especially Cronus. Her brother was too caught up in his obsession with power and taking his father's place as leader of the Titans.

Life under her father Ouranos's rule had been fraught with anguish and terror; he often demanded the tongue of anyone even suspected of speaking ill against him. But Cronus proved to be an even worse ruler. He mandated unrelenting fealty, especially from those like her who had not been born with the brawn to wage a fight against him. He'd imprisoned his own kin and struck down anyone who dared to question his authority.

Mnemosyne had tolerated his rule as long as he agreed not to bring the death and destruction of an all-out war upon their land. But the Titan gods never kept their word. They were a miserable, ill-tempered lot set on keeping the world mired in chaos.

War was upon them now, and for anyone who only wanted peace, there was no place to go.

Just as she was about to take off again, Mnemosyne caught a flash of gold out of the corner of her eye. She squatted behind the thick trunk of a holm oak.

"Who goes there?" someone called from a few yards away.

Mnemosyne crouched down lower, cautious of even taking a breath lest she be heard. Had Cronus sent someone after her? What had he instructed them to do if they found her? Would her own brother have her killed?

Of course he would. Cronus had already proved that he was willing to destroy any entity that threatened his power.

Mnemosyne's breath caught as she heard her pursuer approaching.

"Reveal yourself!" the strident voice called.

The snap of twigs underfoot preceded Mnemosyne's first glimpse of the warrior who had tracked her down.

She reared back in shock at the sight: the tallest woman Mnemosyne had ever encountered in her life. Dressed in head-to-toe armor, with a gold shield strapped to one arm and a gleaming gold helmet covering her head, she had the carriage of a seasoned warrior, her body tense, as if she was prepared to do battle at a moment's notice. Something about her seemed familiar.

Mnemosyne lost her balance and fell to the ground. The woman warrior was upon her in no time, pointing a spear directly at Mnemosyne's face.

"Who are you?" she demanded.

This was it. The end. She'd thought her demise would come at the hands of her own kin, but it seemed as if this warrior would complete the deed.

"Answer my question," the warrior said.

"Mnem—Mnemosyne."

"What are you doing here?" the warrior asked her.

"Escaping the war," Mnemosyne answered honestly.

"You do not look like a fighter."

"No, the last thing I want to do is fight. I just want peace," Mnemosyne said. Her shoulders drooped with the weight of the fate she now faced. "Maybe now I will finally get it."

The warrior snapped her fingers, and moments later, an owl swooped in and landed on her shoulder.

Mnemosyne suddenly recalled what she'd recognized in the warrior. She was the goddess Athena, Zeus's fiercest soldier, known for her prowess in battle and for the wise owl she kept as a companion.

An Olympian.

Mnemosyne had escaped her traitorous Titan family only to get caught by an Olympian goddess. Her family considered them their enemy in this battle, but for Mnemosyne, they were all the enemy.

"Peace belongs to the victor," Athena said. "But as one who remains neutral, you are at the mercy of the victor. Are you prepared to be at the mercy of the mighty Zeus? He shall prove victorious in the end. Mark my words."

Mnemosyne considered her choices. She could go back to her family, where she faced certain death, or she could yield to the Olympians, which would also likely lead to her death.

But would her death be a certainty if she were to choose the Olympians? They seemed to be the lesser of her two enemies.

"If I can live peacefully under Zeus's reign, then that is what I prefer," Mnemosyne finally answered.

Athena looked down her nose at her, then cracked a small smile.

"Very well," the warrior goddess said. "Come with me. Zeus will be very interested in meeting you."

Though that had been a terrible day in many ways, Mnemosyne could not help smiling at how afraid she had been of Athena when she first met her. She could have never imagined that day in the forest that Zeus's goddess would become such a close friend. Athena was one of the only gods she'd trusted during her time on Olympus.

There was much she could not have imagined on that fateful day that now brought tears of joy to her eyes. Without her hasty escape from her family and her eventual capture by Athena, her girls would never have existed. Still, she regretted how things ended with Athena. Only the love of her precious daughters could have compelled her to sacrifice so dear a friendship.

As she sat in Hades's prison, one thing became clear. If she wanted to continue to protect her girls, she would have to stage another escape.

She had done it before. She would do it again.

XI

CALLI

Calli wove a scarf around her head, then loosely belted a rope at her waist, securing it around a shapeless, ankle-length brown tunic. Clio had suggested they don the disguises of eremites on their way to the temple in Thebes, and all the sisters had agreed. No one would question their traveling by foot if they thought they were just a group of religious recluses in prayer. And as much as she would love to hire a coach, she did not want to field questions from a nosy coachman.

Based on the map Clio had purchased from a merchant in the village square, if they traveled the mountain pass through Ritsona, they should reach the city of Eleon by daybreak. From there, they'd journey to Thebes almost entirely on flat, easily navigable land.

Mel came into the bedroom, her tunic draping over her slim hips like a barley sack. "I know we have more pressing matters to tend to, but I cannot believe *this* is how I have to dress the first time I visit Thebes. People will think we are paupers."

"We do not want anyone to think anything when they see us," Calli reminded her. "We need to be as inconspicuous as possible.

Remember, we do not know who took Mother, so everyone we encounter is a suspect until they prove differently."

"You're right." Mel perked up. "What if we make even more elaborate disguises? We can dress as thespians on our way to the grand theater."

"Um, I am not sure thespians are inconspicuous," Calli said. "People would then expect us to perform, and according to Mother, it was our performance that alerted those ruffians who kidnapped her, remember?"

"Oh, yeah. That's right." She shrugged. "Eremites it is."

"Have the others gathered their things?" Calli asked.

Another nod. "We're ready. Let us go rescue Mother."

Calli followed Mel out into the common room, where Clio, Ree, and Thalia had gathered.

"Are we sure this is going to work?" Thalia asked, fiddling with her robe, which seemed to be at least two inches too long.

"No one knows, but we have to do something," Calli said. "Come here."

She adjusted Thalia's belt and tugged the robe so that it wouldn't drag under her feet.

"And I think the gods are already working in our favor." Calli nodded toward the window. "They've provided a clear night and a full moon to illuminate our path. Certainly, they will grant our wishes once we petition in the temple. After all, Mother is one of them."

"Allegedly," Ree added.

"No, not just allegedly," Calli argued. "The more I read through Mother's journal, the more I'm convinced that she really is a goddess."

Calli opened the journal to the pages she'd read just before donning her robe.

"Look," she said. "There are parts that are written more like regular journal entries than riddles." She pointed to the page. "Right here, Mother recounts planting a garden with the goddess Artemis."

"She is the protector of nature and the hunt, isn't she?" Clio asked.

Calli nodded. "So far, she is the only resident of Mount Olympus that Mother mentions by name. There are vague references to others, but I haven't studied the gods as much as you have, Clio. You'll have to help me interpret Mother's writings."

Clio plucked the journal from Calli's fingers. "I could have told you that from the very beginning."

"Careful," Calli told her.

"We cannot assume that anything mother told us is true," Ree said. "That's why we need to find her. Then maybe we can get her to be straight with us, once and for all."

"Why do you insist on painting Mother as a deceiver?" Mel asked her.

"Because she *did* deceive us!" Ree retorted.

"Okay, that's enough," Calli said. "Mel, I understand why Ree is still distrustful of Mother. I'm having a hard time processing what she told us today, too. And, Ree, we must also keep our wits about us and not lose sight of the reason we are headed to Thebes. We are on a mission to save our mother. That is what is most important."

They all nodded.

"Well, let us be on our way," Clio said. "We need to get moving if we're going to make it through the mountains by daybreak."

Calli lifted the journal from her hands. "I'll keep this for now."

"Calliope!" Clio said.

"For safekeeping," Calli said.

Clio's eyes narrowed. "Fine. Let's go."

A combination of tension, anticipation, and fear permeated the air around them as they quietly made their way out of the house. Calli realized how ridiculous they must look, sneaking out of their own home when their closest neighbors were more than a mile away. Yet she continued with the stealthy escape, viewing it as practice for the covert searching they'd need to do for their mother.

Had they taken her somewhere near Thebes? Could it be possible that they would travel right past her on their way to the temple?

Calli shook her head to clear it. She didn't need to plague herself with such questions. The gods would guide them directly to their mother. Hopefully.

Anticipation of a different sort began to thrum through her

veins as they put more distance between themselves and their home. Calli had dreamed of going to Thebes so often, especially in the past few months, as her belief in her writing had grown. She'd never expected that *this* scenario would finally bring her to Thebes . . . but secretly, she felt a bit excited.

Maybe once their mother was safe and secure in Krymmenos, Calli could return to Thebes to pursue her dream. Maybe she could even take some of her sisters along—certainly Clio, and perhaps Thalia or Mel, too.

She and her sisters moved in a straight line, walking along the trail that led to the outskirts of the village. As the ground beneath their feet turned from fine sand to rocky pebbles, it became a touch more difficult to travel.

"Should we have bought sturdier sandals for this trek?" Mel asked, as if she had read Calli's mind.

"We knew the path through the mountains would not be easy. Just be careful where you step and all should be fine," she said.

They reached the edge of the mountain pass and, using Clio's map, carved out a path forward. Calli considered it yet another gift from the gods that Krymmenos sat at the tip of two mountain ranges. Between the two lay a shallow valley that led straight to the main road that would take them to Thebes. The terrain would be more rugged than the beach and soft grass they were used to, but at least they would not have to climb the mountainside. There were small hovels peppered throughout the pass, undoubtedly set up by merchants who sold supplies to travelers during the day.

As they made their way through the pass, Clio pointed out the Olympian gods in the night sky.

"There's Orion, the great huntsman," Clio said, gesturing to the cluster of stars resembling a man holding a bow and arrow. "He is the son of Poseidon and was considered the best hunter in the world."

"Surely not better than Artemis," Ree said.

"Who do you think was more powerful, Artemis or Orion?" Thalia asked.

On and on the discussion went, until Mel asked quietly, "Do you all think Mother was a powerful goddess?"

They were silent for several moments before Clio answered, "She must have been very powerful in her day. How else would she have managed to keep us hidden from the other gods all this time?"

"If only we had not held that performance, Mother may have continued to keep us hidden," Thalia replied with a nod.

"It isn't my fault," Ree said with a defensive huff.

"No one is blaming you," Calli assured her. "How were you to know that the performance would lead to all of this?"

"If anyone is to blame, it is Mother," Clio said. "She should not have kept this from us."

"I agree," Ree added.

"I'm sure Mother had her reasons," Mel said. Her voice held more heat than usual.

"Why are you always so quick to make excuses for everyone, Melpomene?" asked Ree. "Clio is right. If Mother had simply trusted us with the truth about who she really is and about our own creation, we would have been more careful."

"Stop blaming my mother!" Mel screeched, her voice echoing throughout the pass. "Who knows what is happening to her at this very moment! Yet her daughters are laying all the blame at her feet."

"At who else's feet should we lay the blame, Mel?" Ree asked.

"Girls, please!" Calli said. If she did not put a stop to their bickering, it would go on all night. "What good does it do any of us to assign blame?"

Although Calli could see both of her sisters' points. Her mother's distrust hurt her deeply. She could even understand Mnemosyne keeping the truth from the younger girls, but Calli and her mother operated more as partners than mother and daughter. Why hadn't she confided in her?

"It does not matter who is at fault," Calli continued, trying her best to keep the bitterness out of her tone. "All that matters is that we convince the gods to help us so that we can get Mother back."

Duly chastised, Mel and Ree moved to either side of Calli and continued walking silently along the rocky path.

"We shouldn't have tried to travel so far today," Clio said. "This day has been too eventful. Our bodies need to rest. That is why we are so testy. Should we find a place to stop?"

"I'm tired, too," Calli agreed. The desperate need to rescue her mother, along with the anticipation of finally seeing Thebes, had sustained her thus far, but the monotony of the barren mountain landscape made her realize just how exhausted she was. "It will put us behind to stop and rest—but I think you are right."

They had passed a tiny inn about two thousand paces back, but the thought of going in the reverse direction did not sit right with her. However, Calli did not want to make this decision for her sisters.

"Should we continue in hopes of finding another inn, or do you all want to go back to the one we passed?" she asked the group.

"What do you think we should do?" Thalia asked.

Calli released an exasperated breath. She wanted them to think for themselves.

This was the result of years of her sisters turning to her for every little thing. How could she have ever thought she would be able to leave her family and set out on her own?

The longer she thought about it, the more Calli was convinced that this had been her mother's goal all along. She had made it so that her younger sisters relied on Calli to the point where she felt as if she could never leave them.

A streak of defiance raced down her spine. It was unfair of her mother to lock her into such an existence. Calli had a mind and dreams of her own. It was time she weaned her sisters off their reliance on her so they could start thinking for themselves.

"I think we should put it up for a vote," Calli said. They looked at her as if she were the snake-haired Medusa, a villainous creature their mother had told them about in bedtime stories. "By show of hands, who thinks we should travel on in hopes of finding another inn?"

None of her sisters raised their hands.

"Did you hear me?" Calli asked.

"Yes," they said in unison.

"And not one of you thinks we should continue on?" Again, silence. "But if we go back, it will only add to the amount we have to travel."

"But what if there isn't another inn for five thousand paces?" Mel asked. "I will collapse if I have to walk that much!"

"Me too," Thalia said. She gestured to a rough-looking boulder. "I am ready to lay my head on that rock and go to sleep right this second."

Clio pulled out her map and laid it flat across the rock. She positioned it so that the moonlight illuminated the entire right side, then pointed to a spot at the midpoint of the lower mountain range.

"According to the map, Hyria is right here. There is no indication of how big the settlement is, but if it is important enough to be named on the map, then it is within reason to think that it is important enough to have an inn. It would take less time to reach Hyria than it would take to go back to the inn we passed."

Thank goodness for her levelheaded sister.

"How much time?" Thalia asked.

"If we start walking and stop complaining, we can possibly reach it in the next half hour."

"Then let us walk," Mel said.

"And quickly," Ree added, catching up with Mel. It seemed as if all had been forgiven following their previous squabble.

They walked for several more minutes. As they rounded an outcropping jutting out from the base of the mountain, a soft light flickered in the still night. Thank the gods! They were near an inn, just as Clio had predicted.

When they reached it, Calli was relieved to discover there was a single room available. It did not contain any beds, but there were enough mats made of rushes, straw, and horsehair for each girl to have one. At that point Calli would have slept on the packed earth.

If the innkeeper thought it strange that five young eremites were traveling through the mountain pass so late at night, he did not voice it. He likely did not care, as long as their coin was good.

Once her sisters were settled, Calli asked the innkeeper for hot water for tea. She and her sisters ate bread and drank the tea before turning in for the night.

The moment Calli closed her eyes, she heard Thalia whispering her name.

"Yes, Thalia?" Calli asked.

"Do you think the gods will comply with our request?"

The concern she heard in her normally cheerful sister's voice pulled at Calli's heart. She reached over and captured Thalia's hand.

"Yes, I do," Calli said. "Everything will work out, Thalia. I promise."

"And you always keep your promises," Thalia said.

Calli swallowed deeply and fought off the pressure suddenly weighing on her chest.

"Get some sleep," she whispered. "You want to be well-rested for tomorrow when we get to Thebes."

XII

CALLI

The sky was still dark, with only a hint of the deep blue and rich purple indicating that twilight would soon become dawn. The girls had awoken early and left the inn in the same way they'd left their home the day before: soundlessly and stealthily. Clio took the lead as they continued their journey, an updated map tucked underneath her arm.

"It won't be long now," she said. "Remember, keep your head covered and your eyes in front of you. No one should bother us if they believe we are eremites. Pretend we are in prayer as we walk."

"Maybe we *should* be in prayer," Mel said. "Mother can probably use it. Who knows what those ruffians are doing to her at this very moment."

"Calm down, Mel," Ree told her, taking her hand and giving it a squeeze.

Calli was relieved to see the two of them getting along again. Of all her sisters, Ree had the most trouble tolerating Mel's excitable nature. Calli often wondered if it was because they'd spent so much time together that they'd begun to rub each other the wrong way. Maybe coming together for this common goal would bring them all closer.

They quietly made their way along the more heavily traveled road to Thebes. Merchants selling bread, dried meats, and fruit to weary travelers dotted the roadside.

Calli estimated they had traveled about three thousand paces when she caught sight of a man walking with a familiar gait, pulling a mule loaded down with animal hides. It was Mr. Samaras, the saddlemaker from Krymmenos.

How foolhardy to think they could make this entire trip without encountering anyone from their village. The saddlemaker was a known gossip and the last person Calli wanted to see. She knew if he recognized them, all of Krymmenos would know that Mnemosyne's daughters had been seen traveling alone on the way to Thebes.

She still didn't know if someone from their village had something to do with her mother's kidnapping. And what about when the kidnappers returned for them and discovered they were gone? What if they started offering coin to anyone who had information about their whereabouts?

Calli spotted a merchant on the side of the road, surrounded by baskets filled with figs, dates, and pomegranates.

"Girls, follow me," Calli said, starting for the fruit stand.

"But we have plenty to eat—"

"Just follow me, Thalia," Calli said. "And don't look at the travelers. Mr. Samaras is walking toward us."

"That nosy saddlemaker?" Ree asked.

"Yes, now shhh," Calli said.

"On your way to Thebes?" the fruit seller asked.

Calli nodded and brought her clasped hands in front of her chest, indicating they were on a silent pilgrimage to the temple.

"Oh, these figs do look good," Thalia said in a deep male voice, scampering over to the basket of plump fruit.

"They do!" Mel said, following her. Her voice acting could have used some work. "I'll bet they're sweet."

"Men!" Calli groused. They were not supposed to be shopping, or speaking for that matter. "Over here."

They all huddled together in front of the bushel of deep pink pomegranates. She listened, waiting to hear the *clomp clomp* of the mule as he and his owner walked by. Instead, she heard the merchant call out to someone approaching.

"Hey there, fella! Nice mule you have there."

Calli's eyes fell shut. Of course the saddlemaker *would* choose to stop at this particular fruit stand.

"On your way from Thebes?" the merchant asked.

"Yeah," said Mr. Samaras. "I hate that crime-infested city. A man isn't safe there. Nothing but thieves and ruffians. But that's where you find all the best tanners. I can't dye this hide by myself."

Calli caught him looking their way out of the corner of his eye. "Say there, don't I know you?"

"No," she replied in a deep voice.

She felt like a fool, but better to let the saddlemaker think she was a man he didn't know than one of the daughters of the strange woman who lived by the sea.

"No, no, I think I do," he said.

"You don't," she said in that same low, ridiculous voice. She plucked two pomegranates and a handful of figs from the baskets and handed them to the merchant. "We'll take these and be on our way."

Calli quickly paid for the fruit they didn't need, keeping her profile turned as far away from him as she could.

"Come, men," she said to her sisters.

The saddlemaker continued to stare at them with a puzzled frown as she guided the girls back to the road.

"Do you think it worked?" Mel asked.

"Of course it did," Thalia said. "Didn't you see my acting? Even I thought I was a man."

Calli rolled her eyes. "Let's hope it worked. The fewer people who know about our comings and goings, the better. We cannot trust anyone."

"Do you think we can put our trust in the gods?" Clio asked.

"At this point, we have no choice," Calli replied. "We need their guidance."

She could barely swallow past the lump that formed in her throat. The pressure to get this right was immense. What if she was leading her sisters into danger? They were counting on her to guide them, as they always did. One mistake on her part could lead to a disastrous outcome, not only for her and her sisters, but for her mother.

Calli felt a hand on her shoulder. She turned, surprised to find a much calmer Mel staring back at her.

"Everything will be just fine," Mel said. "I know you're scared. We all are. But it will all come together, you'll see."

Calli covered Mel's hand and gave it a squeeze. "Yes, it will."

She was constantly stunned by Mel's uncanny ability to know just the right thing to say at just the right time.

Bolstered by her sister's optimistic outlook, Calli joined Clio at the front of their short procession. They had walked another five thousand paces when Calli noticed a large edifice off in the distance. Its walls had to be at least ten stories high and were made of gleaming marble and smooth limestone. The closer they got to it, the easier it became to make out exactly what she was seeing.

"It's the hippodrome," Calli whispered in an awe-filled voice.

She had read about the stadium where chariot races were held. During a certain time of the year, they carried out contests to determine the best archer, fastest runner, and strongest citizen of Thebes. The structure was said to be a true marvel, with an ingenious design that allowed every person seated to have a clear view of the activities. And she was seeing it with her own two eyes!

"We're here!" Calli said, unable to contain her excitement.

"This is Thebes?" Thalia asked, sounding unimpressed.

"No, no. This is the great hippodrome. It is said to be about a thousand paces outside of the city walls, which means we are almost to Thebes."

"Well, why are we standing here staring at this bunch of rocks? Let's get to Thebes and rescue Mother."

Calli wished she could tour the gargantuan structure, but Thalia was right. She could not lose sight of their mission. There would be time to see all that she had spent so much time dreaming about *after* she was sure her mother was safe.

Knowing they were close to the city compelled them all to move faster. In no time at all they were standing before one of the huge gates that allowed entry into Thebes.

Calli's heart pounded with anticipation as she stepped into an entirely new world.

She had never seen so many people gathered in one place. More people stood along this one street than lived in all of Krymmenos. She and her sisters bumped into one another as they made their way down the street; they were so busy taking in the sights around them that they'd stopped paying attention to where they were walking.

They reached one of the arched entries into the agora. From what Calli had read, the open square was the heartbeat of every city, and it certainly seemed to be the center of everything in Thebes. It teemed with people of all ages and sizes, from small children kicking around a ball made of what looked to be tightly woven straw, to older gentlemen griping at each other.

"Look!" Calli gasped, her pulse quickening at the collection of performers in front of what looked to be the theater. Several played instruments while the actors, resplendent in their costumes, acted out a scene.

Thalia huffed. "Is that supposed to be *Medea*? I can play a better Princess Glauce than that scrawny one they have playing her."

"Do not," Calli said, putting a hand to Thalia's shoulder before she got any ideas. "I'm sure we would all like to explore the city. It looks . . . it looks amazing."

Her eyes fell on a young Theban who sat on the steps of another building with papyrus and a reed pen. A writer! That young man was living out her dream right before her very eyes.

"But we cannot forget why we're here," she continued. "We must go to the temple."

They walked a few more yards and encountered a massive structure with arches positioned every ten feet or so all along the facade. Inside the arches were marble statues of the great writers and actors of their time.

"It's the theater!" Clio pointed.

They all gasped.

"It's beautiful," Ree said.

"Can't you picture us performing there for everyone to see?" Thalia said. "And me, as the star!"

"We can all share the spotlight, Thalia," Mel chastised. "Calli, we must see the theater."

"Not yet," Calli said. "The temple. We have to go to the temple first."

"Yes, yes. Calli is right," Clio said. "You've all heard the stories about the gods. If they were to hear that we did not come directly to them, they may hold it against us. They will find offense in any little thing."

"So let us continue to the temple," Calli said.

She and her sisters collectively took a step forward and immediately hopped back as a chariot raced past them, whipping up the hems of their robes.

"What are you, an animal?" Thalia yelled. "Learn how to drive!"

"Shhh," Mel chastised. "You're going to get us in a heap of trouble before we ever reach the temple."

"We won't reach the temple if we get run over by a chariot," Thalia pointed out.

"Girls, please," Clio said.

But her focus was on the massive buildings bordering the square. Excitement and awe danced in her eyes as they roamed the structures.

"Look at how intricate the cornices are." Clio pointed. "Do you understand the craftsmanship it takes to carve the marble into such complicated designs?" She glanced at Mel with an excited smile.

"The cornices are not only ornamental, you know? They serve a practical purpose by directing the rainwater away from the building."

"Ugh, will we have to listen to her talk about buildings all day?" Ree asked.

"We have to listen to you talk about dance," Clio said defensively. "Don't you think this is fascinating?" She stretched her arms out toward the theater to their right. "Look at the elaborate volute at the top of each column! They are—"

"Ahh!" Ree placed her hands over her ears. "Calli, make her stop!"

Calli would do no such thing. Clio adored architecture; she could only imagine what it meant to her sister to see these amazing structures with her own eyes. She was probably feeling the same thing Calli felt as she finally set foot in Thebes.

She took several tentative steps toward the center of the agora. Merchants and traders hawked their wares from the back of wagons and barrels that had been wheeled into the square. Those who could afford it sold their goods from underneath the covered colonnade of the stoa that surrounded the square. Hundreds of marble columns lined both sides of the gallery.

It was everything she had anticipated and more.

And it smelled. It smelled dreadfully bad.

Calli held her arm up to her nose, preferring the stench of the robe she had just traveled thousands of paces in to the foul odor that pervaded the air.

A man with matted hair and a torn tunic barreled his way past them. "Outta my way," he said, before spitting on the ground.

Mel squeaked. "Ew!"

"*This* is the big city everyone is dying to come to?" Thalia said.

A rat scurried across the dirty marble, eliciting another squeak from Mel.

Her sisters were repulsed, but Calli could see the beauty and potential beneath Thebes's rough edges.

"Where do we find the temple?" Ree asked.

"Over there," a woman dressed in a crimson peplos and carrying a live chicken said as she passed them.

She pointed the chicken toward the far end of the agora to a set of stairs that had to number in the hundreds.

"Tell me we don't have to climb those stairs," Thalia said.

"Come on, Thalia. Do it for Mother," Ree said, capturing her sister by the elbow.

Yes, they were all doing this for their mother. With any luck, the gods would be eager to help them locate Mnemosyne. Once Calli was certain her family was safely back in Krymmenos, she would return to this bustling city and start her new life as an epic essayist. After just this small taste of Thebes, she knew there was nowhere else she wanted to be.

XIII

HADES

Hades paced back and forth in front of the door to the cell where his newest guest currently resided. He'd been correct in his suspicions regarding the group of singers that were the talk of the town. They'd led him directly to Mnemosyne.

And now he had her in his clutches.

It would have been nice if he also had those daughters of hers locked up in their own dungeons, but somehow, he'd miscalculated the potency of the potion he'd given to Pain and Panic. When the two imps had returned to Krymmenos for them, the girls were no longer at their cottage.

No, it wasn't his mistake. Those numbskulls had done something wrong.

He would figure out a way to get the daughters later. It was Mnemosyne's powers he wanted to harness.

But first he had to get her to speak. The Titan goddess had yet to utter a single word.

She stood tall, her wavy black hair draped around her shoulders and her chin defiantly in the air. He hated when people did that!

He had incinerated mortals who dared to look at him with such insolence.

But he couldn't strike her down, and she knew it, which only infuriated him more. His hair flashed orange before he managed to get ahold of himself. Hades passed a hand over his head and felt it cool.

If he couldn't frighten her into bending to his will, surely he could reason with her.

"I know we parted on bad terms when you left," Hades said. "I can't remember everything about it, only what I wrote in my notes, but that is *your* fault." He pointed an accusatory finger at her. "Don't I get points for thinking ahead? No one else was smart enough to recognize what you could do with that gift of yours and take precautions the way I did. I deserve some credit for my caginess, don't I? Get it? *Cagey*? You're kinda in a cage."

Her face remained as cold as a block of ice in the middle of winter. Hmm . . . humor wasn't her strong suit, was it?

"Come on, Mnem. No hard feelings, huh?" Hades held his hands up. "Look, I'm willing to put the past behind us. Why waste time holding grudges when there are so many more productive things we can do together, like finally settling the score against Zeus?"

She looked on the verge of responding but remained silent.

"Ah, so you *do* have a score to settle with Zeus," he continued. "I knew you were too smart to believe that my brother is this benevolent being that saved the world from the big bad Titans." Hades went in for the kill. "Zeus banished your family to the deepest regions of the Underworld and made you as much his prisoner back then as you are mine now."

Her eyes flashed with anger, and Hades could tell he was getting under that lovely bronze skin. Good! He wanted to push her to the brink.

He had always known the Titan goddess had a powerful gift, but he hadn't fully grasped just how powerful until she had used it on everyone in Olympus. An entire season had passed before he'd run across the journal he had written about Mnemosyne. Even as he'd read the words, he couldn't be certain if what he'd recalled were actual memories or just his mind creating them in his head. That was just how good she was.

He'd dropped hints to the other gods over the past two decades, trying to discern if anyone else remembered her, but it seemed that no one else had had the forethought to record their dealings with a goddess who was known to control memory. How could his fellow gods have been so naive?

But their naivety would prove to be one of his greatest assets. No one would be prepared for what would happen when he finally convinced Mnemosyne to join him.

He'd hatched his plan long ago, well before he'd gotten word that Mnemosyne had been found. He hated that so much of this scheme that would finally put him in a position of power hinged on another's cooperation, but when had anything ever come easy for him?

Hades closed in on her, a sinister smile curving up the corners of his lips. It was time to sell this to her, and he was an excellent salesman.

"Payback is simple, Mnemosyne," he said. "All you have to do is wipe out the memories of all on Olympus and replace them with new memories. You could change how the gods view Zeus. You can make it so that they see him as the enemy." He paused for dramatic effect. That had always worked well for him in the past. "And me as their savior."

She still didn't respond.

"Come on, Mnemosyne, you know that I would be better at this than Zeus. All he does is hurl those lightning bolts around when someone gets on his bad side. He demands loyalty from everyone at all costs. It's all about Zeus, Zeus, Zeus." He pointed to his chest. "I, on the other hand, would never treat my people in such a way. If I ruled, you and your girls would not have to live in a dinky little shack near the sea in order to feel safe. Pain and Panic told me about the place. It sounds awful." Hades held out his hands. "What do you say?"

She turned her nose up in the air yet again.

He stomped both feet, barely able to contain his rage.

"Why are you making this so difficult?" Hades screamed, his

entire body turning red. "My blockhead of a brother wiped your kind out of existence. *Your* kin are stuck in Tartarus because of him. Why would you not want your revenge? It's not natural! You should want to kill Zeus with your bare hands!"

She wrapped her arms around her waist and turned to stare at the grimy wall.

Hades resumed his pacing. He was not leaving this dungeon until he had secured her cooperation. He didn't care how long it took.

Just then, a haggard woman with a hump in the middle of her back came running into the room.

"Boss, I've got some news you can use," the woman said.

She disappeared in a puff of smoke and was replaced by Pain.

"Can't you see that I am busy?" Hades asked him.

"But you're gonna wanna hear this," Pain said. "Guess who I saw walking around Thebes just a little while ago, dressed up as eremites?" He gestured toward their prisoner. "Her daughters. I guess it doesn't matter that the potion wore off before we could get to them."

Mnemosyne's eyes widened in terrorized shock. "My girls? Where?"

"Oh, she speaks!" Hades said. "Finally."

"Right there in the agora. They tried to disguise themselves, but the youngest one is too sassy for her own good," Pain said.

"Thalia," Mnemosyne said with a gasp.

Fear shimmered in her eyes. He knew using her daughters would be the best way to get to her.

"Well, well, well," Hades drawled, sauntering back to where she stood. "Isn't this an interesting turn of events?" He tapped the tips of his fingers together. "I wonder how those daughters of yours would fare if I brought them to see their dear mother locked up like an animal. You think they would like that?"

"Stay away from my girls," she said.

"Five words! You've been so tight-lipped since you arrived, I didn't think you could speak five whole words."

Hades rested his chin against his balled fist. "Hmm . . . I wonder what kind of threat it would take to get ten words out of you."

"Don't you dare put a hand on my daughters, Hades!" Mnemosyne said.

"Or what?" he asked. He quickly closed the distance between them, getting right in her face. "I will tell you what will happen. You will help me defeat Zeus the way you should have done twenty years ago, and I'll let you and those daughters of yours go about your boring little lives. Or, better yet, I can become their protector."

"My girls do not need someone like *you* as their protector," said Mnemosyne. "You're the kind they need protecting from."

"I am a changed god," Hades said. "I give you my word that I will protect them."

"I will never trust the word of a god. I have been burned too many times."

Stubborn. She was so stubborn!

"You will not harm a single hair on my daughters' heads," Mnemosyne said, her words dripping with contempt. "If you do, there is no chance that I will *ever* help you."

Hades squeezed his hands into fists and let out an ungodly scream.

His ire had reached cataclysmic levels, more because of what he couldn't do than because of what he could.

He stopped short.

He wouldn't do anything to Mnemosyne's daughters physically, but he could wreak havoc in their lives until they were as miserable as he was.

"Pain! Get Panic and get in here. Now!"

Hades began to pace again, but not to blow off steam. No, he needed to think. There were only a couple of reasons that Mnemosyne's girls could have gone to Thebes. Someone had told them that's where their mother had been taken, or they were planning to ask the gods for help in finding her.

Good luck with that! Because of their mother's actions years ago, the gods didn't know she existed. If any of the gods bothered to respond to their plea, they would likely lump her daughters in with the dozens of others who had gone mad while living on the streets of Thebes.

Just in case they bypassed the gods and went straight to searching for their mother, Hades was going to make sure that whatever they had in mind did not go as planned. He would stall them, and he would use their plight to blackmail Mnemosyne into bending to his will.

Pain and Panic arrived in their normal imp forms.

"Reporting for duty, boss," Panic said, raising his hand to his head in salute.

"Gather around," Hades said, flaring his robe out so that it encircled his two minions. "I've got a task for you." He looked over his shoulder at Mnemosyne, who glared at him as he walked out of the room. "I think you'll like this one."

XIV

REE

"How . . . much . . . farther?" Mel asked, panting. "My legs cannot take it. I think they're about to break."

"Can . . . climbing too many stairs . . . break your legs?" Thalia asked through labored huffs of breath.

"Mel, Thalia, please," Ree said. She looked back over her shoulder at her sisters. They had both taken to crawling on all fours up the marble steps leading to the temple. Despite being in remarkable shape herself, Ree had to admit this climb was testing her endurance.

"Just keep going," she called down to Thalia and Mel. She repeated those words over and over to herself as she followed behind Clio and Calli.

Ree was now convinced the route to the temple had been designed this way specifically to kill any mortal who dared to bother the gods with their insignificant little mortal problems. She could not fathom making this journey unless it involved a life-or-death situation. Was this really such a good idea?

She jogged up a couple of steps to catch up with Calli, who led the pack. "Calli, wait. Before we go any farther, I think we should be certain we are doing the right thing by petitioning the gods here in Thebes. Remember, Mother distrusted the gods, or at the very least, she did not feel as if she could ask them for help."

"We went over this—we have no other choice," Calli replied. "She did say we could trust at least some of them, so this is our best option. Are we supposed to search the skies looking for the bird Mother mentioned? And then what? We ask it to guide us? We look around for the flowers she wrote about and hope to find some clue hidden within their petals?"

Terpsichore didn't have the answer, but she couldn't shake these sudden doubts that their mother would disapprove of their asking the gods for help. If it were that easy, why wouldn't her mother have turned to the temple at Thebes years before instead of trying to keep them safe on her own?

Something about this didn't sit right with her.

"Come on, girls! We can make it," Clio said as she breezed past Ree and Calli. "Just take it one step at a time."

"Easy for you to say," Thalia called. "You can take *two* steps at a time with those long legs."

Despite being sure that at least one of them would pass out before they reached the temple, Ree and her sisters finally made it to the pinnacle of the hill. Her breath stopped for another reason. Tilting her head back to take in the magnitude of the building, Ree was in absolute awe of its sheer size and beauty. The sun glinted off the pristine white marble threaded with veins of gold and onyx. Its columns were as thick as the trunk of their mother's favorite oak tree. And there were so many of them! There must have been over a hundred columns stretching the length of the immense structure.

"Clio," she said, waving at her sister while still looking up at the temple. "What style are those columns?"

"The Corinthian style," Clio answered, her attention focused on the building. "You can tell by the acanthus leaves carved into the capital of the columns. I plan to visit Corinth one day. Their designs are said to be the most beautiful in the world."

Ree finally understood her sister's obsession with history and architecture. This was unlike anything she had ever seen before.

"They are stunning," she whispered.

"We can't stand out here staring at the temple all day, as much as I want to," Clio said. "The gods are extremely temperamental. One wrong move and they will toss us out of the temple. Or worse."

"Worse?" Thalia asked.

Clio hunched her shoulders. "You never know how the gods will respond. It is the price one pays for seeking their assistance."

"Maybe we *shouldn't* ask for their help," Ree said. "Maybe we should try to find Mother on our own."

"You telling me we climbed all those steps for nothing?" Thalia asked.

"No," Calli answered. "I believe in our original plan. We just have to be respectful in our approach." She looked to Mel and Thalia. "Do you have our sacrificial offers?"

All Ree could do right then was trust Calli's instincts.

Thalia gestured to Mel. "She has the bag of stuff for the gods."

Mel held up the two small sacks. "They're right here. Are we ready?"

All eyes turned to Calli. She stiffened her spine and stuck her shoulders back.

With her chin in the air, she said, "Let us go and plead our case."

One by one, they filed into the pantheon. It featured a surprisingly simple design, with more columns evenly spaced throughout, each topped with a carved statue depicting one of the gods of Olympus.

"Oh, oh, that must be Artemis," Thalia said, pointing to the striking woman with a small deer next to her.

"And this one must be Dionysus," Clio said. "Mother has told us stories of his penchant for wine."

"Do you really think Mother knows all of the gods?" Mel asked. "That she lived among them?"

"There is only one way to find out," Calli said.

She stretched her hands out and motioned for them to all gather near. Then, as a group, they made their way to the center of the temple.

Ree had thought she'd been anxious before their performance

the previous day, and she often felt on the verge of fainting whenever Sivas was near. But neither of those experiences could compare to the nerves dancing in her stomach right now.

"Remember what I told you," Clio whispered to Calli.

Calli nodded, then cleared her throat.

"Great gods of Olympus. Zeus, Hera, Apollo, Demeter, and all the others. We come on behalf of our mother, Mnemosyne, who once lived among you as a goddess from the Titan era."

"No. Don't tell them she was a Titan," Clio whispered again. "They went to war with the Titans. They may still hold a grudge against her for that. They can be both volatile and vengeful."

"Why didn't you tell her that before?" Thalia said.

"I did!" Clio replied.

"Shh . . ." Calli admonished. "It isn't as if the gods don't know that Mother was a Titan." In a louder voice, she continued. "Your fellow goddess is in severe trouble, and we, her daughters, are in need of your assistance."

She stopped and looked around. Ree did the same. So did Mel, and Thalia, and Clio.

"I don't see any help coming," Thalia said.

As the temple remained deafeningly quiet, Ree wondered if maybe Clio had been right about the gods holding a grudge against her mother, despite Zeus's not banishing her to Tartarus with the other Titans. Maybe that was why her mother had fled—because the other gods on Olympus didn't approve of her living among them.

Just then a brisk, cold wind swept through the temple.

A voice boomed out. "Who goes there?"

Ree squinted as a figure emerged from behind one of the columns. He was one of the largest specimens Ree had ever seen. His deep purple skin was radiant, and his thick locks as gorgeous as Mel's hair—but the symbol emblazoned on the pendant at his breastbone literally shone the brightest. It looked as if he had reached up, grabbed the sun, and stored it in his pendant.

She looked up at the statue resting atop the column from where he'd come.

"Apollo," Ree whispered under her breath. "He's really here."

"Yes, I am the sun god," he said, still a distance away. "I also have excellent hearing, which is why there was no need for the tall one to project her voice. You nearly woke up every god on Olympus."

Calli's head snapped back in affront, but before she could respond, Thalia said, "You're real," then promptly fell to the floor in a dead faint.

Apollo peered down at her limp body, his brow creasing with a hint of annoyance.

Ree and Mel both rushed to Thalia's aid. Ree set her head in her lap while Mel fanned her face.

Apollo turned his attention to Clio and Calli. He crossed his arms over his astonishingly large chest and said, "You did climb all those steps to request favor from the gods, did you not? Did you believe you were climbing those steps only to call on fake gods?"

Up until that moment, Ree had harbored serious doubts that they'd speak to actual gods. They seemed out of reach for mere mortals like her and her sisters.

But *were* they mortals? What were they, exactly? She understood that they were her mother's creations, but what did that make them?

That betrayal she'd felt when her mother first told them her secret washed over her yet again.

"We knew you were real," Calli said hastily, her voice shaking slightly. "And we need your help."

Ree's eyes widened at the unease in Calli's voice. She rarely saw her sister get rattled, but it was obvious an encounter with an actual god was something even the fearless Calliope could not face with her usual imperturbability.

"It sounds like you need *our* help!" said a new voice. "How's it going, Apollo?"

They all whipped around to find another being, this one much smaller than Apollo, floating toward them. There were wings on his sandals that fluttered rapidly.

"Yes, Hermes, it appears we have been summoned," Apollo said.

Of course! Hermes, the messenger.

Ree's heart started to do that banging thing in her chest again. Would she wake up and discover this was all some elaborate dream? It seemed too fantastical to be real, yet it was.

"Eremites?" Hermes asked.

"We are not eremites," Calli said, whipping off the hood of her robe. "These were only disguises. We have traveled from Krymmenos, a small town on the shore of the archipelago. We require the help of the gods in order to rescue our mother, who was kidnapped yesterday. Her name is Mnemosyne."

Ree held her breath as she waited for the two gods' reaction to hearing their mother's name.

Except there was no reaction. They both continued to stare at Calli without a hint of recognition.

"I said her name is Mnemosyne," her sister repeated. "She is a Titan goddess."

"A Titan, you say?" Hermes tilted his head to the side. "Does she have long black hair?"

"Yes!" Mel said, springing up and running to stand alongside Calli. "Like mine, but not as long. And she is tall and willowy, but not as tall as Calliope or Clio."

Hermes shrugged. "Still no idea who she is. Those Titans all had long hair. What was she the goddess of?"

She and her sisters all looked at one another. Their mother had not specifically told them what her role on Olympus had been.

"Dance?" Ree said uncertainly.

"And probably song," Clio added. "She told us that she created us to mirror the things she held most dear, like music and art."

"Those are *my* areas of expertise," Apollo said in his deep voice.

He narrowed his eyes, then smiled a smile that was so radiant it made Ree's breath catch in her throat. Thalia finally started to come to, so Ree helped her sit up.

Apollo pointed at Clio. "I thought I recognized more champions of song as I looked at the five of you." He glanced over at Hermes. The two seemed to be communicating, though they spoke no words. After a few moments, Apollo continued. "I am not sure what the mortals in your little town—"

"Krymmenos," Clio provided.

He brushed that off. "Whatever. As I was saying, I'm not sure how much you know about how things work here, being from such a small town, but one does not simply come to the gods for help without giving something in return."

"We brought offerings," Mel said. "Hair and incense. Along with garden roots and our best olive oil."

One would think Mel had offered him horse dung with the way Apollo peered down his patrician nose at her.

"No, thank you," he said. He turned to Calli. "You say your mother was a goddess of dance and song. As her daughters, I would assume you possess such talents as well, am I right?"

"Um . . . yes," Calli answered.

Apollo folded his arms over his massive chest. "Prove it."

XV

REE

"What?" Ree asked, certain she had misheard him.

"Prove that you are the daughter of this alleged Titan goddess of dance and song," said Apollo.

"You want us to sing?" Clio asked. "Right here, right now?"

"And dance," Apollo said. "That is my price for offering assistance. My initial price," he corrected. "The terms are subject to change at my whim."

"Temperamental and unpredictable, just as I knew the gods would be," Clio muttered.

"What was that?" Apollo asked, putting a hand up to his ear, a smile tugging at the corner of his mouth. He looked over his shoulder at his fellow god. "What is your price, Hermes?"

Hermes shrugged. "I don't know just yet. But I do love a good song and dance. Let's see what they've got. Maybe the entertainment will be enough for me."

Apollo rolled his eyes. "You could have at least asked for a year of devotion and allegiance." He gestured to Ree and her sisters with his chin. "Well, go on. Sing and dance."

Ree had never imagined being put on the spot, ordered to perform for Olympus's chief expert in the arts. A cold knot of apprehension formed in her stomach, but there was also something else.

Excitement!

They were about to perform for *the* Apollo. The God of Music, Dance, and the Sun.

"Girls," Clio called, motioning for them to come in close. "Mother's birthday performance from four years ago. Do you remember?"

Ree gasped. "You really are a genius." Turning to the others, she asked, "Does everyone remember their part?"

Thalia wiggled her arm like a serpent. "That one?"

"That's the one," Clio confirmed.

The sisters quickly got into their respective positions, and then Calli stepped into her role as the narrator.

"The great Apollo and Hermes," she opened, bending in her deep curtsy. "Please sit back and relax as we, the daughters of Mnemosyne, present to you the story of a mighty warrior who slew the nasty dragon-serpent Python at Delphi."

"Hey, I know that story," Hermes said. He nudged Apollo with his elbow. "And I think *you* know it too. Good choice, ladies."

Their mother said she'd appealed to Zeus's ego when she made her deal with him. Clio must have realized there was no better way to cater to Apollo's ego than to present one of his most celebrated feats in song. And they all knew their mother loved this story—she had told them numerous times over the years, and Ree remembered how much she had enjoyed it when they'd performed it for her birthday.

Calli, who had written this dramatic retelling, guided them through the story as they all performed their individual parts: Clio in the role of Apollo, Thalia acting as the craven Python, and Mel and Ree as the nymphs at Delphi who cheered the god to victory. The dragon-serpent had been sent by Gaea to stand watch over the oracle at Delphi, but Apollo wanted possession of it, and he fired over one hundred arrows into Python, killing the monster and laying claim to the oracle.

Other than a couple of missteps by Mel—she always had the hardest time with turns—their performance was near flawless. Yet as they stood before Apollo at the end of their number, he only appeared indifferent, his arms still crossed over his chest.

Finally, he nodded once. "Impressive. I question a few of the artistic choices, especially with the dance, but it was still enjoyable."

Ree's head reared back, but before she had the chance to foolishly respond, Calli stepped in.

"Does that mean you will assist us?" she asked.

He glanced over at Hermes, and together they hunched their shoulders as he said, "Very well."

The sisters' collective sighs of relief echoed throughout the temple.

"Settle down," Apollo said. "I am still not convinced your mother is a goddess, but I like the five of you. You've got talent. With a little practice, you will be even better."

"We will sing your praises from the highest hill if you help us find our mother," Clio said.

"Are you sure you don't remember her?" Mel asked.

"I do not remember her at all," Apollo answered.

"But she said she lived among the gods."

"I don't know her," he repeated. "But we said we would help, didn't we? Be grateful."

"We are," Clio said, clamping a hand on Mel's shoulder and pulling her back.

"We need to figure out what is going on with this Mnemosyne character," Hermes said. "It would help if you had something of hers that—"

"We do!" Calli interrupted. She reached into her satchel and retrieved their mother's journal. "My mother left us with this. It is supposed to help us, but it is very old, and the writing is very faint and cryptic."

Hermes fluttered to her side and read over Calli's shoulder. "Hmm . . . some of this is in the old language. Maybe that mother of yours is a goddess after all. I don't see too many people using these expressions anymore." He wiggled his fingers at the journal. "Flip the page."

Calli obliged, gingerly turning the frail page. A moment later, Apollo plucked the book from her hands. He closed it and held it between his flattened palms, his eyes shut.

After a moment, he handed it back and said, "Nothing. Usually, having something of the one you are seeking will elicit a connection, but I feel nothing."

"What does that mean?" Mel asked.

"It means it's going to take a lot more to find your mother than I first thought," Hermes said. "My suggestion is to start at the Elektrai Gate. If she was brought to Thebes, that is likely the gate she entered through. Maybe someone saw something."

"That's it?" Thalia asked. "That's your advice?"

"It's more than you had before," Hermes retorted.

"Thank you," Calli said, shooting Thalia an angry look. "How exactly do we get to this Elektrai Gate?"

"Well, you've got to go back down to the agora," he said.

"Not the steps again," Mel and Thalia said together.

"Nah. There's an easier way down." He looked to Apollo. "Do you mind giving the girls a lift?"

"No," Apollo replied.

Hermes put two fingers in his mouth and released a loud whistle.

A moment later, a chariot pulled by four extraordinarily large horses flew inside the temple. They went directly to Apollo, who produced shiny apples from somewhere inside his robe.

"That's not a golden apple, is it?" Hermes asked.

Apollo shook his head. "We don't want that kind of trouble again."

"Hop in," Hermes said, pointing to the chariot. "Apollo's mighty steeds will get you down there in no time."

"You mean we don't have to worry about those steps?" Thalia asked. "Oh, honey, you just went from zero to hero." She snapped her fingers. "Just like that."

"Thalia!" Clio chastised.

"Well, thank you." Hermes preened. "Just keep in mind that the horses can only take you as far as the base of the steps. From there, you'll walk straight that way." He motioned with both arms, pointing in the direction of the Great Sea. "The Elektrai is the most ornate of the seven gates leading into Thebes. You can't miss it."

When Ree looked at each of her sisters, she saw the same apprehension that she felt staring back at her.

"Well?" Thalia said. "Are we getting in?"

Did they have a choice?

As always, Calli led the way, climbing into the waiting chariot and helping each of her sisters to come in behind her.

"One minute," Apollo said. He reached inside his chiton and

produced a small flute. “If you need to get in touch, just blow out a little tune on this. It will save you from having to climb these steps again.”

“Ah, good idea,” Hermes said. “I’m always flittering around. I’ll come to you. Now, go on. If I find out anything else, I’ll let you know.”

With a wave, Apollo and Hermes sent them on their way.

XVI

CALLI

Calli's stomach dropped as the chariot glided past the hundreds of steps that had taken them hours to climb. Her queasy stomach wasn't the only thing to contend with on their swift journey down to the agora. Her head was still reeling from what had just taken place in the temple at Thebes.

The gods had answered their call!

Well, two of the gods had answered their call, but that was more than Calli could have hoped for. Clio constantly reminded them about how fickle the Olympian gods could be, and how they barely tolerated the mortals who worshipped and revered them. But both Apollo and Hermes had offered their assistance.

No, they had not just offered their assistance—she and her sisters had earned it! Apollo had tried to remain impassive, but Calli had caught the gleam in his eyes several times throughout their performance. She'd even noticed a flicker of a smile when she had dramatically recounted the moment he shot Python with the bow and arrow.

It was disappointing that neither remembered her mother. That made Calli question if what their mother had shared with them was true. If she *had* been a goddess, wouldn't the gods have remembered her?

She abhorred how distrustful she now felt toward her own mother, but the only way to gain that trust back was to hear Mnemosyne's explanation. To do that, they had to find her, and now, with the help of Hermes and Apollo, they would. She could feel it.

Their chariot landed at the base of the steps, in a spot hidden away by one of the larger columns.

"Thank you," Mel said, brushing each stallion's gorgeous mane as she climbed out of the chariot. They all responded with excited neighs.

"They like you," Thalia said.

"All animals like her," Ree pointed out. "The chickens lay more eggs for Mel than for any of the rest of us."

"It's because I take the time to get to know them," Mel said.

Once they had all alighted from the chariot, they made their way around the base of the massive column and back into the frenetic fray of the square. It seemed as if even more people now swarmed around the area.

"Before we go any farther, we need a plan," Clio said.

"I thought the plan was to go to that gate," Thalia said.

"And then what?" Clio asked. "We have no idea what we are looking for at the gate. Do we begin asking random people if they saw our mother? That is nonsensical. We must be deliberate in how we go about this." She pointed to Calli. "Hand me that journal."

Calli hesitated only a moment before complying. She knew better than to get in Clio's way when she was like this.

"I keep going back to Mother's last words to us," Clio said. "She said this will tell us everything we need to know. There must be more to her writing than what we've uncovered. We need to figure out what we are missing."

She returned to the steps that led to the temple and sat with the journal in her lap. Clio's forehead creased in concentration as she studied their mother's words.

"What do you think she means by this? 'Beware the one whose flame burns hot and cold. He knows more than he should.' Do you think she was trying to tell us to beware of the blacksmith?"

Calli hunched her shoulders. "I've never known mother to have an issue with the blacksmith in any of the towns or villages where we've lived."

Clio's forehead furrowed with concentration as she went back to reading. A few moments later, she pointed to a page with a sketch of a reed pen.

"Look at this one. It says that the flower's skill with a pen will help her to conquer anything. What flower uses a pen?"

Calli frowned as something occurred to her. "Doesn't she mention flowers in other parts of the journal? I remember something about a flower using its voice."

"And knowing when to laugh and when to be serious," Mel said. "I remember you reading that part."

"Maybe she wants us to look for the garden she planted with Artemis," Ree said. "It must be a flower garden."

"No," Clio said. "I don't think those are the flowers." She looked around at them, a curious smile tilting up the corners of her lips. "But I think I know who the flowers are."

"Did you hit your head while we were in that chariot?" Thalia asked.

"Think about it, Thalia!" said Clio. "What do you do with flowers? You plant the seeds, then you tend to them and nurture them and watch them grow. And whom has Mother tended to and nurtured and watched grow?"

"We are her flowers!" Ree, Mel, and Calli said at the same time.

Clio pointed to the journal. "The flower's skill with a pen? Who is skilled with a pen?"

They all turned to Calli.

"Mother said the journal has everything we need to know. I believe she left clues about each of us. We just have to figure out what they mean."

"Well, can't we figure it out while we're walking to that gate Flutter-Feet told us to go to?" Thalia asked.

"Thalia's right. We need to head to the Elektrai Gate," Calli said. "But I think you may have unlocked the most important clue, Clio. That journal has something to do with all of us, not just

Mother." She reached over and captured her sister's hand. "We'll figure it out together. But now let us go to the gate."

Once again, they headed for the center of the square. It teemed with people, more people than Calli had ever seen in her life.

"Remember, we are not in Krymmenos anymore," she told her sisters. "Be vigilant. Keep your eyes open."

Just to the right of them, two men dressed in the soot-covered garments of charcoal burners began to argue. Their verbal squabbling quickly escalated, and they soon appeared to be on the verge of a physical fight.

"Stay close together," Calli said. She took Thalia by the hand, suddenly overwhelmed by the need to protect her sisters. "Hermes said we are to head in the direction of the Great Sea. It looks as if this road will take us there."

Shoulder to shoulder, they trekked through the crowded street. They were jostled back and forth by the crush of bodies. Out of the corner of her eye, Calli noticed that Mel had stepped away from them. She thought maybe she had caught sight of a stray dog and had gone to pet it—something she often did—but then realized that she was heading straight toward an elderly man with deeply wrinkled skin and sunken eyes. He stood just under the portico surrounding the square.

"Mel!" Calli called. She took off for her. "What are you doing?"

Mel stuck her hand out toward Calli, staving her off.

"Melpomene!" Calli said. "Get back here."

Mel shook her head. She shrugged off the hand Calli tried to clamp onto her shoulder.

The rest of the girls caught up with them just as Mel reached the old man.

"Hello," Mel said to him. She tipped her head to the side. "Are you well, sir?"

The man looked to his right and to his left. He then reached inside his robe and withdrew a small marble jar, like the one their mother kept her most prized perfumed oil in.

"Here. Take it," he told Mel.

"What is that, Mel?" Calli asked.

She shook her head. "I don't know. Why are you giving this to me?"

"Just take it," said the old man.

"Do I open it?" she asked.

"You will know when it is time to look inside."

"Give it back to him," Calli said, reaching for the jar so that she could return it to its owner. But Mel extended it just out of her grasp.

"No!" Mel said.

"Mel, it is dangerous to take things from strange people," Ree said.

"We were considered strange people once, remember?" she shot back. In a calmer voice, she said, "Let it be. I . . . I don't know why, but I get a sense that this is important. Something about him called to me. I didn't hear it, but I felt it."

"Well, if it's important, open it," Ree said.

"Not yet." She held the small jar against her stomach. "It's too soon."

She took the bags that held the items they had brought as sacrifices to the gods and placed the jar in one. Then she hauled the strap on her shoulder and wrapped it around her torso until the jar sat secure against her stomach.

"We should continue," Mel said.

Calli had a bad feeling about this, but trying to reason with Mel when she got into one of her stubborn moods was useless.

They continued toward the Elektrai Gate. Calli could tell when they reached their destination by the four large towers anchoring each corner. The towers were built into the fortified wall to allow for the best vantage point to spot those who might dare invade Thebes. They were connected by balustrades with evenly spaced battlements that Calli was sure hid soldiers ready to defend the city.

"What now?" Ree asked.

"Look for merchants," Clio said. "Anyone who looks as if they are near the gate on a regular basis. They would have a better idea if something out of the ordinary recently occurred, like a strange woman being dragged by force into the city."

Genius! Calli had always known her sister possessed an acute intellect, but Clio's insight since their arrival in Thebes seemed even sharper.

Calli was about to respond to her when she heard a slightly familiar voice making its way through the crowd.

"Excuse me. Pardon me. Make some room." A short man with unusually large ears, ears that looked almost like wings, walked up to them. "I've got some information for you."

Calli's eyes widened, then narrowed. "Hermes?"

"Shhh . . ." He looked over each of his shoulders. "Not so loud." He leaned toward her and, in a lowered voice, said, "We gods like to keep a low profile when we're walking among the masses here in Thebes. Anyway, according to the information I was given, what you're seeking will be on the other end of that white door."

He pointed at a door just across from where they were standing.

"What we're seeking?" Calli asked. "Do you mean our mother?"

"Based on the intel I gathered." He nodded. "Well, what are you waiting for? Get moving."

"Let us rescue Mother," Calli said, excitement pulsing through her as she flattened her hand against the door and pushed it open. She walked over the threshold and stopped so quickly that Mel and Clio both bumped into her.

She stood face to face with a limestone wall. To her left was a narrow passageway that seemed to lead to nothing but blackness.

"Hey, what's going on here?" Thalia asked. "I thought Mr. Flutter-Feet said that what we were looking for was on the other side of this door."

"He said the other *end* of this door," Ree reminded them. "So where does this end?"

"Maybe there is another clue in Mother's journal," Calli said. She pulled it out and flipped through the pages, but there was nothing about narrow passageways.

"Well, Hermes sent us here," Thalia said. "He's going to have to explain this one to me."

She turned and pushed on the door they had just entered through, but it did not budge.

"Oh, nuh-uh," Thalia said. She banged against the door. "I know we're not stuck in here. Open up!"

The five of them began pushing against the door but could not get it to move in the slightest.

"There's no going back," Calli said. "We can only go forward."

"Where?" Thalia motioned around them. "Where are we supposed to go?"

Calli noticed Clio staring at something just beyond her shoulder. She turned to see what had caught her sister's eye.

"What is it, Clio?" she asked.

Clio pointed at the wall. "There's something etched there." She moved in closer and read aloud: " 'There is only one path, amazing as it may be. If you don't veer from it, daylight you will soon see.' "

"That doesn't make one bit of sense," Thalia said.

" 'Amazing as it may be,' " Clio repeated slowly. She closed her eyes and repeated the words. "Amazing as it may be. Amazing." Her eyes popped open. "A maze! It's a maze, girls!" She tapped a finger against the side of her head. "Actually, a labyrinth seems more likely."

"I'm confused. I thought this was the gate," Ree said.

"It is," Clio said. "It's the Elektrai Gate *and* a labyrinth. It makes sense. Rulers often have labyrinths built within the city gates and the walls connected to them as a means of confusing the enemy. I thought everyone knew this."

The four of them just stared at her.

"Never mind," Clio said. She grabbed Calli by the arm and positioned her toward the corridor. "It says there is only one path—which is why I think it is a labyrinth as opposed to a maze, which would have multiple paths. We just need to stay on the path, and we'll eventually get there."

Calli took the lead, guiding them through the narrow corridor. It was a peculiar space, with the halls narrowing so much that the girls had to walk sideways to get through several patches, and then expanding to where the sisters could walk side by side.

"What is the rationale behind the expanding and contracting walls?" Ree asked.

Clio shrugged. "I don't know everything." Then she tacked on in a cheeky tone, "Just *almost* everything."

A few days before, Calli would have called her on her arrogance, but so far Clio's smarts had taken them further than the help they'd received from the gods.

"How much longer are we going to walk around this place?" Thalia asked.

"Until we reach the—" They came to another door. "End," Calli finished.

"Well, open it," Mel encouraged.

Calli did as they asked, opening the door and revealing a small boxy room with no other way out.

"Well, this wasn't the right path," Ree said.

"There was only one path," Clio said.

"Maybe we just didn't see the other path," Mel said. "Should we head back the way we came?"

That was when Calli noticed more writing on the walls.

"Wait a minute," she said. "What does that say?"

Clio went up to the writing. " 'Do not dither, do not delay. If you take too long, you will never see the light of day.' "

"Is that saying what I think it's saying?" Mel asked.

Calli's stomach dropped. "I think it's saying that we may get stuck here if we take too long to get to the end of this labyrinth."

"Stuck?" Thalia asked. "In here? No. No, no, no, no, no."

She bolted, running back the way they had come. The rest of them took off after her.

Thalia made her way back through the corridors much more quickly than she had on the first pass, dipping low to the ground so she could squeeze through the narrow parts and sprinting through the rest. But when she reached the door where they'd first gained entrance, she found only the outline of a door etched into the limestone. A mere drawing.

"Why is this happening!" Thalia yelled. "We cannot get stuck in here."

"We will never reach Mother," Ree said. "What if she dies?"

"We're all gonna die," Mel screamed.

"Calm down!" Clio shouted. She brought her hands to her temples and rubbed them. "I need to think. I can get us out of this if you give me time."

"We don't have time," Thalia said.

"Thalia, shush," Calli said. She stepped up to Clio and braced her hands on her shoulders. "Do you think you can get us out of here?"

"Is there something in that journal about a flower that knows its way around a labyrinth?" Thalia asked.

"No, there's nothing like that in the journal," Calli said. She stopped short. "Wait a minute!"

She retrieved the journal from her satchel, her fingers trembling with anticipation. Flipping through it, she searched for a passage she remembered reading before going to bed at the inn the night before.

Perception will blossom as a thirst for knowledge blooms. Feed it and watch it grow. The world will harvest wisdom if this flower is allowed to glow.

"Right here," Calli said. She showed the passage to Clio. "This is you. You are perceptive, and knowledgeable, and wise beyond your years. You can get us out of here. Mother gave you the ability to do this when she created you."

Clio's forehead furrowed with her frown. "Do you really think so?"

"Absolutely." Calli nodded. "You figured out that this was a labyrinth. I know you can solve this puzzle."

Calli could see her sister's confidence growing with each word she spoke to her. Clio tightened her hands into fists and nodded.

"Follow me," she said.

With a determination Calli had never seen in her before, Clio took over, leading them back through the corridors. When they arrived at the first expanded passageway, Clio held her hand up, halting their forward progress.

"Wait," Clio said. "I've seen this before. Theseus and the Minotaur. Of course!"

"Clio, what are you talking about?"

"It's the labyrinth from the myth of Theseus and the Minotaur. It has been quite some time since I read the story, but I see it clearly in my mind. But how can that be?"

"What?" Calli asked.

"I don't understand how I can see it so clearly. Something has shifted in my mind, and I can see the picture as if I were staring at it this very second. And the story, as well. I remember it word for word.

"This is the labyrinth that King Minos commissioned. The

fluctuating width of the corridor is an illusion meant to confuse us, but we will not fall for it. And that room we thought had no exit . . ." she continued, sprinting toward the small room that had stumped them the first time. "There *is* a way out."

The words echoed, as if they were spoken from far off. When Calli arrived at the entrance of the room, it was empty.

"Clio?" she called.

"This way!" her sister said.

Calli looked in the direction of the voice and noticed Clio's hand waving them forward. It appeared to be floating in the middle of the wall.

"Wait," Calli said. "Is that—?"

"It's two walls," Clio said, poking her head out from behind what Calli could now see was a shorter wall. "From a distance it looks as if it's one solid wall, but it isn't. The path continues this way. Come on."

"What madman built this thing?" Thalia said.

"It's making me dizzy," Mel added.

"Just keep moving," Ree said. "Follow Clio. It looks as if she knows what she's talking about."

They continued through the narrow passageway.

"I see light!"

Clio's excited yelp made them all jump, but when Calli looked in the direction her sister pointed and made out the tiny speck of light herself, she could not contain her glee. They ran toward the light.

CALLI

When they reached their destination, Calli was surprised to find a room like the one they had first entered in this labyrinth, except this one was even smaller. And their mother was nowhere to be found.

"This is the end, isn't it?" Ree said. "There's nowhere else to go."

They all spun in a slow circle, looking up at the ceiling and at the floor. Thalia began patting down the walls, and Calli immediately joined her. Soon all five of them were running their hands along the walls of the small room, searching for a trick wall like the one they had encountered in the previous room.

"Nothing," Mel said once they had covered every bit of the area. She put her back against the wall and slid down to the floor. Covering her face in her hands, Mel began to sob. "We'll never find Mother."

"Don't say that," Ree admonished.

"Girls, over here," Clio said.

She left the tiny room and returned to the corridor. That was when Calli noticed a thin line in the limestone wall. Clio pushed at it, and it moved the tiniest bit.

"Help me!" she called, and they all ran to the wall and began pushing. It took great effort, but soon they were able to move the stone far enough to escape the labyrinth.

They tumbled out and back onto the streets of Thebes.

"There you are!" Calli looked up to find Hermes staring down at her and her sisters. "I've been looking all over for you girls." His mouth pulled down in an apologetic frown. "I'm sorry to have to tell you this, but it turns out I got some bad information."

"What makes you think you were misinformed?" Calli asked.

He leaned in close. "I pride myself on my ability to deliver the correct message—after all, I'm the messenger, it's what I do—but when I returned to my source after talking to you and your sisters, he was adamant that it was the first time he'd spoken to me today." He shook his head. "I thought it was strange that he'd changed out of the crimson robe he'd been wearing earlier."

"Crimson robe?" Calli asked.

"Where did you see a crimson robe?" Thalia asked. "Take us to him."

Hermes held his hands up. "Wait, wait, wait. Why are you ladies so worked up about a crimson robe?"

"Because one of the ruffians who took our mother wore a crimson robe," Ree said.

The people who took their mother knew they were here to find her. And it would seem they were one step ahead of them.

XVII

MNEMOSYNE

An overwhelming sense of distress startled Mnemosyne out of her fitful sleep. The feeling washed over her like a wave, stealing the breath from her lungs.

"Girls," she said in a frantic whisper, pushing herself up from the floor. Her girls were in trouble.

She could feel them, despite the barriers separating them. The dungeon Hades had stashed her in couldn't stop that connection, a link hewn out of pure love.

Mnemosyne began to pace back and forth inside the tiny cell. She had never tried to reach her girls through the power of their bond, but she had never had a reason. She had always kept them close to her.

She thought to call out to Mel, her most empathetic daughter, but then she stopped. Even if she could reach her, Mnemosyne could not be sure if Melpomene would know how to accept the call. Would Mel even understand what was happening?

She had caused such turmoil already with her hasty, incomplete explanation of their creation. To cause even more chaos by invading Mel's mind was unthinkable.

At least she could still feel them. And because she felt the connection even though she was certain Hades had done everything he could to cut her off from both the divine and mortal realms, Mnemosyne could only deduce that her girls were close.

They were searching for her!

Did that mean that they had discovered the journal Mnemosyne kept hidden in her favorite tree? She had been too afraid to hope that they would be able to follow the vague instructions she'd shouted as she was dragged out of her home by Hades's henchmen, but she should never have doubted her girls. She had created them to be the most intelligent, most compassionate, and most creative beings either world had ever known.

Once they figured out how to harness the unique gifts she had bestowed on each of them, Mnemosyne was certain her girls would find her. But finding her was only the first task. If Mnemosyne could not figure out a way to break out of this dungeon, her girls would have to get past Hades to rescue her.

They would need assistance. There were few Olympians she would trust with her girls, and only one she had enough faith in to have left clues that, with luck, would guide her daughters to her. She was counting on their quick wit to decipher what she'd written in the journal about Athena.

Would her old friend be willing to help, or had she moved on, caring so little that she wouldn't even give her daughters a second glance?

"Please don't hold my past actions against me," Mnemosyne whispered.

Athena had been eager to help Mnemosyne once—maybe she would do the same for her girls.

Mnemosyne relished the feel of the cool dirt as she glided her fingers through it. When Athena asked if she wanted to join her in a garden she and Artemis kept in Thessalia, a region of the mortal world in the valley of Olympus, Mnemosyne's first instinct had been to turn down the invitation. She still had a hard time trusting anyone, even the gods who had gone out of their way to befriend her. She was trying to let go of her misgivings, though, especially around Athena.

She also had never gardened before and did not want to cause any harm to Artemis's beautiful flowers. But Athena assured her that the blooms were sturdy and could withstand whatever Mnemosyne did to them.

It turned out that she enjoyed it and had become quite good at it.

"My lilies are progressing nicely," Mnemosyne said over her shoulder. "Maybe it is time I attempt to grow roses."

"With Artemis's tutelage, you can grow anything, my friend," Athena called to her. "Just look at me. I had no interest in gardening until she dragged me to this part of the mortal world. Now I have my hands in the dirt whenever I can."

Mnemosyne laughed at Athena's confounded expression before she resumed tending to her lilies. The deep green shoots were at least two feet tall, with blooms that flourished under the sun's warm rays.

Suddenly, Mnemosyne heard the snort—and in an instant, a wild hog appeared just steps in front of her. Its sharp tusks looked as if they could pierce her with barely any effort. Her limbs stiffened.

"Stay back," Athena ordered in a fierce whisper.

With precision that both fascinated and terrified Mnemosyne, the goddess quickly threw the spear she carried through the air, directly into the animal's side. The wild hog dropped to the ground.

Mnemosyne's jaw dropped along with it.

"That was amazing," she said.

"It is what I do." Athena shrugged, then went back to picking flowers as if she hadn't just saved Mnemosyne from certain death. "You should arm yourself with a bow and arrow for the occasions when you are tending to the garden alone."

"A bow and arrow would not be of any use to me," Mnemosyne said. "I have never held a bow."

Athena gasped. "Are you saying no one ever taught you how to wield a bow and arrow?"

"My brothers did not consider it important," she explained. "Although I believe the real reason I was never taught to hunt is because they were concerned I would try to use a weapon on them."

She would have been tempted. Some of her brothers were harsher than the others, but they were all ogres when it came to her.

"Well, your brothers have done you a grave disservice, one we will rectify this very moment." Athena set down the flowers she had just picked and lifted the hem of her gown. "Where is Artemis? This is a job for the two of us."

"But . . ." Mnemosyne looked to where the wild hog had first emerged, fearful that the animal had friends nearby.

But she hadn't needed to worry. Minutes later, with her trusty owl perched atop her shoulder, Athena returned with Artemis.

"What is this I hear? You never learned to use a bow and arrow?" Artemis asked.

"It is unacceptable," Athena said, stomping her foot.

Mnemosyne fought to hide her grin. The goddesses' outrage on her behalf both tickled and touched her. Her own siblings did not hold her in such regard, but these two did. She had never known the joy of having true friends until she came to Olympus.

"You should learn to protect yourself," Athena said. She

retrieved her spear from the dead boar's side and gripped the weapon in both hands. "Pay attention to my movements."

Mnemosyne could not deny her excitement. The Goddess of the Hunt and Goddess of Wisdom and Warfare were preparing to teach her how to fight! Athena wielded the spear with stunning ease, slicing through the air and piercing the imaginary foes attacking them. Using a spindly branch, Mnemosyne tried her best to mimic her actions, but spear fighting was much harder than it looked.

After she'd dropped the stick for the third time, Artemis scooped it from the ground and said, "If you're this bad with the spear, I don't think you are ready for the bow and arrow."

"Am I really that bad?" Mnemosyne said.

"Yes," Artemis and Athena answered. Then Artemis added, "But you will get better with practice. For now, observe."

Mnemosyne studied Artemis's posture, determined to glean as much as she could so that she could impress her friends.

"What do we have here?"

Mnemosyne, Artemis, and Athena whipped around simultaneously at the sound of Hades's voice. The strange feeling Mnemosyne got whenever she was around Hades began to settle in her bones. Maybe she was being unfair, but intuition compelled her to keep an eye on him.

"Ladies, ladies, ladies." Hades tsked *as he neared them. "We just ended a decade-long war. Why are you asking for another?"*

"No one is asking for war," Artemis said. "We are teaching Mnemosyne how to defend herself."

"Teaching a Titan to shoot? That is an . . . interesting choice." He came to stand next to Artemis. "However, if this is what you choose to do, at least do it correctly."

He held his hand out. Artemis rolled her eyes as she placed the bow and arrow in his hand.

"It's been a while since I played around with such toys," Hades said.

"Well, while you play, we'll continue our lesson," Athena said.

She once again wielded her spear, twirling it like a small baton instead of a six-foot, pointed-edge weapon. Mnemosyne was mesmerized. She was also certain that, no matter how much she practiced, she would never have such command over a spear.

"I guess some would consider that impressive," Hades drawled.

Mnemosyne looked over to see him aiming his arrow at an oak tree, but then she gasped when he quickly turned his aim toward Athena.

"What are you doing?" Mnemosyne screamed.

"Oh, nothing. Just practicing my aim," he said. He shot the arrow at the tree as if nothing had happened.

To her dismay, both Artemis and Athena brushed it off in that same way she'd noticed many of the gods dismissing Hades's antics, but Mnemosyne could not shake the unsettling feeling that came over her. She didn't buy Hades's excuse and in that moment knew she would never fully trust him.

"I was right to be skeptical of you," Mnemosyne whispered.

Hades had shown his true colors to her a long time ago. But so had Artemis and Athena, and several of the other gods on Olympus. They had shown themselves to be true friends. Mnemosyne could only hope that her friends would come through for her again.

XVIII

REE

A pall had fallen over the sisters, much like the dark clouds that hovered over the city of Thebes that day. They sat in a row on the stone steps that led to the grand theater, their shoulders slumped. Clio had not even mentioned Calli's previous promise about looking inside the theater, and she never passed up the chance to explore structures like this one. But none of her sisters seemed capable of doing anything right now, other than reflecting on the disappointing outcome of their journey through the labyrinth.

Ree did not want to even entertain thoughts of their failing to find their mother, but if her captors could use such deception to confuse them—trickery that could fool even an Olympian god—they were facing an even bigger challenge than they'd expected.

They had endured that confusing ordeal for nothing, and that made her ill. Then again, at least their journey through that complicated labyrinth had helped her recognize the breadth of Clio's amazing ability to problem-solve. She wasn't sure Clio had truly recognized it until then, either. She'd sensed her sister's own surprise as she'd puzzled out each of the riddles.

Even so, Clio's hidden talent didn't make up for the fact that they were right back where they started in terms of finding their mother.

"This is just a minor setback," Thalia said with a conviction Ree couldn't bring herself to feel. "We've had our chance to wallow, but now it's time to keep our chins up!"

She pushed herself up from the steps and stood in front of her sisters.

"Why the sad faces?" Thalia asked. "Just look at where we are: Thebes, the grandest city of all. Why, even the rats that crawl in the gutters are grand. The one we passed earlier even smiled at me."

Ree couldn't help chuckling, and next to her, Mel laughed, too.

"You think I'm joking?" Thalia asked. "It looked at me just like this."

She made a funny face, fitting her two front teeth over her bottom lip and wiggling her nose.

Calli and Clio guffawed as well.

"And what about this odor?" Thalia asked. "Oh, wait, I think they call it an aroma. Who needs the pleasant scent of the sea when you can spend all day smelling garbage and sweat?" Thalia breathed in a healthy dose of air and began coughing. "See . . . what . . . I mean?"

Calli wiped tears of mirth from her eyes. "It's not as bad as all that."

Thalia laid the back of her hand across Calli's forehead. "Are you well, my dear sister? Or have you just lost your sense of smell?"

A woman with a collection of fat fish hanging from a string walked up to them.

"I don't smell anything, either," she said. She held the fish up to Thalia. "Can I interest you in mackerel? Caught fresh today."

Thalia shook her head. "I no longer eat anything that can look back at me."

"Not a problem," the woman said. She promptly plucked out the eyes of one of the fish.

Mel yelped, and Ree burst out laughing, along with a woman and child who must have heard their chatter and had come to investigate.

Count on Thalia to wrangle a laugh from her, even after the heartbreaking conclusion of their journey through the labyrinth.

Her sister continued her humorous musings about Thebes, making fun of the city's less than desirable traits, but in a way that had the local citizens stopping in the middle of their daily routines to listen and laugh.

After the day they'd had, Ree was grateful for her sister's ability to turn even the most depressing situations into a reason to smile. For a moment, she forgot about how upset she had been about their mother.

When Thalia picked up a stray feather from the ground and

began parading around, waving it back and forth in a dramatic fashion in an ode to the goddess Hera, who was known to have a pet peacock, the entire crowd erupted in good-natured laughs. Then she pretended to be Zeus so that she could strike down a pottery maker who had come out of his shop to see what all the ruckus was about, and the crowd nearly had a collective apoplexy.

Ree laughed so hard at the poor man's confused expression that she developed a stitch in her side. As she stretched out, she looked up at the sky and noticed something strange.

The low-hanging clouds had begun to dissipate.

Ree leaned over and said to Clio, "Have you noticed the change in the sky since Thalia began entertaining the crowds?"

Clio tipped her head back. "Ah, *that's* what's different. I could not put my finger on it. I just felt this . . . I don't know . . . this lightness."

"So did I," Calli said from where she sat to the right of Clio. "But it wasn't until you mentioned it that I made the connection between Thalia and the clouds. It is almost as if she is moving them away with her words."

"It's not just the clouds," Clio said, gesturing to the crowd that had gathered. "Look at what is happening here. These are the same people who seemed to be drowning in despair. Now they are filled with merriment."

With each joke Thalia delivered, the gloom waned, and joy swept into its place.

Ree pointed to two men covered in soot. "Aren't those the same two men who had been on the verge of fighting while we were on our way back from the temple? Look at them now."

One man had his arm draped over the other's shoulder, and they were both leaning on each other, physically having to hold themselves up or risk falling over from laughing.

"What is happening?" Ree asked.

"I'm not sure," Calli said. "It is very peculiar, though, isn't it? Thalia's penchant for joking can be a pleasant distraction on occasion—when she isn't annoying me," Calli added. "But when the emotion you make people feel has the power to chase the clouds away, it isn't something to take lightly. Something very special is happening here."

"It is extraordinary," Clio agreed.

"It's remarkable," Mel said. She gestured to the crowd. "Just look at their faces. They're all so happy." She brought her hand to her chest. "I can *feel* their happiness."

"It is like you said," Ree told Calli. "Thalia's ability to distract people from their troubles is most significant. It's powerful to forget about your trials for even a short amount of time." She hunched her shoulders. "I will confess that I temporarily forgot about Mother's predicament."

Ree looked over at Thalia, who continued to entertain the crowd as the few lingering clouds floated away. Then she bowed to her audience and accepted applause. Once the crowd dispersed, Ree and her sisters ran up to Thalia and enveloped her in a hug.

"You were sensational," Ree said.

"Spectacular," Mel added.

"Outstanding," Clio said.

"I *was* all those things, wasn't I?" Thalia replied. But then, in a more serious voice, she said, "I am not sure how to describe what just happened. I looked at the people who had gathered and saw how much they needed to smile. And the words just came to me."

Clio snapped her fingers. "The journal. What did it say about the flower learning when to laugh and when to be serious?"

"You're right!" Calli said as she retrieved the journal. She found the page and pointed to it. "My *young* flower," Calli said. "Thalia, you are Mother's youngest flower. Your humor is your gift!"

"Do you really think so?" Thalia said.

"Of course," Mel said. "You lifted their hearts." She cocked her head to the side. "It was the strangest thing, but it was as if I could feel their burdens drifting away."

"Just as the clouds have." Ree pointed upward.

"I found my gift," Thalia whispered, her voice colored with wonder and awe.

"And it is an unusual gift you have," Calli said. "Unusual and powerful. I'm sure we all felt it."

The other sisters all nodded in reply.

Calli put her hands on both of Thalia's shoulders. "I am proud of you. And I know Mother would be proud, also."

Ree wasn't sure where the feeling came from, but she suddenly had an overwhelming sense that Thalia's ability to distract them all with laughter would eventually work in their favor.

XIX

CALLI

They were all still laughing at Thalia's shenanigans as they made their way back toward the center of the agora, but Calli noticed that Mel seemed a bit distant. Instead of sharing in the fun, she had that peculiar look on her face again, the one she'd had when approaching the man who had given her the jar she still carried in its sling close to her chest. She would focus on people as they passed, her expression shifting from sad to fearful to surprised and even to disgusted.

"Mel, are you okay?" Calli asked.

Her sister looked at her. "I'm not sure."

Calli's chest tightened with worry. "Do you feel ill?"

"No, no. It's nothing like that," Mel said. "Just . . . I'm fine. Don't worry about me."

They came upon a young mother holding a baby. When Mel spotted them, she placed her free palm over heart.

"What's wrong, Mel?" Calli asked, her concern growing.

"I . . . I don't know," Mel said. "I don't know why she is hurting, but she is."

"Who?"

"The mother," Mel said, gesturing with her head to the woman and child. "She is trying to be strong for her baby, but she is going through a very hard time. So many of these people are, Calli. I can feel it deep in my bones. It is like the sadness I sensed in the crowd before Thalia began entertaining them."

Calli was tempted to brush this off as her sister being her normal dramatic self, but there was something different this time.

"You do not seem like yourself, Mel."

"I don't feel like myself," she said. "It is difficult to describe, but it is as if I can look inside someone and feel everything they truly feel." She shook her head. "Maybe I am just tired."

Calli wasn't so sure about that. It was obvious something strange was going on with her and her sisters here in Thebes, and it made her wonder if this was why their mother had always been so adamant about their never coming here. Maybe it was never about the danger of the big city. It might have been a danger of a different kind.

They kept walking, and Mel continued to point out people who seemed to be indifferent on the outside, but who she insisted felt deep turmoil on the inside.

"I wish there were something I could do for them all," Mel said.

"What about the jar?" Calli asked. "Maybe the answer to their problems lies within it."

Myriad emotions moved across Mel's face before her sister finally shook her head. "No. Not yet. It does not feel right."

"Are you sure, Mel?"

She hesitated, then nodded. "Yes, I'm sure."

They arrived at a small park in the middle of the agora and decided to stop and have a meal. The five of them sat underneath a tree, eating bread, honey, and the figs they had bought from the roadside merchant on their way into the city. As hungry as she was, Calli found she was even more in need of sleep, but for now, she must gain whatever sustenance she could from their meal so that she could figure out what to do about their mother next.

She licked a bit of honey from her fingers, then reached inside her satchel for her mother's journal. She pored over the pages once more, searching for some clue as to what she should do, where they should go, whom they should reach out to. As she examined the faint writing, one line caught her eye.

My flowers will be a gift to the world, one that will bring joy and help the masses to forget all their trouble.

She looked down at the sentence, then up at Thalia, then back at the sentence again.

Ree had mentioned that, while listening to Thalia, she'd forgotten about the problems they faced for a time. Calli realized that the same had happened for her, and it was obvious the residents of Thebes—the masses—had found Thalia's performance diverting, too. She thought back to their singing for Apollo and Hermes, and how much the two gods had enjoyed it.

Calli drew her fingertips across the writing. Had her mother known they would one day come to provide such entertainment for crowds of people? Had she designed it to be that way? If so, why had she forbidden them from performing outside of the house?

Calli's back went ramrod straight.

Every time they shared their talent, they discovered that one of them had a unique gift. Clio had always possessed a keen mind and an ability to remember and recite facts after hearing them only once, but after they performed that skit for Apollo and Hermes, Clio's powerful intelligence had amplified. Just as Thalia's ability to make people laugh and forget their troubles had intensified so much that it cleared the clouds away and brought in sunshine. Calli gingerly flipped back to the pages she'd read earlier, reading over the other clues they had uncovered regarding her mother's *flowers*, searching for something that would explain the peculiar sensation Mel was feeling.

The heart can be as delicate as the petals of a rose, but strength lies in the empathy and kindness it possesses.

Empathy.

Mel had described sensing what strangers around her were *really* feeling, and not just the image they projected to the world. That must be her gift.

They had already established that they indeed were the flowers her mother had written about, but the more she thought about it, the more things started to fit together. The journal was not just a guide to how her mother had created them, but to *why* she had created them.

She recalled Mnemosyne's parting words.

It will tell you everything you need to know.

"Girls," Calli called, gesturing for her sisters to all scoot closer. "I think I have figured out why Mother wanted me to find her journal."

"I already figured that out," Clio said. "It contains the story of our creation that she never got the chance to tell us."

"There's more to it," Calli said. "We were created for a reason."

"Because Mother wanted daughters?" Mel asked.

"Yes, but it's more than that," Calli said. "We were not created to just exist; we are meant to do more. Something remarkable happens every time we perform. Think about it. . . . All of this started with our very first public performance. That is why Mother never wanted us to sing outside of the house—because she knew there was power in our gifts."

"But how do any of these gifts help us find Mother?" Ree asked.

Calli's shoulders sagged. "I'm not sure yet. However, there must be a connection. Why else would Mother have told us to look for her journal?"

Clio leaned over and pored over the pages along with her. Calli flipped a page and Clio pointed to a drawing.

"Wait a minute," she said. "Is that a sunburst?"

"It appears to be," Calli said. "Almost looks like the one . . ."

They both looked at each other. "On Apollo's pendant," they said in unison.

"He's connected to Mother, even if he doesn't realize it," Calli said.

"Maybe that is why he enjoyed our performance as much as he did. He pretended he wasn't all that moved by it, but I can tell he was."

"Of course he was," Calli said. "He was so moved by our talent that it inspired him to offer help. But what if we put on an even more elaborate performance? I think we could entice even more of the gods to help us!"

"Hmm, I'm not sure about this," Clio said, pulling her bottom lip between her teeth. "When you think about it, how much help have Apollo and Hermes really provided?"

Her sister had a point. But Calli wasn't ready to give up on the gods just yet.

"Maybe we haven't found the right one," she said. "If we could get the attention of more of them, we may discover that one of the gods actually remembers Mother."

"That's a possibility," Clio said. "It still feels as if I'm missing something. What was it that Mother said about the bird? The one that flies at night?"

Calli had forgotten about that. "I'm still not sure what she meant by that, but maybe one of the gods will know." She scrambled up from the ground. "We have to go back to the temple, girls. We need to call on Apollo."

"We don't have to go anywhere," Thalia said. "We have this, remember?" She reached in her bag and brought out the gleaming gold flute Apollo had given them. "Shall I do the honors?"

Mere moments after Thalia played a few notes on the flute, a broad-shouldered man dressed in garb usually worn by farmers appeared.

"You called?" Apollo said. He motioned to his clothing and explained, "I cannot very well be seen in my normal attire."

"I like it," Ree said.

He smiled at her. "I wondered when I would hear from you little songbirds again. Hermes told me about the way things went at the Elektrai Gate. That was unfortunate. But it sounds as if you are not letting it get you down." He pointed to Thalia. "You must be the jolly girl everyone has been talking about."

"Me?" Thalia pressed both palms to her chest. "*I'm* being talked about?"

He nodded. "You made quite an impression on the people of Thebes. Even Dionysus noticed, and he's usually so wrapped up in himself that he doesn't pay attention to anyone else."

"Dionysus?" Thalia screamed. "He's the fun one!"

"Thalia, please," Ree said.

"He knows how to have a good time, just like me!"

Apollo folded his arms across his massive chest and rolled his eyes, but then his mouth tipped up in a grin.

"I like you, despite your questionable opinions of the gods." He looked at each of them. "In fact, I like all of you. You have a certain style, a presence."

"We do," Calli said with conviction. "I have an idea that I think you may be able to help us pull off. We would like to attract more of the gods on Olympus to help in our quest to find our mother, and I believe a concert would do it."

"Do you now?" He brought his fingers up to his chin and rubbed. "The gods do love a good show."

"Now, I know that *you* are the one who is usually doing the entertaining—from what I have heard, your voice is incomparable," Calli said. "However, I don't think the gods would mind something a little different."

"And just what are you seeking from this concert?" Apollo asked.

"We hope that one of the other gods remembers our mother from her time on Olympus. If they do, maybe they could give us some insight into who kidnapped her. Too much time has passed already. We must do something drastic."

"Summoning all of the gods down to Thebes for a concert is

drastic," Apollo said. "Because if you fail to entertain them, the consequences may be a bit . . ."

He wiggled his hand.

"We're willing to take the risk," Calli said.

"We are?" Thalia asked.

"Yes," Calli said. "So, Apollo, will you help us pull off the biggest concert Thebes has ever seen?"

XX

MNEMOSYNE

Mnemosyne rehearsed the words she would say when Hades next came to interrogate her, practicing until the deal she would offer him sounded enticing rather than forced. Hades was not stupid; he would see right through her sudden desire to join his quest to overthrow Zeus.

But she could not simply sit there in hopes of being rescued. If she convinced Hades that she was willing to use her powers for his benefit, perhaps he would let his guard down—and she could wipe his memories clean yet again. But she could not touch his memories until she figured out where he'd brought her and the best way to escape.

Mnemosyne thought back to the last time she'd made a deal with one of the Olympians. But that deal had given someone else the upper hand. She replayed the memory in her head, vowing not to make the same mistakes again.

BEMUSED

A warm, comforting breeze blew across Mnemosyne's face as she picked wildflowers from the field near her tiny home on Olympus. The heavy rain showers of late had nourished the thirsty lands, providing refreshment to all who lived there.

It felt as if they were finally entering a time of new growth, something that had been promised at the conclusion of the Great War. Athena had also promised her eventual freedom, but Mnemosyne had known better than to hold her breath. The warrior goddess, who had proven to be a loyal friend over the years, was not in a position to make her any promises. The only one who could grant her freedom was the one who ruled over them all.

"Mnemosyne."

She froze at the sound of his voice. It was as if she had conjured him by merely thinking about him. She put away the foolish thought. Her mind was powerful, but it wasn't that powerful.

She turned and allowed a small smile to grace her lips.

She knew she was expected to bow in his presence, but her mind immediately rejected the thought. Her gratitude for his sparing her in the Titanomachy only went so far. She was still his prisoner, no matter how quaint the jail he had provided.

"Hello, Zeus," Mnemosyne greeted. "I'm surprised to see you here in my little corner of Olympus."

"I rule this land," he said. "I take it as one of my duties to see that all is well."

"Oh, I thought that is why you dispatched Hermes," she said,

plucking a purple hyacinth from the patch growing at her feet. "Is it not his role to bring back news of all that is happening throughout the lands?"

"I rule this land," Zeus repeated. After a moment, he continued, "Tell me, Mnemosyne, how are you enjoying this freedom you have been granted?"

She could not fight the tight smile that drew across her lips. She had not had much contact with Zeus since the end of the war, but whenever their paths did *cross, he was sure to remind her that she was here only because of the grace he had given her and the six Titans who had sided with the Olympian gods during the war.*

Mnemosyne had lost contact with her family, although Athena told her that many of the residents in Athens sang the praises of her nephews Prometheus and Epimetheus for being champions of mortal causes. She wished she could speak to her sisters Themis and Phoebe, but it was probably for the best that she did not know where they were. They would all bring up memories that Mnemosyne did not want to recall.

"I very much enjoy my life here on Olympus. It is peaceful," she answered. She twirled the hyacinth around by its stem, looking intently between the bell-shaped blooms. "But I would not call the life I am currently living a free one."

"No? You have your own home, do you not?"

His tone had changed. Hardened. Mnemosyne recognized that she must proceed with caution.

"That is true, but I feel eyes upon me," she said, motioning around herself. She knew Zeus dispatched multiple guards to look in on her throughout the day. "If I were truly free, there would be no need for such."

"You are a Titan." His answer was spoken in that same curt tone. "A Titan with a powerful gift, at that. If you are not watched closely, you could use that gift against Olympus."

Zeus's keen insight demonstrated why he was such an effective leader. But he was also a man. And having grown up surrounded by male egos, Mnemosyne knew catering to his ego was one way to break through his tough wall.

An idea had been swirling around in her head for quite some time, and this seemed like the perfect opportunity to test it.

"What would it take to prove my loyalty to you and the other gods?" Mnemosyne asked, holding the hyacinth out to him. He stared at it but did not accept it. She tucked the stem behind her ear.

"You said it yourself," she continued. "I have a powerful gift, but I do not believe in using it for harm, especially against those who rescued me."

Zeus folded his arms over his chest. "You have my attention. What do you propose?"

"There is peace here on Olympus. The problem is everywhere else." She clasped her hands behind her back and walked slowly back and forth. "There has been such turmoil experienced by both

gods and mortals since the Titanomachy. I believe I can do something about it."

"I am the ruler of this land. What can you offer the people here that I cannot provide for them?"

"Solace," she answered. "And a diversion."

Zeus's forehead furrowed. "A diversion?"

"Yes. To help ease the pain of the war and bring joy. I can create a pleasant diversion that is powerful enough to vanquish even the strongest of bad memories. And I can credit it to you," she finished.

His brows arched with interest. She knew the proposition would appeal to him. The male ego never failed.

"Not only will the masses forever sing your praises for saving them from Titan rule, but they will associate you with feelings of warmth and safety and pleasure and all things good. It will be beautiful, Zeus. I promise."

Technically, she had delivered on that promise by creating the most beautiful, most compelling, most delightful beings the world had ever seen. She'd gifted them with the ability to bring joy to everyone, both god and mortal. She just hadn't granted Zeus control of them as she'd pledged, because she'd received information that made her doubt everything.

And since she'd broken that part of the deal, she had been

forced to shield her girls' extraordinary gifts from the world. During those early years, it had bothered her that others could not be entertained by Ree's dancing, or have their spirits lifted by Thalia's indomitable sense of humor. But Mnemosyne eventually came to accept that sharing the gifts that had been meant for the world was not as important as keeping her daughters safe.

Now, because of Hades, her girls were putting themselves at risk trying to find her.

She would break free from this cage before her girls endangered themselves any more than they already had. This should not be their fight. It should be hers. And she would win it by beating Hades at his own game.

XXI

REE

After their second meeting with Apollo, the girls had decided to turn in for the night and found lodging at an inn on the outskirts of the agora. They rented two separate rooms, one for Calli and Thalia and one for the other three.

Ree fell asleep the moment she lay on the soft bed.

Hours later, she felt the warmth of the sun on her face. She opened her eyes but immediately closed them. The clouds that had lifted during Thalia's impromptu comedy special on the steps of the theater had yet to return. She wondered how the people of Thebes felt about that. Did they welcome the sun, or did they enjoy the gloom because it was what was familiar to them?

She had started to have those same thoughts about Krymmenos. Her hometown was familiar, but surprisingly, she had taken to Thebes, too. The vibrancy of the city captivated her, outweighing the troubling despair that seemed to loom around every corner.

A thick braid flapped across her face, covering the sunbeam.

"Mel, move your hair," Ree said, pushing her sister on the shoulder.

"It is time for you both to wake up," Clio said.

Ree twisted on the surprisingly comfortable klinē she and Mel shared, pretending not to hear Clio.

A feather pillow connected with her head.

"Wake up," Clio repeated.

Ree groaned, but she knew she could not spend all day in bed. There was something important they must do today.

She popped up.

Their mother. They had to find their mother.

Ree scurried out of the bed, searching the room for her sandals.

"What do you think about Calli's concert idea?" she asked Clio.

"It's our best chance at summoning the other gods on Olympus," Calli said, stepping into the room.

Going by her haggard look, her sister hadn't gotten much sleep last night. Yet, despite the overall exhaustion on Calli's face, her eyes shone with an unmistakable zeal.

Calli held up the bound book they'd found in that tree back home.

"I've been reading through Mother's journal all night. There's still so much in here that does not yet make sense, but I ran across a drawing of an amphitheater—at least I think it's an amphitheater."

"And?" Ree asked.

"And don't you see?" Calli said as Thalia walked into the room. "It is our sign to put on the concert."

"We're putting on the concert?" Thalia asked, an excited smile stretching across her lips. She shimmied her shoulders. "Let's do it, honey. I'm ready."

"Ready for what?" Mel asked, rubbing her eyes.

"We're holding a concert for the gods of Olympus," Thalia answered.

"We are?" Mel sat up in bed, all vestiges of sleep gone. She pulled the braid she'd twisted her hair into the night before over her shoulder and began unfurling it. "When should we do it? And where?"

"It has to be the amphitheater, and the sooner, the better," Calli answered. "After spending last night reading, I am more convinced than ever that Mother's journal is the story of how she created us. There are clues about the gifts she instilled in each of us, and I believe those gifts, like Clio's extraordinary intelligence and Thalia's comedic talent, were activated once we began performing in public."

She walked over to Ree. "I think your dancing is by design. By our mother's design. She gifted you with that talent, which is why it comes so naturally to you."

Her dancing did come naturally to her, much more so than it did to any of her sisters or her students. Ree often found herself getting frustrated with how long it took others to catch on when she tried to teach them a new dance move. It wasn't the healthiest trait for a teacher to possess, but she was trying to work on it.

Was what she always thought of as an innate skill actually a gift from her mother?

"Like I suggested yesterday, we should use these talents to gain more of the gods' attention," Calli was saying. "Apollo and Hermes haven't been able to help us as much as we hoped they could, but maybe one of the other gods can."

"Is there a clue in the journal about what my talent might be?" Mel asked.

"Probably caring *too* much," Thalia said.

"You say that as if it is a bad thing," Mel told her.

"Actually, I think Thalia is right," Calli said. "But it is *not* a bad thing. From what I can tell, your gift is that you feel deeply. You can read the hearts of those around you."

"That is not a real talent," Mel said, her voice laced with disappointment.

"It is too," Calli said. "What is more significant, the mask people wear on the outside or who they truly are on the inside? You can look beyond the mask. That is not only a talent but also a precious, precious gift, Mel."

Ree grabbed Mel's hand. "She's right. We all jest about how dramatic you can be at times, but I envy how you're able to connect with everyone you meet. I probably would have more students enrolled in my dance school if I was better at connecting with people. It is a gift, Mel."

"Oh, Ree," Mel cried. And, in her dramatic way, her sister nearly knocked her to the floor with her fierce hug.

"You're . . . welcome," Ree said, peeling Mel's arms from around her neck. "What does the journal say about your talent, Calli?"

Calli pulled her bottom lip between her teeth and chewed. "I'm still trying to figure that out. I'm beginning to think it has to do with my love of storytelling, but I can't be sure."

"I'm sure it's in there somewhere," Mel said. "Maybe it's your ability to guide us the way that you do. You're so good at leading us in the right direction."

Calli hunched her shoulders. "Maybe."

"Well, I'm still uncertain about holding a concert," Ree said, getting back to the matter at hand. "Considering Mother's outburst at my studio, I would think it is the last thing she would want us to do."

"You've got a point there," Thalia said. "I've never seen Mother so upset."

"But *why* was she upset?" Clio asked, a look of understanding making its way across her face. She stood and, like their mother, began to pace as she spoke. "Mother was upset because she said our performance would bring attention."

"Which it did," Mel pointed out. "It is very likely how those awful men found her."

"Exactly!" Clio said. "Our performance in Krymmenos brought unwanted attention, but this time we *want* the attention. The attention of the gods."

"That doesn't make . . ." Thalia cocked her head to the side. "Actually, that *does* make sense."

"Of course it does," Calli said. "Now, let's go! We have a concert to prepare for. If we start rehearsing as soon as possible, we can put on the same performance we did in Krymmenos by this evening."

Ree's blood began to pound in her veins. The chance to put on their entire performance without their mother interrupting it? The thought thrilled her!

"Yes!" Ree said. "Let's go! But I think we should tweak it a bit. I have some ideas."

She and her sisters dressed, then had a small meal to break their fast. They returned to the park where they'd eaten the day before and began rehearsing for their performance. Ree incorporated a special dance set to a dithyramb they would sing to honor Dionysus. Once she was certain her sisters had learned their parts, they each broke away to practice other aspects of the performance.

Thalia and Mel stood off to one side, rehearsing a comedy routine Thalia had hastily put together that morning. Calli and Clio were working on a song Calli had written. They tried to keep their voices low, but Clio occasionally got excited and belted out notes loud enough to draw stares.

Meanwhile, Ree had moved a short distance away so that she could rehearse her favorite dance routine. She'd considered performing a more elaborate one, but now that she'd added the dithyramb, she didn't want to further complicate things. It was better to stick with one that she knew well. Besides, she loved this routine. It was elegant and graceful and sure to attract the attention of the gods.

As she executed a perfect twirl, Ree caught sight of two young girls trying to mimic her movements. She fitted her heels against each other, her toes pointed outward, and bent her knees while bringing an arm over her head in a graceful arc. The girls tried to re-create the move, but the smaller one fell backward on her bottom, much as her students had at the studio when she first began teaching them. It had taken Cressida weeks to find her balance, but she eventually did under Ree's tutelage.

Ree laughed and ran over to the girls. "Do you want to join me?"

They both nodded enthusiastically.

She instructed them on how to properly stand, then on how to stand on one leg while supporting it with the other. They both begged her to show them how to twirl, and even though they were not ready for such a move, Ree obliged. Both girls tumbled to the ground mid-twirl, but their infectious giggles spoke to how much they were enjoying themselves.

She felt both delighted and somewhat melancholy as she stared into their cherubic faces. She realized that there was life outside of Krymmenos, yet at the same time she missed her home and her students. And Sivas.

As if she had conjured him simply by thinking about him, Ree caught sight of a tall olive-skinned man who looked remarkably familiar. He was walking with purpose toward the park, maneuvering his way through the crowded streets. Their eyes locked and they both froze.

Ree gasped.

Sivas.

She took off toward him, wrapping her arms around his waist when they collided. Inwardly, she rejoiced as he returned the hug.

She quickly let go, looking over her shoulder to make sure her sisters had not witnessed her display. She didn't know what had come over her. But then Sivas grabbed her by both hands and brought them to his lips.

"I am so happy I found you, Terpsichore," he said. "I have been so worried about you."

Ree's heart swelled to at least twice its normal size. He had been worried about her! He cared about her!

"You had nothing to worry about," she said. "I am with my sisters."

"But Thebes is no place for any young woman to roam without protection," he said.

"Ree?"

Her eyes fell shut at the sound of Calli's voice. How had she snuck up on her? Ree turned to find her sister marching toward her with fierce determination.

"Hello," Calli greeted in a voice that held both suspicion and agitation. "What a pleasant coincidence to run into a fellow villager from Krymmenos here in Thebes. One would think this city was too big for such a meeting to occur."

"It is no coincidence," Sivas said. "I came here to find Ree."

Calli's brows rose. So did Ree's. Sivas had never called her by the pet name only her sisters and mother used before.

"I was concerned for her safety," Sivas continued.

Calli reached over and pulled Ree's hand away from his. "I can assure you that she is quite safe. She is also in the middle of a very important task."

Ree's heart sank, and her face warmed with embarrassment.

"Now, if you do not mind, we must get back to it," Calli said. "Come on, Terpsichore."

Without another word, Calli turned and started for where her sisters were gathered. Ree had no choice but to heed her directive. She gave Sivas an apologetic smile. "I am so sorry about that."

"I'm sorry if I caused you trouble," he said.

"No—" she started, but stopped when Calli called her name again. Her older sister waited for her a few yards away—and behind her stood her other sisters, staring with eyes wide and mouths hanging open.

"I have to go," Ree said to Sivas.

She took off toward Calli.

"How could you?" Ree cried once she reached her.

"Me? How could *you*?" Calli asked. "I knew there was

something going on between the two of you when I caught you back at your studio with him."

"There is nothing going on between us," Ree said. And there probably never would be after the way her sister had treated him.

"You cannot trust anyone, Ree," said Calli, and she started to march across the park. "We still are unsure who had a hand in Mother's kidnapping."

"Sivas did not kidnap Mother," she protested. "He is—"

"He is what?" Calli said. She stopped walking. "How much do you know about him? *Really* know about him? You are smarter than this, Ree. We have lived in Krymmenos for two years, and suddenly Sivas Anastasios is interested in you?"

It felt as if her sister had slapped her in the face. She was not some naive child. Did Calli really believe that Sivas was feigning interest, using her to gain something else?

They returned to where the rest of her sisters were, but Mel, Thalia, and Clio all remained quiet.

"Let us take a break from our rehearsal," Calli said. "I saw a merchant selling honey cakes in the square. I think we all deserve a treat."

Ree followed her sisters to the merchant whose wagon was filled with the sticky, sweet cakes she usually loved. But as she took a bite, Ree could barely taste it. Calli had embarrassed her in front of Sivas, and worse, she had implied she was too guileless to know when someone was misleading her.

Just because she was older, it did not mean that she knew everything.

She was probably jealous. Ree had never heard Calli make mention of anyone she was romantically interested in from their village, but her sister still might wish to catch someone's eye.

Calli called on them to continue their rehearsal. As they started for the park, a chariot rolled past and splashed muddied water all over them.

"My hair!" Mel screeched.

"Does no one in Thebes know how to drive?" Thalia asked, wiping grimy water from her brow.

Ree had managed to dodge most of it since she had hung back behind her sisters.

She pointed. "There's a fountain over there."

As Ree washed away the few specks of mud that dotted her forearms, a strange sensation prickled at the back of her neck. She spotted Sivas standing partially behind one of the columns that surrounded the lawcourts. She looked over her shoulder at her sisters, who were all preoccupied with cleaning the muddy spots from their robes.

Before she could talk herself out of it, Ree slipped away and ran for the lawcourts.

"Sivas!" she said. She hugged him once more. "I am so sorry about what happened with my sister."

His eyes held a blankness that caught her off guard.

"Sivas?" Ree asked. "Is everything all right?"

He stared as if not really seeing her, but then he nodded and slowly said, "Yes. All is well." A peculiar smile drew across his lips, and he said again, "All is well."

She frowned and tilted her head to the side. "Are you sure?"

He nodded again. "I have some exciting news to share about your mother."

Ree's breath caught. "My mother?"

"Yes." He took her by the hand. "Let us be on our way."

She glanced back at the fountain, then took off with Sivas.

XXII

HADES

Hades leaned his shoulder against the smooth stone facade of the library in Thebes, unrolling the papyrus scroll he'd taken from inside—part of the disguise he'd donned for his foray into the mortal world. He'd dressed in a hooded robe and presented himself as a cartographer. He would rather eat his own eyeballs than breathe the same air as the riffraff that roamed around Thebes, but he didn't have a choice. Not anymore. The job that lay before him was too important.

Hades didn't mind relying on Pain and Panic for wreaking normal havoc, but he had to force the stubborn Mnemosyne's hand. Maybe she would be less inclined to fight the inevitable if she knew just what he was capable of.

Because his victory *was* inevitable.

He intended this as his last attempt at revenge against Zeus. He would not have a better opportunity, and he had never developed a more ingenious plan than to have Mnemosyne manipulate the memories of both the gods and mortals. Only his headstrong captive and her refusal to cooperate stood in the way.

But he had finally found a way to make her bend to his will.

Hades chuckled as he watched the dashing lad and willowy young beauty make their way through the crowded square.

He'd been spying on Mnemosyne's daughters near the park when he caught sight of the boy approaching one of them. Hades had a hard time believing his good fortune as he'd listened to the two prattle on, then seen how things had shifted when another of Mnemosyne's girls invaded their little reunion. He could not have designed it better himself.

The moment the two girls had left, Hades approached the boy and sprinkled him with a potion more powerful than the concoction Pain and Panic had used to immobilize Mnemosyne's daughters. The purple dust put the boy in a trance, and Hades now controlled his every move—and he had quite the plan in store for him. He had still been contemplating how to orchestrate another meeting between the starry-eyed couple when the girl had reappeared and the two had run off.

Now all he had to do was tell Mnemosyne of the true peril one of her dear daughters had landed herself in, and he would have her exactly where he wanted her.

Hades pushed away from the library building and tossed the scroll he'd taken on the ground.

By the time he returned to the dungeon where he'd stashed Mnemosyne, he could barely contain his excitement. His long-standing plot to defeat Zeus was just one part of this; Hades just as badly wanted to teach Mnemosyne a lesson. Her defiance was a direct insult, and for that she must pay.

He entered the suffocatingly small room and found her huddled in a corner with her arms wrapped around her bent knees. Her head was back against the wall. Her eyes were closed tight.

"Meditating?" Hades asked.

She lifted one eyelid and eyed him with leery apprehension.

"What can I do for you, Hades?" Mnemosyne asked.

"You know what you can do," Hades answered. "Are you ready to help me?"

She pushed herself up from the floor and stood before him.

"Yes," she answered.

Hades reared back at her unexpected response. "Yes?"

She nodded. "You were right, Hades. Zeus destroyed my family. He destroyed my life. And he didn't pay the slightest price."

Hades's pulse quickened as excitement filled his chest. He knew there was a streak of vengeance running through her after all.

Hades rubbed his hands together. "Fantastic. With the two of us working together, Zeus won't know what hit him."

Mnemosyne held up a hand. "Not so fast."

Was she making demands already? Did she not realize she was *still* his prisoner?

"You said that you would help keep me and my girls safe," she continued. "Do I have your word on that?"

For what his word was worth to a Titan goddess to whom he owed no loyalty.

"Of course," Hades said with a shrug.

Wait a minute. What had she told him?

I will never trust the word of a god. I have been burned too many times.

His eyes narrowed as he studied her face.

"You're lying to me," Hades said.

"You're too smart for that," she said in a smooth voice. "You would see through any lie."

Hades knew when he was being hoodwinked.

"You *are* lying!" he said. She lifted her hand as if to cast a spell, but Hades caught it. "No, you don't. Not this time."

She was not erasing his memories ever again.

"Are you sure you want to continue defying me, Mnemosyne?" Hades asked. "It may prove to be very costly. For you and for those you love."

She turned her head away.

"Ah, ah, ah," Hades tsked. "You'll want to hear this. You see, I just had the pleasure of meeting your five lovely daughters in person."

Her head shot up, her eyes glaring at him.

"I knew that would get your attention," he said.

"What did you do to my girls?" she asked.

"Me?" He clutched his hands to his chest. "Why, nothing. I didn't have to do anything. The one who moves with the gracefulness of a dancer fell for my plan all on her own."

"Ree," she whispered.

"Ah, is that her name? Lovely name for a lovely girl. Her beau thinks she is lovely, too. They are rather smitten with each other."

"You have no idea what you are talking about," Mnemosyne said. "Ree is not smitten with anyone. The only thing she is concerned about is her dance school."

Hades shook his head and grinned. "Teenagers fooling their naive parents. It is a tale as old as time. Your precious little Ree has a sweetheart, and her sweetheart is now under my command."

Mnemosyne stuck her nose in the air. "I don't believe you."

"Is that so? How sure are you that I'm not telling you the truth?" Hades hissed. "So sure that you are willing to risk your own daughter?"

"I trust my daughters," she said. "I created them to be compassionate and intelligent. They would never fall for your games."

Her obstinance would be her downfall. No, it would be her daughters' downfall.

He whipped around and stalked toward the door.

"You're going to regret trying to trick me," Hades said between clenched teeth as he exited the dungeon and slammed the lock into place.

He would make sure of it.

XXIII

MNEMOSYNE

Mnemosyne's heart beat savagely against her ribcage as she paced the length of the small room. She couldn't seem to catch her breath, despite sucking in huge gulps of air. She wrapped her arms around her middle as if she could physically hold herself together when all she wanted to do was fall apart.

She could not even *think* about falling apart. She had to stay strong for her girls.

Her plan to trick Hades into believing she was willing to join forces with him was an abject failure. She should have better prepared herself; she knew one as cunning as Hades would be able to see through a lie.

Mnemosyne pounded her fists against the rough-hewn wall.

Had she blundered her one chance at getting out of this prison? Had she put her girls in even more danger by trying to deceive Hades?

"I'm not giving up on you, girls," she whispered.

Mnemosyne refused to believe the story he'd fed her about her sweet Terpsichore. Ree often became preoccupied with her dancing, but she had a good head on her shoulders. She would not fall for any of Hades's devious schemes. He was only trying to scare Mnemosyne into doing his bidding, but she wasn't falling for it, either.

She'd made that mistake before.

Mnemosyne settled her back against the smooth trunk of a towering cypress tree, the delicate fragrance of a nearby oleander shrub permeating the air around her. She turned to a fresh square of papyrus in her journal and, tapping the ink-filled reed against it, contemplated the virtues she wanted to instill in Terpsichore.

She sketched the figure of a dancing nymph, capturing the rhythmic flow of her movements with precise detail. This one would be headstrong, but her energy and passion would balance well with Melpomene's sweet nature.

You shouldn't have named them already.

Mnemosyne brought a hand up to her temple and rubbed the ache that had formed there. She'd felt herself getting attached to her girls—even though they were simply ideas written on papyrus, she still thought of them as her girls*—back when they were just a bunch of obscure thoughts floating around in her head. The maternal protectiveness she felt over these exquisite entities she'd been creating these past few weeks was unlike anything she had ever experienced.*

But they were promised to do Zeus's bidding.

Mnemosyne's throat grew tight as she tried to swallow down the anguish that overwhelmed her whenever she thought about relinquishing her girls to Zeus.

"You're being foolish," she chastised.

It was not as if she would have no contact with her girls. She planned to persuade Zeus to allow her to serve as their guardian. After all, someone would have to take charge of nourishing and molding them. Who better to fill that role than the one who created them?

As long as she remembered not to refer to them as *her* girls while in Zeus's presence, all should be well.

"But you will be *my* girls," Mnemosyne said, a broad smile traveling across her lips as she quickly scribbled on the papyrus.

As she continued to sketch, a shadow fell over her. At first, she thought a dense cloud had drifted overhead, but when she glanced up, she was startled by the ominous scowl blanketing Hades's face.

Mnemosyne had been even more hesitant to trust the God of the Underworld ever since that day in the flower fields when he'd aimed an arrow at Athena. She did her best to avoid him during his infrequent visits to Olympus, and on the occasions when she couldn't avoid him, she kept a close eye on him. There was something about the way he assessed the other gods when they were not looking, with thinly veiled contempt lurking in his eyes.

She hastily stood. "What do you want?"

"Oh, nothing much," came his nonchalant reply. "I just thought we should . . . you know . . . chat."

"I am sorry, but I cannot." She gathered her journal and held it against her bosom. "If you do not mind, I am busy."

She started to walk away, but a hand on her shoulder stopped her. Hades turned her to face him, a sneer replacing his earlier scowl.

"I do *mind," he said. "You should not be so quick to leave. After all, I came here to warn you."*

"Warn me? Warn me of what?"

"I know about the special project you're working on for Zeus."

She immediately went on guard. Zeus was not known for sharing his intentions, especially with the likes of his crafty brother.

"What of it?" Mnemosyne asked, sticking her nose in the air.

"He no longer approves. He has changed his mind, as is Zeus's way."

"No, he has not. He would have told me."

Even as she said the words, trepidation skittered down Mnemosyne's spine. She'd lived among the gods all her life. Whether Titan or Olympian, they all could be fickle at times, which was how she knew never to fully trust them.

And she certainly did not trust Hades.

A low chuckle rumbled from deep within his chest. "You are so naive. It's not difficult to see how the Titans were so easily defeated."

Mnemosyne flinched at the unprovoked barb. "Zeus and I have a deal."

"And now he no longer wants any part of it."

"He would have—"

"I believe I know my brother better than you do," Hades cut her off. "He is no longer in favor of this little . . . thing you're creating for him. He's decided it's an unnecessary waste of time. And when something falls out of favor with Zeus, there is only one solution in his mind." He leaned in close. "He will destroy it the same way he destroyed the Titans."

"No," she whispered. She began backing away, but Hades kept in step with her. "You do not know what you are talking about."

"I, of all people, know how my brother operates," he said. "But Zeus doesn't have to get the last word on this. Not if you make a partnership with me instead."

Mnemosyne continued to shake her head. Hades was wrong. Zeus would not *destroy her creations. They came from a place that was too pure, too beautiful, for him to ever consider such a thing.*

. . . the same way he destroyed the Titans.

And the way he'd held her prisoner, even though he wanted to pretend that she was free.

And Hades's words held some truth: Zeus was *the reason her family had been banished to Tartarus and remained there to this very day. They belonged there, but she could not forget which god had put them there and what he was capable of.*

What if Zeus had *changed his mind? Would he banish her girls, as well? Destroy them before they ever had the chance to come to be?*

"You know that I am right," Hades told her. "That is why your face suddenly became ashen and your eyes expanded with fright. You know that Zeus will—"

Mnemosyne stuck out her splayed palm, holding it up to his face. Just like that, she erased all memories he had of this conversation. And of her. It was the only thing she could think to do.

She must go. If she wanted the beautiful creations that still only existed in her mind to ever come to being, she must leave Olympus. And she must erase all traces of herself from all who knew her.

Mnemosyne thought of the bonds she'd made with some of the gods on Olympus, the friendships that had come to mean so much to her since the end of the Titanomachy. She conjured images of Athena and sucked in a painful breath at the thought of never seeing her again. She would be alone, forced to start over, with only her memories to provide comfort.

No!

No, she would not be alone. She would have her girls!

Her remarkable daughters would provide all the love and companionship she could ever need. As long as she kept them safe and ensured that the gods knew nothing of their existence, all would be well.

Mnemosyne ran to her home. She gathered her belongings,

packing up what she could carry. She took a moment to commit her surroundings to memory. Then she left the humble dwelling that had been more of a prison than a home, embarking on a journey with an uncertain destination.

Mnemosyne made her way around Mount Olympus with one goal in mind: to erase the memory of herself from every being that resided there.

She encountered Hephaestus and Aphrodite on a stroll around the golden lake just on the outskirts of the temple.

"Hello, Mnemosyne!" the God of the Forge exclaimed. "How have—"

Before he could finish his question, Mnemosyne arced her hand in the air and wiped both their memories of her clean. They continued their stroll, walking past her as if she were invisible.

She did the same to Demeter and her daughter Persephone. And again to Hermes and Apollo.

She came upon Artemis, tending a wounded stag in the golden stable of her palatial home. Pain sliced through Mnemosyne's chest. As she had of all the gods, she had been leery of Artemis when she first arrived, but the goddess had become a true friend. Mnemosyne would miss her dearly.

She silently walked up to Artemis, and with the goddess's attention still focused on the stag, Mnemosyne erased all memories her friend had of her. She left the stable as quietly as she had arrived.

Rubbing the center of her chest, she tried and failed to relieve the ache that had settled there. She never would have expected to experience such hurt, but it did *hurt to leave the friends she'd made.*

"Mnemosyne?"

She startled and turned, her breath hitching in her throat.

"A-Athena, I did not expect to find you here. I thought you went out for a hunt?"

"I am done with my hunt," she answered. Athena gestured to the sack Mnemosyne had tossed over her shoulder. "Are you going somewhere?"

"I . . ."

Mnemosyne was at a loss for words. She knew leaving her friends would be the most difficult, and of the friends she'd made during her time on Olympus, there was none she had connected with more than Athena.

"I must," she said.

She could not lie, but then, it did not matter. In just a few moments Athena would not remember this conversation. She would not remember Mnemosyne at all.

It's for the best.

"Thank you for everything you have done for me. I treasure you as a friend and will always be thankful for the day you found me in the woods," Mnemosyne said.

Before she could talk herself out of it, she lifted her hand in the air and erased all memories Athena had of her.

Then she fled.

She'd fled Olympus and so many other places over the years but had always strived to give her daughters a sense of home. They had found one in Krymmenos. An overwhelming wave of panic crashed into Mnemosyne at the thought of her and her girls never seeing home again.

But there was something more to this distressing feeling that had engulfed her. She sensed it deep in her gut.

Her girls were in trouble. Their emotions were in a frenzy. She felt it in her every heartbeat.

Was it Ree? Had Hades been telling her the truth?

"Oh, Ree," Mnemosyne cried, bringing her fist to her mouth. "Your sisters will be there, Ree. They won't leave you. And don't forget how strong you are."

She'd created her girls to be strong, resilient forces in the world. Ree would remember to tap into that strength. She would get through this.

She had to. The alternative was incomprehensible.

XXIV

REE

Ree held on tightly to Sivas's hands as they raced from the agora. Her heart pumped with excitement and just a tiny smidge of guilt. It was a rash decision to leave her sisters the way she had, but Sivas told her he had information on their mother's whereabouts. If *she* could be the one to rescue their mother, then it would show Calli what Ree was capable of—that she wasn't a little girl anymore.

She was so distracted by her one-sided internal argument with Calli that she hadn't noticed where Sivas was taking her.

"Why are we at the dock?" she asked him.

He remained silent, staring out at the water as if he had not heard her.

"Sivas?" Ree tugged on his arm. Her head reared back slightly when he turned to her. There was something about the look in his eyes that didn't seem right. He seemed to look straight through her.

"Sivas, is everything okay?"

"Yes," he answered. He looked back to the water, then started walking toward the end of the dock. "Follow me."

Ree tried to ignore the trepidation that began to race down her spine. She was being foolish. It was probably just lingering disquiet following her argument with Calli. But her alarm intensified when Sivas motioned for her to climb into a boat.

"Where are we going?" Ree asked.

"Somewhere special," he said.

Her head reared back again, her eyes narrowing. "Are you taking me to where my mother is being held?"

"Yes. We are going to find your mother."

His voice was still . . . off. He seemed distracted.

Something told her not to get into the boat, but Ree batted the thought away. The voice in her head sounded like Calli, and she refused to allow her sister to make her decisions for her any longer, especially when she wasn't even there.

She climbed into the boat and settled in for her adventure.

Sivas untied the boat from the dock, and they were soon off, drifting away from the teeming streets of Thebes. Despite living along the seashore, Ree hadn't taken a boat ride in quite some time.

"This is nice," Ree said. "Maybe when we return to Krymmenos we can take Cressida on a boat ride."

"Cressida?" Sivas asked in that same flat voice.

Panic gripped her, sending her heartbeat racing. "Sivas, what is going on with you?"

He didn't answer, just continued steering the boat.

"Sivas?" Ree called. Then she screamed, "SIVAS!"

Something was wrong. This was not same person who came to her dance studio.

Ree searched around, but there was nothing but a vast expanse of water surrounding them. They had already traveled too far for anyone to hear her.

"Wait!" Ree scrambled for the bag she'd brought with her. While Mel was washing the muddy water from her robe, she'd handed Ree the bag filled with the offerings they'd brought for the gods. If she remembered correctly . . .

Her sisters had picked stems from the bergamot tree as part of their offering. She knew the oils were regularly used to revive someone who was suffering from the vapors.

Ree tapped Sivas's cheek and held the bergamot underneath his nose.

"Sivas! Sivas!" she called. "Are you there?"

His head jerked back, and he blinked several times. His glassy eyes seemed to clear up.

"Terpsichore?"

"Sivas! Is it you?" Ree asked.

He frowned, shaking his head. "Of course it is me. What do you mean?" He looked around. "Where are . . . Why are we on a boat?"

"I knew it," Ree said. "Sivas, I am not sure what happened, but I think someone must have put you in a trance of some sort."

"A trance?"

She explained what had happened over the past few minutes, and how he had not even known his own sister's name.

"Did someone give you something to eat or drink?" Ree asked.

"I don't think so," he said. "I recall a tall man wearing a hood. He approached me in the square just after your sister came over to collect you."

"Do you remember me coming back to you after Calli dragged me away?" Ree asked. He shook his head. "What about us traveling through the streets of Thebes and to the dock?"

Again, he shook his head.

"Do you know where we are going? And what about my mother?" Ree asked.

But she knew the answer to that before he could voice it. She felt it in her gut. They were not going to her mother.

He held his palm against his forehead. "I am sorry, Terpsichore. I . . . I do not know."

Ree thought about what Calli had said regarding their mother's kidnappers, and how they could not be sure that it wasn't someone from Krymmenos. Could Sivas have had something to do with it?

"Are you lying to me?" Ree asked, her voice shaking.

His head shot up, his eyes wide. "No! Terpsichore, I would never lie to you. I do not know what happened. I am so sorry. I never should have come to Thebes."

Ree hoped she wasn't making a mistake by believing him, but

what other choice did she have? They were alone together in the middle of the sea.

"We must make our way back to Thebes," Ree said.

Sivas stood and looked around. "I don't know the way. I have only traveled to Thebes through the mountain pass."

Were they really lost at sea? Could this really be happening? Ree's skin heated up, and she struggled to catch her breath.

Why had she left her sisters? Why hadn't she listened to Calli?

She had to calm down. It would do them no good if she flew into hysterics.

"We just have to turn the boat around and go back the way we came," she said.

"It isn't like traveling along a straight road, Terpsichore."

"I know that," Ree said. "But maybe—" She stopped. Was that . . . ? Ree squinted, looking past Sivas's shoulder. "I think I see land. Look, over there!"

There was a tiny island sparsely dotted with trees.

"Yes, I think you are right," Sivas said.

Suddenly, a violent wind rocked the boat from side to side, then started to blow them away from the island.

"No," Ree said. "We need to go there. Maybe there's someone who can help us."

But the wind continued blowing them in the opposite direction. Just when she thought things could not get worse, a loud crack resounded and the skies opened up. The pounding rain came with such ferociousness that Ree could barely see two feet past the boat.

She dropped her head into her hands, feeling utterly defeated. She would never, ever leave her sisters again.

XXV

CALLI

As she wiped away the last of the mud that had splattered onto her face and arms, Calli told herself that every day in Thebes would not be like the two they'd had so far. Surely there was joy in this city—joy that was not dependent upon her younger sister holding an impromptu comedy hour on the steps of the theater.

She would make Thebes her home, just as she had Krymmenos. It would just take her a little time.

Maybe if . . .

"Calli, have you seen Ree?" Mel asked her.

"What do you mean? She was just—" She turned in a full circle, scanning the area. "She was just here."

Mel pressed her palm to her chest. "I have a bad feeling about this."

This time, Calli knew Mel wasn't being overly dramatic, because she had a bad feeling too. Ree had been so upset after she'd snatched her away from Sivas Anastasios. Had her sister run off with that boy?

No. Ree would not do such a thing. She knew they were here

to rescue their mother; the thought of Ree abandoning their family in this time of upheaval was too far out of the realm of possibility for Calli to even suggest it.

Or . . . was it?

"Maybe Ree went in search of the facilities," Thalia said. She wiggled. "I need to make a trip there myself."

"That has to be it," Calli said. "Mel, Thalia, go to the latrines and look for her. Clio and I will ask around."

The moment she turned, an old woman with a crooked, pointy nose and a turquoise shawl covering her head pulled on Calli's robe—her cream robe with silver threading, like the ones all the girls had donned this morning.

"Are you looking for the one wearing a fine peplos like this one?" she asked.

"Yes! Have you seen her?" Calli asked.

The woman nodded.

"Please, tell me where she went," Calli begged.

The woman held out a wrinkled palm. "Do you have any coin, my dear?"

Calli pinched her lips together. She should have known better than to expect anything for free, but it was worth her coin to get information on Ree's whereabouts. She reached into her pouch and produced a hemiobol.

The woman shook her head. "Drachma."

"A drachma?"

"You want to know where the girl went, don't you?"

Calli searched her bag. She would not be able to afford two rooms in the inn after giving this woman all her coin, but all five of them could share if they had to spend another night in Thebes.

"There," Calli said, dropping a silver coin bearing Dionysus's likeness into the woman's waiting palm. "Where did my sister go?"

She looked furtively over each of her bony shoulders. "She and her beau took off for the port."

Calli's head snapped back. "But there are no ports near Thebes."

She should have known the old woman was a scammer.

"Of course there is a port. The channel will lead you straight to the Aegean. But I wouldn't go there if I were you," she warned. "Many sailors have tried to cross those waters in search of fortune, but none return."

Her warning sent shivers down Calli's spine. She tried to shake them off, but something told her that ignoring the old woman's advice would be to the detriment of both her and her sisters. Yet the thought of leaving Ree out there without searching for her was not one that Calli could stomach.

Calli knew what she had to do. She motioned to Clio and went to retrieve Mel and Thalia from by the latrines.

"Thalia, where is that flute?" Calli asked.

She would be so indebted to the gods by the time this ordeal was over that Calli was unsure if she would ever have the chance to live the life she wanted. But that was something for her to consider at another time.

Thalia took the instrument out of her bag. "I hope we don't have to sing again for Apollo to help us. I need to save my voice for the concert."

Thalia blew on the flute, and moments later, Calli heard someone whistle. She spotted two men leaning against one of the columns that surrounded the library. One was short, with ears that seemed a tad too large for his head. The other was tall, with broad shoulders and radiant purple skin.

Hermes and Apollo, still in disguise.

"There they are, girls," Calli said to her sisters as she took off for the library.

"I wasn't expecting to hear from you so soon," Apollo said in greeting. "Shouldn't you be rehearsing?" He held a hand up, stopping her before she could answer. "Were there not five of you?"

"That's why I had to play that little ditty on the flute again," Thalia said. "We need your help. Our sister ran off with her new man." She propped a hand on her hip. "And do you think she bothered to tell her own sisters that she even *had* a new man? No!"

"We need help locating Ree," Calli said. "I have learned that she and her beau—a boy from our village—have taken off in a boat. And that boat is heading in the direction of—"

"Aeaea," Apollo said. "It does not matter where they were

headed; if they left through the channel near Thebes, Aeaea is where they will find themselves. I hope you were not very fond of your sister."

All four of them gasped.

"Why would you say that?" Mel cried.

"Because she will soon become one of Circe's prisoners," Apollo said.

Calli frowned. "Who is this Circe?"

"I've never heard of her," Clio said. "And I know everything there is to know about Olympus. I've read every book I can find."

"Well, it appears you don't know everything," Apollo said. "May that be a lesson for you."

Clio's head reared back in affront.

"What about Circe?" Calli asked. "Who is she?"

"She's bad news, that's what she is," Hermes answered. "There's still enough of you to put on the concert Apollo told me about. That's what you need to concentrate on."

"How do you expect any of us to concentrate when our sister is possibly heading toward this person you say is bad news?" Thalia asked.

"Circe is a goddess, not a person," Apollo said. "Technically, she's an enchantress."

"I'd say more of a sorceress," Hermes interjected.

"Enchantress. Sorceress. Doesn't really matter," Apollo said.

"What *does* matter is the havoc she can cause. Circe charms unsuspecting victims onto her island, which is so beautiful they do not want to leave it, and then turns them into swine."

Calli's head began to swim with images of her sister rooting on the ground like a filthy pig.

"We must rescue Ree," she said. "We cannot allow her to fall into the hands of this Circe."

"That's if she makes it to Aeaea," Hermes said. "She and her fella first have to get past the Sirens."

"No," the girls said collectively.

Their mother had relayed the story of the Sirens to them many times. Their sweet singing was purported to lure men to a watery death.

"Ah, so you understand that to reach your sister, you will need to make it past the Sirens, too. Now, I can help protect you against Circe," Hermes said. He snapped his finger and produced a white flower seemingly out of thin air. "This here is moly. If Circe manages to poison you, just chew a bit of this herb and you should be fine. As for the Sirens . . . I can't help you there."

She turned to Apollo. He, too, hunched his shoulders.

Calli closed her eyes and sucked in a deep breath. They had no choice: they had to find a way to save Ree, even if it meant delaying their rescue of their mother. Calli knew that her mother would not have it any other way.

"I will not expose my horses to the Sirens," Apollo said. "But I will allow them to take you as far as the port."

He whistled, and moments later, his chariot appeared.

"This may be your toughest battle yet," Hermes said. "But you've figured out a way to make it this far. Keep doing whatever it is you're doing."

As they left the library, Calli replayed Hermes's words in her head. Searching through her mother's journal for clues to their gifts had sustained them so far. Trusting that Apollo's horses would take them where they needed to go, she pulled out the journal and began thumbing through the pages once more.

Just as quickly, Calli shut the journal.

She didn't have to search within its pages to figure out what she needed to do next. She already had the answer.

"Girls," Calli called. "I know how to get past the Sirens, but we will all have to work together to get it done."

"We won't have to fight them, will we?" Thalia asked.

"I can't fight!" Mel said.

"We're not going to fight them," Calli said. "But we *are* going to beat them at their own game."

XXVI

REE

Ree gripped Sivas's hand, urging him to keep up as she navigated the unfamiliar terrain of the island where their boat had run ashore. They had tried to dock on another island, where Ree had spotted several women who she could have sworn looked as if they had wings. It reminded her of a fairy tale her mother used to tell them as children. They were waving to them on the edge of the seashore, but the tranquil sea had turned violent. The sudden storm had been so loud that it drowned out all other sound, including whatever the women on that island were saying.

But Sivas had seen this island in the distance and had guided their boat here.

It was so very different from what Ree was used to. Krymmenos's coastal landscape boasted sand and rock, grassy weeds, and a few trees here and there. Foliage abounded in this place: lush green grass, thick wild brambles filled with berries that she had never seen before, trees with branches that stretched so far out they curved downward and then back up again.

Despite the apprehension pulsing through her veins, Ree could not dismiss the beauty of this island.

"Terpsichore, I hope you can understand how sorry I am for all that has happened," Sivas said.

"I asked you to stop apologizing," she said. "It isn't your fault."

Ree tightened her grip on his hand. She wasn't sure what she would encounter on this island. She recalled her mother reading them tales of seafaring men washing ashore on desolate islands teeming with creatures. Whether those stories were real or just fairy tales, Ree knew they were likely not alone.

"You never told me how you ended up in Thebes," she said to Sivas.

"I came to check on you," he answered. "It does not matter that you told me not to worry. I cannot help it. I worry about the people I care about."

Ree's breath caught. "You care about me?"

"Of course I do," he said. "I told you as much back in Krymmenos. I regretted not accompanying you and your sisters on your journey from the moment I left your studio."

She was amused that he thought her sisters would have just allowed him to join them.

"That is very sweet of you, but— Did you hear that?"

She searched for the source of the unmistakable growl she'd just heard.

"I—"

The rest of his words were drowned out by an awful roar.

Ree grabbed him by the hand again and took off through the dense foliage. They climbed over gnarled tree roots that protruded from the ground and slithered underneath the canopy of overgrown leaves.

They arrived at a tiny clearing. A narrow beam of sunlight made its way through the stand of trees.

"I think we've eluded whatever that was," Sivas said. "Hopefully, we are safe for now."

"Hopefully," Ree repeated.

Sivas went off to relieve himself while she walked a few yards in the opposite direction, toward a gurgling sound.

"Yes, thank the gods," Ree whispered upon finding a narrow, shallow brook. She had avoided soiling her robe when that chariot splashed muddy water on her and her sisters but had made up for it by traipsing through this jungle.

She crouched low and scooped up a handful of water, using it to clean her face and arms. She would not bother with her clothes. They were likely to get even dirtier as they made their way out of these woods.

Ree scooped a bit more water and sipped it. Then she looked up and found herself nose to nose with the biggest lion she had ever seen in her life.

Her entire body went rigid with fear. The hair at her nape stood at attention, and what little breath she had left in her lungs after their run rushed out in a terrified gasp.

The animal's yellow eyes narrowed as his massive body advanced on her. He leaned forward.

And gave her a playful lick on the nose.

Ree was too stunned to move.

The lion rubbed his head against her chin, his deep purr rumbling in her chest. Then he nudged her hand with the top of his head, urging her to stroke it.

She tentatively passed her fingers over his head. He nudged harder.

Ree couldn't help laughing at his cheek. "Oh, was I not rubbing to your liking?" She smoothed her palm over his head, marveling in how his soft fur felt against her fingers. "You are a beautiful cat, aren't you? But I think you already knew that."

"Don't move," Sivas said, holding a thick branch overhead.

"No," she called. "Don't. He's friendly."

"That beast is dangerous, Terpsichore. Just look at him."

"Yes, look at him," she said, massaging the lion's head. The animal released a satisfied moan, then turned on his back so that his head was cradled in her lap. "Have you ever seen such a docile lion before?"

"No, he hasn't," someone called. "No one has."

Ree spun around, her eyes widening at the sight of a gorgeous woman with thick black hair that rivaled Mel's, and a stunning robe made from flowers and thick vines.

"Welcome to Aeaea," the woman said. "I am Circe. I see you have met Queen." She snapped her fingers, and the lion immediately went to stand alongside her. "I have been expecting you."

"You have?" Ree asked.

Circe put a finger to her chin. "Oh, maybe I should not have mentioned that." She laughed, the musical sound carrying on the wind. Circe captured the hem of her robe and turned. "Why don't you join me?"

An odd, unsettling sensation tickled the back of Ree's neck. She caught Sivas by the wrist and pulled him close.

"Do you think something nefarious is afoot?" he whispered.

"Why would she have been expecting us?" Ree asked. "We were not supposed to be here."

Circe glanced back at them. "Why aren't you following?"

Her voice held less welcome and more command. Ree's alarm intensified.

She held on to Sivas's wrist, afraid to let go for even a second. Too much had happened for her to trust their host's friendly greeting. She searched her mind, trying to remember if her mother had ever told them stories of someone named Circe, but she drew a blank.

"You must be famished," Circe said. "You needn't worry. The fruits of this land are bountiful. There will be much to eat and drink once we arrive back at my dwelling." She glanced over her shoulder again and, with a chuckle that raised the hairs on Ree's arm, added, "So much that you may never want to leave."

XXVII

CALLI

Calli pressed a hand against her upset stomach as the kaiki hit another wave on the choppy waters. The traditional wooden fishing boat was the only one available to them, though the more Calli thought about it, she realized anything bigger would have probably moved slower. Speed was essential.

So was Clio's knack for figuring out how to do just about anything with very little instruction. Her sister had taken command of the boat and expertly guided them out of the channel and into the open waters.

When they asked the fisherman who'd rented them the boat how to get to Aeaea, he warned them not to travel to the island. But when Clio told him they would venture on their own, with or without his help, he conceded.

At Calli's request, he reluctantly drew them a map, even though Apollo had assured them that if they left by this channel, they would eventually end up at Aeaea. She felt safer with the extra guidance. Clio had glanced at the map once and had not referred to it since. She told Calli she could see the route in her mind, just as she had while navigating them through the labyrinth yesterday.

Calli, however, scrupulously followed the map. They still had some time before they encountered the tiny island that "called men to their deaths," according to the fisherman. Calli presumed it was the island the Sirens called home.

She tossed about ideas of how to get past the creatures without suffering the same fate as the many who had met their death in these same waters. She could not explain why, but she had a feeling deep in her gut that this was the time for *her* gift to shine. Calli was certain her gift was her ability to tell a story.

She looked at her sisters. Mel sat in the very center of the hull of the boat, clutching the bag with the jar and resting her forehead against her bent knees. Thalia sat with one arm over the starboard side; she looked close to losing her breakfast.

Calli hoped this worked.

"Gather around," she called to her sisters. After huddling around where Clio steered the boat, she asked, "Do you all remember the stories Mother used to tell us about the half woman and half bird creatures when we were younger? She said the Sirens would sing magnificent songs that lured their victims into the sea. But we're going to sing a magnificent song of our own. I have been working on an epic song—"

"Is that what you have been writing when you go down to the seashore?" Thalia asked.

"Yes, it is," Calli said. It was time she shared her dreams with her sisters. No more holding back. "It is what I want to do for the rest of my life. I want to write epic tales, and I am good at it. I *know* that I am. I believe it is the gift that Mother gave to me. Remember what mother's journal said—'the flower's skill with a pen will help her to conquer anything'?"

"Oh, that's why *you* always carry around that journal," Mel said.

Calli nodded. "The song that I have been working on is the perfect story to lull the Sirens into bending to our will instead of the other way around. Do you all trust me to get this right?"

"Of course we do," Mel said. She grabbed Calli's hand and gave it a firm squeeze. "I trust you to get this right, the same way that Mother trusted you to figure out her journal. You've never led us astray, Calliope."

And she wouldn't this time, either.

Calli spent twenty minutes teaching Clio, Mel, and Thalia the song she had written; she could only hope it was enough time for them to learn and retain it. They were used to performing made-up songs at a moment's notice, but not under such circumstances. A knot formed in her stomach as they neared the island where the Sirens were purported to reside.

"It's time to start singing!" she called to her sisters. "Remember, sing as loud as you can and don't stop until I tell you to."

The most gorgeous voices Calli had ever heard reached her ears just as she and her sisters began singing the lyrics to the song she'd written, telling the tale of Andreia, the courageous mother who loved her daughters so much that she would do anything for them. The closer they got to the island, the louder the beautiful voices became.

But she and her sisters were louder.

The strength of Thalia's lungs was on full display as she belted out the notes. Calli, Mel, and Clio joined in, and together they powered through the song.

Calli glanced toward the island and saw the winged women standing along the shoreline.

Her breath caught at the sight of the unbelievably stunning creatures. They were too far to make out the details of their faces, but she could tell even from this distance that they were beautiful, with long flowing locks of shiny titian hair.

And those wings! Their glittering, majestic wings captivated her the most. The sleek feathers extended out at least six feet on either side and came in an array of colors, from dark purple to deep pink, brilliant yellow to rich green. They shimmered under the sun, mesmerizing her.

"Sing, Calli!" Thalia hollered.

She looked away from the shore and continued singing with her sisters, but the Sirens' voices were even more enchanting than their beautiful wings. Calli could feel the melodious sounds pulling her toward the edge of the boat. She didn't even realize she had moved until she heard Clio scream her name.

"Calli, no!" her sister screeched.

Mel encircled her, wrapping her arms around Calli's waist. Thalia came over and plugged Calli's ears with her fingers. She tried to wrestle away, but her sisters only held on harder.

Calli fought off the wave of lightheadedness that washed over her. She must focus. Her mother had not given her this gift only to let it fail her when she needed it the most. She closed her eyes tight and concentrated on the words to the song she'd written.

She removed Thalia's fingers from her ears and disengaged from Mel's hold. Standing tall, Calli filled her lungs with air and belted out the words as loud as she could.

After several moments, she heard a splash, then another, and another. The winged creatures were diving into the sea.

They'd done it! They'd turned the curse back on the Sirens.

Calli gathered Thalia and Mel in a hug. They danced in a tight circle, celebrating their victory.

"Enough of the jumping," Clio said. "That was the first obstacle. The real test will be getting to Ree."

"And convincing her to come back with us," Thalia said.

Calli wasn't so sure that would be an issue. She'd had this strange feeling ever since they started searching for Ree, as if a taut string stretched between them, linking them together.

"She will," Calli said. The connection she felt was too strong to deny. Had Mnemosyne designed them to be linked this way?

The farthest Calli had ever been from her sisters was when she went down to the sea while one of the other girls went to the village square. She remembered this same strange feeling niggling at the back of her mind. It had always been faint but had been there.

With what she now knew about her mother and her reasons for creating them, Calli would not be surprised if she had designed them so that they would always be connected as sisters, no matter how much physical distance separated them.

They were silent as they continued on the choppy seas. After some time, Calli spotted a tiny dot off in the distance.

"Over there, Clio." She pointed. "That has to be Aeaea."

XXVIII

REE

As they followed the dark-haired woman and her pet lion, Ree could not shake the uncomfortable feeling that had settled into her bones. Why would Circe be expecting them? They were strangers to her.

She glanced at Sivas. Had he brought her here on purpose? Or had the person who put him under a trance done so?

Ree's stomach dropped.

This was a trap. She was sure of it.

"Ah, here we are," Circe said.

They had arrived at a stone grotto. The same varieties of flowers and vines that made up Circe's robe covered the walls of the structure. In its center stood an ornate throne.

She gestured to the area around them. "Please, make yourselves at home. I insist."

Ree took a step back. She did not want to show her fear; she had a feeling their host would pounce on it. She should pretend to go along with whatever it was this Circe had planned for them.

And who had planned this? Was it the same person who'd put

Sivas under a trance? Were they the same men who'd kidnapped her mother? Had they gotten to Circe as well? Or, what if Circe had orchestrated the kidnapping? Could her mother be on this very island, a prisoner of this strange woman?

While Circe raved about the beauty of her island, Ree's shoulders stiffened as a peculiar but familiar sensation washed over her.

Her sisters!

They were singing. She couldn't hear it, but she could feel it. Feel *them.*

It didn't matter who had trapped her here, because she had a plan of her own—and with her sisters nearby, she knew she could pull it off.

Since their arrival in Thebes, the gifts their mother had bestowed upon them had emerged exactly when they needed them the most. Ree didn't need to look in their mother's journal to figure out her gift. She had known it ever since she was a little girl.

She would dance.

"Oh, my dears." Circe stopped abruptly, turned, and flattened her palm against her chest. "Forgive me for being such an inconsiderate host. I did not offer either of you a refreshment. Don't you go anywhere. I will be right back."

Ree waited until Circe was out of earshot, then motioned for Sivas to lean closer.

"This is what we will do," she whispered. "I will distract Circe, and you will return to the boat."

"What?" he asked, his eyes widening in horror. "No."

"Yes," Ree said. "Listen. My sisters are on the way. I can feel them."

"How?"

"I don't know how, but I do. I know they are coming for me. For us."

Calli would not leave Sivas here, despite her reservations about him.

Ree sucked in a deep breath, and a staggering sense of guilt overcame her. How could she have deserted her sisters the way she had back in Thebes? Ree would not blame them if they'd decided that they were done with her. But their mother had instilled a sense of family and loyalty in them—her sisters would never turn their backs on her the way she had turned hers on them.

"How do you plan to distract her?" Sivas asked, gesturing with his head toward where Circe had gone.

"With a dance," she answered.

He frowned.

"Trust me," Ree said. "I know this will work." She felt it deep in her gut. "I will offer a dance as a show of gratitude for her hospitality. Once I have gained her full attention, that is when you go in search of my sisters. They are near. I promise they are."

He clasped both her hands in his and gave them a squeeze. "Are you sure about this, Ree?"

She smiled. "I'm sure." Then she pressed a swift kiss to his cheek and turned just as Circe reemerged carrying goblets hewn out of wood.

"Here we are," their host said.

"Oh, dear Circe," Ree said with a sweet smile as she accepted the drink. "You must let me repay you for your warm welcome."

XXIX

CALLI

Calli's heartbeat raced as the lush island came into view. The abundant foliage was unlike anything she had ever seen with her own two eyes. Trees of all sizes, from stout to towering, were laden with deep green leaves that swayed in the breeze. Flowers of every color imaginable grew from the rich soil, their delightful fragrance imbuing the air.

"This is beautiful," Calli whispered on an awe-filled breath. She wished she could explore it all. Then she reminded herself of the danger that lurked here. They needed to find Ree and get away from this island as quickly as possible.

As they pulled closer, she noticed a male figure waving at them.

"I think that's Sivas!" Mel said. "But where's Ree? My goodness, where is our sister!"

"Calm down, Mel," said Calli. "Let's wait until we get there."

They couldn't get there quickly enough for Calli. Even though she could feel that her sister was close by, she too was worried that she did not see her.

CALLI

She had been suspicious of Sivas Anastasios, and she would never forgive him for carting Ree off to this island, but Calli felt deep in her gut that he had not harmed her. She would know if Ree were hurt. She still could not understand *how* she would know; she just knew that she would.

Sivas ran into the water, grabbing hold of the boat's bow. Calli, Mel, and Thalia climbed over the side of the boat, and the four of them dragged it onshore while Clio steered from her place at the helm, making sure the boat remained straight.

"Terpsichore was right," Sivas said, greeting their arrival with an exhausted sigh.

"Where is she?" Calli asked. "Why isn't she with you?"

Sivas explained that Ree had instructed him to leave and go in search of her sisters, who she'd insisted were on their way to Aeaea to rescue them.

So Ree had felt this connection, too. This was their mother's doing. She had created them to always feel this bond.

"We were searching for shelter from an unusual storm," continued Sivas. "It was unlike any I have ever witnessed. The waves drove our boat here, and a woman who lives on this island found us."

Calli's stomach dropped. "Is her name Circe?"

His eyes brightened. "Yes!" Then his expression darkened. "But Ree had a bad feeling about her. And so did I."

"And you left our sister with her anyway?" Mel asked.

"She told me to do so," Sivas said. "She said she had a plan. She would distract Circe while I came to find you. And look! I've found you, just as Terpsichore said I would!"

Thalia snapped her fingers and stepped up to him. "For your information, this Circe is an enchantress."

"Sorceress," Clio corrected.

Thalia batted her away. "Same difference. The point is, she is dangerous. How is Ree supposed to distract her?"

"With dance," Calli said, the beginnings of a smile making its way across her lips.

"Yes, that is what she said she would do!" Sivas said.

"Don't you all get it?" Calli asked her sisters. "We have conquered every obstacle we have encountered since we came to Thebes by using the gifts that Mother gave us. Ree's gift is dance. She must have recognized that using it would give her the best chance to escape Circe's wrath." She turned to Sivas. "Take us to her."

They traveled through verdant foliage, with thick vegetation that carpeted the ground and those sweet-smelling flowers that grew in intense, vibrant colors. It was an island paradise, more splendid than anything Calli could have ever imagined.

She now understood Apollo's warning about Aeaea being so beautiful that those who visited never wanted to leave. Circe must use this beauty to lure people in.

Well, her tricks would not work on them.

Sivas led them to a marble grotto. A curtain of vines and moss hid what was inside. Calli crept closer to it and gently parted the moss. She spotted Ree in the center of the grotto, performing a graceful dance. Upon a raised dais sat a stunningly gorgeous woman with thick black hair, olive skin, and lush red lips. At her feet lay a lion that was equally exquisite.

"That's Circe," Sivas whispered near Calli's ear. "How do you suppose we get to Terpsichore without alerting her? She seems to be entranced by your sister's dancing."

Calli did not know how to put anyone into a trance, but Sivas's words brought to mind the next best thing.

She motioned for her sisters to follow her. Once they were a safe distance away, she pulled them into a huddle. "Do you remember the lullaby about the sea nymphs Mother would sing to us when we were little girls?"

"Did it go something like this?" Mel asked before starting the opening strains of the song.

Calli nodded. "That's it. This is how we rescue Ree. We're going to lull Circe to sleep."

"I like that plan," Clio said.

"I just have to make sure *I* don't fall asleep," Thalia said.

"I already thought about that," Calli said. She'd spotted the cypress tree up ahead. It was still young, and its cones were small enough to fit in their ears. Calli plucked several from the tree and tossed them to her sisters and Sivas. "Plug your ears with these."

"How can you sing with your ears plugged?" Sivas asked in awe.

"We're just that good," retorted Thalia.

"Our talents have always been . . . special," Clio agreed.

Calli turned back to Sivas. "Ree may very well fall to sleep, too. If she does, it is your job to carry her to safety."

"I would not have it any other way," Sivas said.

"Hmm . . ." Thalia said. "Is that exomis made of brother-in-law material?"

"Thalia, not now," Mel chastised.

"Come on," Calli said, motioning for them to follow her back to the grotto.

She put the cypress cones in her ears and directed her sisters to sing softly. Gradually, they increased the volume. Calli noticed Ree stumbled a bit and briefly glanced their way, her eyes widening in recognition for just a moment.

Don't give us away, Calli silently pleaded.

But Ree only continued with her dance, and in a brilliant move, slowly began moving in time with the song they sang. Calli could tell she was becoming lethargic. Her movements were not as fluid, and her eyes drooped.

But the same was happening to Circe. The sorceress's head began to bob, and then her pet lion let out a loud snore.

An excited smile broke out across Sivas's face, and he gave Calli a thumbs-up.

Calli nodded to him, still singing. She instructed her sisters to sing louder.

The moment Circe's chin hit her chest, Calli sent Sivas to capture Ree. He scooped her up in his arms and hurried back to where they all hid behind the vines.

"Ree, thank goodness you are okay," Mel said.

"You scared us," Clio added.

"Don't . . . stop singing," Ree said.

"Shh . . ." Calli said, reading her sister's lips. She stuck cypress cones into Ree's ears. She motioned for the others to keep singing.

Moments later, an angry voice called out so loud that Calli heard it despite the cones plugged in her ears. "Where are they? Queen! Go!"

Circe! She was awake.

"Run!" Calli ordered, but her sisters were way ahead of her.

Lifting up the hem of her robe, she sprinted over fallen tree limbs and dense grass. She pulled the cones out of her ears and tossed them aside, then tried to decipher how far Circe was behind them based on the rustling of the foliage.

"There they are! Get them, Queen!" came Circe's call. Calli could hear the lion's heavy panting. They were both much too close. "Hurry!"

Up ahead, she could tell Sivas was struggling to carry Ree as they scurried through the forest. The extra weight would slow him down.

Calli could barely catch her breath, due more to panic than exhaustion. She knew it was impossible to make it back to the boat in time. After all they had been through, it would end with them as a meal for a sorceress's pet lion.

"Over here!" Clio called.

Calli whipped her head around and spotted Clio's head peeking over the thick trunk of a downed tree. She hurried over to her sister, finding Thalia and Mel there with her. Sivas carried Ree, who was becoming more alert.

Clio put a finger to her lips, and they all flattened themselves against the cool earth.

Calli closed her eyes. She was certain Circe and her lion would hear the wild thumps her heart made against her ribcage.

There was rustling, then footsteps.

"Where did they go?" she heard Circe say. "They could not have just disappeared."

Calli could hear the lion sniffing around as the two continued to search, but after some time, she heard nothing. She fought the urge to peek over the tree trunk and instead looked over at Clio. Her sister shook her head, indicating that she didn't think it was safe to move yet.

Calli agreed. Circe and Queen couldn't have gone far.

Countless minutes drifted by as they all remained exactly where they were. Finally, Clio squeezed her hand—the signal they were safe.

Calli closed her eyes again and sucked in a deep breath. As slowly as she could, she turned to look over the tree trunk.

Nothing.

"I think they're gone," Calli whispered.

One by one, her sisters, along with Sivas, emerged from behind the tree trunk.

"We must move quickly," Clio said. "They may still be near."

They hastily continued through the forest. At the first sight of the water, Calli nearly fell to her knees in gratitude. But that would have to wait until they were safely off this island.

Everyone except Calli and Sivas climbed into the boat. The two of them pushed the vessel into the water before jumping in themselves.

"We did it!" Ree whispered. Unable to suppress her excitement, she hugged each of her sisters, then Sivas. "I told you it would work, didn't I?"

"Yes, you did," he said.

He leaned back and smiled at her. Their eyes widened at the same time, as if they were only now realizing how they appeared. They quickly separated.

"It's too late to hide your little romance now," Thalia said. "My only question is, when is the wedding?"

"Thalia, please!" Ree said, her cheeks reddening. She walked over to Calli, tense lines of apprehension creasing her forehead. "I'm so sorry for leaving the way I did. To all of you."

Calli tried to hold her composure. There would be time for reprimands later, after they were all safely back in Thebes. But before she could stop herself, she lashed out.

"You should be!" Calli said. "Look at the danger you put us all through."

"I know, and I am sorry. It was stupid and selfish, but I believed Sivas when he said he knew where Mother was! I see now he'd been a victim of an enchantment, but—"

"It was incredibly selfish," Calli said. "We all have a responsibility to this family—and you failed at yours."

Ree's head snapped back as if Calli had slapped her.

"Girls, don't do this," Mel said, reaching for Ree's hand. Ree jerked it away.

Her eyes blazing with anger, she stepped up to Calli. "Forgive me for having faults, but we cannot all be as perfect as you are, Calliope. We cannot all be Mother's favorite little helper."

"What are you talking about?" said Calli. "That is nonsense."

"Is it?" Ree asked. She looked to the others. "Everyone knows that you are Mother's favorite. You're the one she turns to when she needs anything. It's always 'Listen to Calli,' 'Calli knows best,' 'Calli—'"

"Do you think I *want* to be the one that Mother turns to for everything?" snapped Calli. "You don't think I have dreams of my own, things that I want to accomplish, but I can't do any of it because I'm stuck helping to raise my younger sisters?"

A collective gasp rang out around the boat, and Calli immediately regretted her words. The hurt on her sisters' faces tore at her heart.

"Is that how you feel about us?" Mel asked.

"Are we a burden to you?" added Thalia.

"No. Of course not." She wanted to cry at the sight of their doleful expressions. "That is not what I meant."

Calli took Mel's hand and squeezed it, then did the same with Thalia's. She looked to Clio and Ree.

"Having the four of you as my sisters has been the greatest joy of my life. You are not a burden. But . . . I . . . I *do* have my own aspirations. And I hope that I can count on my sisters to support my dreams when the time comes for me to pursue them, because I need you all just as much as you *think* you need me."

She let go of Mel's and Thalia's hands and walked over to Ree, who stood near Clio and Sivas. "I'm sorry for snapping at you. I love you, Terpsichore. You know that, don't you?"

Ree pulled her trembling bottom lip between her teeth. "I know. And I'm sorry for what I said. I don't think Mother plays favorites—at least, she doesn't mean to."

"Mother loves each of us equally," Clio said. "She gave us each a special gift, which shows just how much she loves us."

"Clio is right," Thalia said, standing and walking over to Ree and Calli.

Mel followed and, with a cheeky grin, said, "Besides, we all know that if Mother did play favorites, *I* would be her favorite."

"You wish," Clio said. She nodded at Ree and Calli. "No hard feelings between you two?"

"Of course not," Ree said. She reached over and wrapped her arms around Calli. "Thank you. I knew you would come. It was so strange, but I could feel you close to me the entire time."

"I felt the same," Calli said. She cupped Ree's cheeks within her palms and pressed her forehead against her sister's. "I love you and I will always be there for you. But Ree, don't *ever* do that to us again."

"I promise," Ree said.

Calli turned to Sivas, who had been quietly manning the boat. "Can you get us back to Thebes, or do you need Clio's help?"

"It doesn't matter what you say—I'm helping," Clio said, taking up a position next to Sivas.

"Well, I guess that answers that," Calli said. "It's time to get back. We've got a concert to put on."

XXX

HADES

Hades sat atop his throne, plucking syrup-soaked figs from the tray that Pain and Panic had brought him and popping them in his mouth. He'd requested ambrosia, but apparently his brother had seized all the ambrosia on Olympus because his dear Hera had requested it. Hades still had no idea what she saw in Zeus. Other than his being the ruler of the gods of Olympus.

Hades spat a fig stem from his mouth.

Well, they could keep the ambrosia, because he would have something even sweeter soon. It was only a matter of time now before his plan succeeded. Once Pain and Panic returned with confirmation that Circe had turned Mnemosyne's daughter and the new beau into swine, Hades would have her exactly where he wanted her. Mnemosyne would bend to his will and change the memories of both the gods and mortals.

He could almost taste victory.

He still could not decide just what he would do with Zeus first. He would make his brother bow to him, of course, but Zeus's degradation would have to go much further. And he still had not decided what he would do about Mnemosyne's trying to deceive him. He could not allow it to stand, but he needed her help first. Her punishment would come after she'd done his bidding.

He heard a ruckus outside his lair.

"That must be my little minions now," Hades said just as his two imps came scurrying into his sanctuary. "I've been awaiting your arrival." He bit into another fig. "So, how did it go?" he asked around a mouthful of fruit. "Did they squeal—literally?"

"Uh, about that," Pain said. He stuck his hands behind his back and inched to the side. "It would appear there was a bit of a snafu on Aeaea."

Hades squeezed a fig in his fist, squashing it into a pulp. "What type of snafu?"

"Well," Panic hedged. "They're no longer there. The other four sisters arrived by boat to rescue them, and they all returned to Thebes."

"What!" Hades jumped up from his throne. "Circe let them go? We had a deal!"

They both hunched their stubby shoulders.

"I don't know what to say, boss," Pain said.

Hades brushed passed them. He'd had enough of this.

His anger was burning so intensely by the time he reached Aeaea that the water underneath his boat boiled like a potion in a witch's cauldron. His body glowed like the sun, his vivid orange skin an outward manifestation of the rage roiling inside of him. Hades whipped through the dense forest, slashing down trees left and right as he marched to Circe's hidden retreat.

"What is the meaning of this?" he bellowed the moment he entered the grotto.

"Hades, what a surprise," she said flatly.

"We had a deal! How could you let her go?"

"I didn't," Circe said, bored and unbothered. "She and the boy escaped."

Her apathy infuriated him even more.

"What. Happened?" he asked through gritted teeth.

She ran her hand along that stupid lion's head. The big cat purred like a kitten.

"I do not know," Circe finally answered. "One minute the girl was treating me to a beautiful dance, and the next I was asleep. I woke up in time to give chase, but they outran both me and Queen."

"So you went to sleep instead of doing your job?"

"Do not use that tone with me, Hades," she stated. "I told you that I woke up and gave chase."

"I'll use whatever tone I want," he said. "And apparently you did not chase them fast enough. I want—"

Before Hades knew what was happening, his body jolted, and then his face was in the mud. He looked down at his feet, but instead of seeing feet he saw hooves.

Hades squealed.

"What did you do?" He jumped at the sound of his high-pitched voice. "Circe! Change me back!"

Her lion sauntered over to him, sniffing the dirt around his feet. Hooves.

"Get your cat!" he said. "And change me back."

Circe casually studied her cuticles. "You understand this is *my* island. I agreed to help you because, as you know, I'm ready for payback on some of the gods of Olympus. But no one talks to me with such disrespect. Even the mighty Hades."

He remained silent, except for the snorts he could not help. He would annihilate her once he was no longer walking around on all fours.

"We can still be partners," Circe said. "You know I have always wanted retribution against Zeus for exiling me to this island." She huffed. "He should have rewarded me for ridding the world of my awful husband, but instead he banished me. Do not let this one hiccup ruin a good thing, Hades."

"Change me back," Hades repeated.

"Oh, very well."

In the blink of an eye, he was once again himself, albeit on all fours. Hades pushed up from the ground and dusted off his tunic.

"For what it is worth, I am sorry she got away," Circe said. "She would have been quite a treasure to have on my island. Her dancing is remarkable."

Her dancing. Of course.

Mnemosyne's little creations were living up to their purpose. They existed to provide a diversion, to make people forget about their troubles.

Well done, Mnemosyne. Well done.

But Hades was done playing games. He didn't need Circe or anyone else. He would take care of Mnemosyne's girls himself.

Then she would have no choice but to do as he commanded.

Once back in his lair, Hades stomped back and forth along the banks of the River Styx. He could barely contain his rage.

At the outset of his latest revenge plot, he thought it would be a simple negotiation between himself and Mnemosyne. After she got over her anger at being kidnapped, of course. But she refused to budge, even when he threatened her beloved daughters, who she just knew would eventually rescue her.

And they had tried. Oh, they had tried their little hearts out, poor dears.

But his attempts at putting up roadblocks to hamper her daughters' search hadn't worked out the way he thought it would, either.

"I have a new strategy," Hades murmured. "And this one *will* work."

Instead of thwarting their search, he would bring them directly to their mother. He would force Mnemosyne's hand by making her watch as he tortured each of those precious daughters.

"Pain! Panic! Get in here," Hades called.

He rubbed his hands together in anticipation of his plan coming together. He'd held on to this tool in case the situation became dire, which was exactly where he now found himself. He'd developed a serum that would temporarily alter Mnemosyne's daughters' minds so that they saw their mother in distress. How could they not come running after seeing her chained to the floor, struggling to break free?

The serum would also bring clarity so that they could finally pinpoint exactly where their mother had been taken, since it was taking them so long to find it on their own. It was his fault, of course. He'd had Pain and Panic ply Hermes and Apollo with false information. Those two little Goody-Two-Shoes were always so willing to help. It sickened him.

They had served Hades well without even knowing it, but he was done with the two Olympians.

Where were those imps?

"Pain! Pan—" The two skidded across the floor, with Pain running into Panic and knocking him over.

"Reporting for duty," Pain said, bringing his hand to his forehead in salute.

"Me too," Panic said as he righted himself.

Hades huffed out a sigh. He questioned the wisdom of sending these two out to do such an important job, but he could not risk another trip to the agora so soon. He'd been lucky no one had recognized him the first time.

"Listen here," Hades said. "I am done playing around with Mnemosyne and those daughters of hers. I'm ready to end this." He walked over to the wall where he kept his potions and serums. He pulled a red bottle from the shelf. "Those girls must be famished after gallivanting from Thebes to Aeaea and then back again. I think we should provide them a little snack."

XXXI

CALLI

When they arrived back in Thebes, a dark cloud hung over the city, along with the oppressing sense of doom Calli had felt when they first arrived. The reprieve Thalia's comedic performance had granted seemed to have worn off during their absence.

Yet Calli felt different, because now she better understood what her and her sisters' roles were in this world. They could alleviate such suffering, even if only for a short time. They could use their talent to remind people that things would not always be as bad as they appeared to be.

They could give people hope.

The realization brought a lightness to Calli's steps, while at the same time compelling her to move faster. She wanted—needed—to get her mother back. She had more questions for her now than ever. Why would she grant them such extraordinary abilities only to keep them hidden for all these years? They could have done so much good in the world up to this point, yet her mother had stifled them.

CALLI

Despite her complicated feelings toward what her mother had done, Calli also owed her a debt of gratitude for her brilliance and vision, and for linking her forever to her remarkable sisters.

Although, at the moment, one of those sisters was testing the limits of Calli's patience.

"You understand that someone placed Sivas in a trance, right?" said Ree. "He doesn't even remember taking me from away Thebes."

"Ree, please! No one is blaming Sivas," Calli told her as they navigated through the throng of Thebans crowding the agora.

Ree had spent much of the journey back from Aeaea defending Sivas. Clearly, she feared that her sisters wouldn't forgive him.

"We were already on the boat by the time I realized that something wasn't right," Ree continued.

"It is clear that someone manipulated Sivas," Calli told her. The story of how the two had landed on Circe's island led Calli to believe that whoever held her mother captive had masterminded this attempted kidnapping, too.

Calli wondered, once again, if someone from Krymmenos was behind this. How else would they have known about Sivas and Ree's budding courtship, and how perfect it was to use the boy that her sister was smitten with as a tool to kidnap her?

"—and I was the one who ran away from you and the others while we were rehearsing," Ree was saying. "So, when you think about it, it really is my fault."

Calli turned and put her hands on her sister's shoulders. "Ree, listen to me. No one is blaming you or Sivas. Yes, I was suspicious of him, but no longer. I see that he cares for you. If he didn't, he would have taken the boat that the two of you sailed on and left Circe's island before we ever arrived. He did exactly as you asked him to do and waited at the shoreline for us. He made sure we found you."

"So you forgive us both?" Ree asked.

She sighed. "You've done nothing that needs forgiving, but if it will help to soothe your frayed nerves, then yes, I forgive you. Now it's time to focus on the concert."

A deep voice sounded from just over her shoulder. "I agree."

Calli spun around. A large man stood with his arms crossed over a massive chest and a glow to his deep purple skin, despite the overcast sky.

"What are you doing here? We didn't use the flute," she said to Apollo.

"I came to see how things are going with your concert preparations," he said. "The gods can be a fickle bunch—present company excluded, of course—so you must make sure you put on the best performance of your lives."

"We are just returning from Aeaea," Calli informed him.

"I see all five of you are back together again," he said. He hooked a thumb at Sivas. "*This* is who she ran away with? I will never understand mortals."

A man shrouded in a black cloak and pushing a wheelbarrow bumped into both Calli and Apollo.

"Do you mind?" Apollo asked with an air of superiority.

"Outta my way," the man said.

He curled his lips in disgust. "Such an ill-mannered lot here in Thebes."

"Not only in Thebes," Calli said, thinking of how they had once been treated in Krymmenos.

"Calli, I need a nap before we start rehearsing again," Thalia said.

"Me, too," said Mel.

Seeing the exhaustion on her sisters' faces brought to mind just how tired Calli was. It had been a rough day.

"I know, Thalia," Calli said. She squeezed her shoulder. "We'll discuss it in just a minute." She turned to Apollo. "Do you think we can hold the concert tomorrow?"

Considering how depleted they all were, she was afraid their performances would not be as good as they could be if they tried to hold it tonight.

But Apollo shook his head.

"Remember what I just said about the gods being fickle? They are also busy, and they are quick to turn their attention elsewhere. If you want to attract as many of the gods as possible, you need to hold the concert as soon as you can."

A sense of foreboding began to overwhelm her.

Calli considered all that had taken place since they arrived in Thebes. Nothing had worked out as planned. Despite all she and her sisters had done, she still had no idea where to find her mother or whether any of this would lead them to her.

Why would this concert be any different?

"Apollo, what do you think are the chances this concert will attract the gods?"

He lifted his large shoulders in a shrug. "It is difficult to predict anything when it comes to my fellow Olympians, but they do enjoy being entertained."

"So you can't ensure that any of the gods will come to our concert?" she asked.

"No," said Apollo. "Hermes is informing them all of the event, but we cannot force them to attend."

Apollo's words hit Calli square in the chest, intensifying her unease. No matter how much they practiced or how amazing they promised to be in their performance, they couldn't guarantee the gods would be there.

If they could not summon the Olympians, where would that leave them?

Apollo jerked forward as someone bumped into him again. This time it was a woman pushing a cart filled with pomegranates. The cloak she wore was the same color as the fruit she sold.

"It is time for me to return home." He dusted off the sleeves of his tunic. "I truly hate being here among the mortals. I know they serve a purpose, but why must they touch me?"

Calli still could not believe her sweet mother originated from the same realm as someone as self-important as Apollo. She could never imagine Mnemosyne behaving in such a way. Then again, maybe she had been that way and living among mortals had mellowed her out.

After Apollo departed, Calli walked over to where her sisters and Sivas perused the various merchant carts displaying wares of all kinds, from delicate pottery to vessels filled with wine and honey.

"Look here!" Sivas said excitedly, rounding a cart loaded with musical instruments. He picked up a double-reeded flute made of polished ivory. "I'm quite accomplished on the aulos."

He brought the wind instrument to his lips and blew out a lively tune.

Thalia snapped her fingers to the beat. "Why didn't you tell us your man was a musician, Ree? You should play for us during our concert."

"That's a wonderful idea!" Mel chimed in.

"Oh, can he?" Ree asked.

Calli and Clio looked at each other and shrugged.

"It couldn't hurt," Calli said. "Unless you mess us up, which means you need to practice. We all must practice."

"Can't we eat first?" Thalia groused. "I'm hungry."

"Did someone say they were hungry?" a frail voice asked. Calli whipped around to find the same pomegranate merchant who'd bumped into Apollo.

"I'm sorry, girls, but we don't have time to eat right now," Calli said.

"But I'm hungry," Thalia repeated.

"You can eat after we rehearse," Calli said.

"But . . . but I will give you a good deal," the pomegranate peddler said.

Calli reached into her satchel. She'd paid most of their money to the old woman who had given her information on Ree's whereabouts. If they wanted a guaranteed place to sleep tonight, they only had a few coins to spare. But they had to eat. She would figure out where they would sleep and how she would pay for it when the time came.

"I'll make a compromise," she said to Thalia. "We spend some time discussing the changes to our routine, and then we can eat." Calli gave the coins to Sivas. "Would you mind purchasing the pomegranates, and find some figs and almonds, as well?"

He stuck the aulos he'd just bought in his bag and took the money from her. Calli then gathered her sisters together.

"We do not have any more time to waste," Calli told them. "I know we are tired, but we must hold the concert tonight or risk losing the interest of the gods."

"It should not be difficult," Clio said. "I remember all my steps from the performance back in Krymmenos."

"Actually, I have another idea," Calli said. "Not that the show you crafted was not stellar, Ree. It was, and we will incorporate most of it into the concert. But I think we should tell our story."

They all just stared at her.

"*Our* story," Calli repeated, reaching into her satchel and retrieving the journal. "Mother has already written it for us. If there is one thing I am certain of, it is that Mother was very deliberate when she created us. There is something in our family's history that will call to the gods. I know there is. We just have to take what is in this journal and put it to music." She looked at Ree. "And dance." Then to Thalia. "And comedy.

"Clio, with your intelligence, I'm sure you can help me come up with clever ways to show how Mother created each of our gifts. And Mel," she said, turning to her last sister. "No one can reach a person's heart the way you can. You can help with the writing, too, can't you? What do you all think, girls? Do you think we can do this?"

Despite their exhaustion, the four of them nodded enthusiastically. Calli and Clio quickly began figuring out the pertinent aspects of the story they should include in their performance, with Mel chiming in about the parts she found most touching.

Sivas returned with the goods he'd purchased, but they were

all too absorbed in their concert preparations to stop to eat. Instead, Ree and Sivas stepped away so that they could figure out where to incorporate his songs on the aulos.

As Calli and Clio mulled over the riddle about the bird that flies at night that had puzzled Calli ever since she first read it, she heard a high-pitched scream that snatched both her and Clio's attention.

"Oh, my goodness!" Ree screeched.

Calli and Clio ran to their sister, who stood next to Sivas. At their feet lay a donkey. Broken pieces of pottery from the small wagon the animal had been pulling had scattered across the ground.

"What did you do to my donkey?" the merchant yelled.

"Nothing!" Sivas held his hands up. "Your donkey snatched my fruit."

"What happened here?" Calli asked.

"I don't know," Ree said. "Sivas was playing a song for me when the donkey nabbed a pomegranate from his bag without him noticing. Moments later, the donkey was on the ground."

"Is it dead?" Clio asked.

The merchant and Sivas knelt on either side of the animal.

"I do not believe so," Sivas said. "It appears to be breathing."

Suddenly, the donkey's eyes opened wide, and it scrambled up from the ground. It began to neigh and clomp around in a circle, carrying on as if a ghost was after it. The more the merchant tried to soothe it, the more irritated the animal became.

"The donkey has gone mad," Ree said.

Calli had never heard of a donkey suddenly going mad, but she immediately thought about what happened to Sivas earlier, before he and Ree took off for Circe's island.

"I don't think that's it," she said. She looked around for the old woman who had been selling the fruit. "Sivas, do you remember the person you encountered earlier, before you were put into that trance?"

He tilted his head to the side. "Not well. I believe he was tall."

"Are you sure it was a man? Could it have been a woman? Like the woman who sold you the pomegranates?"

"No, it was not her. I would have remembered. At least I think I would have."

"Either way—none of us should eat those pomegranates," said Calli. "But don't throw them out. We don't want a child picking one up and eating it. We will figure out a safe place to dispose of them later."

The merchant finally brought his donkey under control, but the animal still looked good and spooked. The feeling of foreboding that had troubled her earlier returned. Calli tried her best to shake it off. There was still too much to do.

"Let us get back to practicing for the concert," she said.

"You can forget the concert." The voice came from just behind her.

Calli whipped around. "Hermes? What are you doing here?"

"Bringing you the bad news," he said, holding his hands out apologetically. "I tried to be proactive, but it backfired."

"What do you mean?" Calli asked.

"Well, I was flying around Olympus, so I decided to invite the gods to the concert. They all declined."

"They declined?" Clio asked, alarm making her voice go high.

He nodded. "Every single one of them."

Ree turned to Calli. "What are we supposed to do now?" she asked.

"I don't know," Calli said, and immediately felt as if she was letting her sisters down. They relied on her for guidance, but she was at a loss. This concert was their one shot at getting the gods' attention.

"Calli?" Mel approached, holding the jar she had been carrying close to her chest—the same one that old man had given her the day before. Her hands shook and her eyes were bright with a mixture of fear and anticipation. "It is time."

Calli stared cautiously at the jar cradled in her sister's palms. "What makes you think that?"

"I just feel it," Mel answered. "I can't explain why, but I know that it is time to open it. Should I?"

It wasn't as if anything else could go wrong on this awful day.

"If you feel it is what you must do," Calli answered.

Mel sucked in a deep breath and slowly lifted the top of the jar.

A bright flash of lightning streaked across the sky—and pandemonium erupted.

XXXII

MNEMOSYNE

Mnemosyne brought her knees up to her chest and wrapped her arms around her legs. The thought of surrendering to Hades's demands tempted her like a honey cake, but she refused to fall victim to it. She would think of another way to free herself from this mess with Hades and reunite with her daughters.

A smile tugged at the corners of Mnemosyne's lips as a memory of her girls replayed in her head.

"Thalia, stand there," Calli demanded.

"Calliope, you mustn't boss your sisters around," Mnemosyne reminded her. "I raised you to be a leader, not a bully. There is a difference."

"Yeah, stop being a bully," Thalia said.

Mnemosyne quelled the urge to laugh. Even though she was the youngest, Thalia was definitely the second biggest bully out of her five daughters.

She knew what she had been getting into by creating such

headstrong girls, but it never failed to amaze her just how much they were alike on that front.

"Pay attention, girls," Mel admonished. "Clio is ready to start."

Her five daughters had summoned her for a birthday "surprise," and now they stood in the center of the common room. Clio had been tasked with narrating today's performance, and of course, Calli served as the mistress of ceremonies. She'd rounded the girls up and made sure they were all in their proper places.

After wishing her happy birthday, Calli said, "And now we present to you this history of the mighty sun god Helios. Clio, you can begin."

As Clio told the story of the Titan god, Ree and Melpomene mimed her words with their dance.

Mnemosyne had been deliberate in what she taught the girls about her kind and their rule. Of course, they had no idea that the gods they spoke of—and whom Clio had studied with fervency—were close relatives of their mother. And, by extension, of them.

Thalia and Calli acted out an amusing scene between Helios and his sisters, Selene and Eos, playing up their opposing views as the sun, the moon, and the dawn. Thalia's hilarious jokes caused Calli to break character several times, and at one point even made Clio stumble across her words.

At the end of the performance, Mnemosyne gave them a standing ovation.

"Bravi, my beautiful daughters. Bravi! As usual, you have

spoiled your mother with an outstanding birthday surprise. Your talent continues to amaze me."

"Wait until your birthday next year," Ree said. "I'm in charge of your surprise, and it's going to be even better."

"I beg your pardon," Clio said.

Mnemosyne held her hands up. "Please, girls." She laughed. "Let me enjoy this *year before making me think about the next."*

Calli walked over and put her arms around Mnemosyne. "Mother already knows that it doesn't matter who is in charge of her surprise. They will always be spectacular because that is what she deserves."

Mnemosyne's smile dimmed before turning into an outright frown. The happiest times of her entire life were those she spent with her girls, but the more she thought about the good times, the more suffocating her guilt over lying to them became. She'd raised them to be smart and self-sufficient. She should have trusted that they would have been able to protect themselves. Instead, she'd kept them hidden, stifling the gifts that were meant to be shared with all.

"I must release them," Mnemosyne whispered.

She pulled her trembling bottom lip between her teeth, stifling the cry that threatened to escape. She loved her girls more than anything, but she had been selfish. They were never meant for one person's enjoyment. They were meant to bring joy to the masses, to one another, and to themselves.

If she ever got away from Hades—no, *when* she got away from Hades—she would let her girls go. They no longer belonged only to her. They had their own lives to live, with dreams and aspirations to pursue. And if any of the other gods came after them, Zeus included, she would do whatever it took to stave them off.

Mnemosyne jolted out of her musings, overcome by an overwhelming sense of dread. She had felt varying levels of unease from several of the girls ever since Hades put her in this dungeon, but the connection had been faint. Not anymore. She felt vivid and visceral terror coming from her daughters.

Something awful had been unleashed. And Mnemosyne had the terrifying feeling that her girls were right in the middle of it all.

XXXIII

CALLI

A windstorm whipped up the dirt and grime from the streets, then swirled around the girls in tight, destructive spirals, demolishing merchants' carts, tossing chariots onto their sides, and blowing away anything that was not tied down or made of stone.

"What's happening?" Thalia yelled.

"I don't know, but we need to find cover," Calli shouted.

She looked around for somewhere to hide from the debris flying around them. Balls of ice began to fall from the sky, pelting all who were not sheltered from the elements.

"It was her!" a woman shouted, pointing at Melpomene.

The same young mother Mel had noticed the day before was standing in accusation of her.

"She unleashed this on us!" the young mother screamed. "I saw it. She opened that jar and released the demons."

"No!" Mel cried.

The mob grew angrier and more terrified as further chaos erupted all around them.

An old man wearing a tattered chiton ran up to her and yelled in her face. "Who sent you here? Go back to where you came from!"

"And take your demons with you!" the woman next to him screamed, shaking her fist.

Their venomous expressions sent a streak of fear down Calli's spine. She gathered her sisters and Sivas, and they ran.

"Look! Over there!" Calli yelled.

She guided them to the library, where they huddled together, using its marble facade as a shield. Calli used her body as a buffer between the elements and her sisters. Keeping them safe was the only thing that mattered right now.

"No, no, no," Mel continued to cry.

She covered one ear with her hand. The other was pressed against Calli's chest.

"It's okay, Mel," Calli said.

A loud bang crackled a few feet from where they were. One of the capitals from a nearby column had toppled to the ground.

She tightened her hold on Mel. With her other hand, she reached for Thalia and pulled her in closer. She had to protect her sisters from the pure mayhem happening all around them.

People continued to scream, running to find cover wherever they could. The spot Calli had found next to the library partially shielded them, but they were still vulnerable to the wind and ice pellets. She used her body to safeguard Mel and Thalia as much as possible, and Sivas concealed Ree and Clio from the madness.

But it was more than just the elements she needed to protect her sisters from. The people on the streets were looking at them in the same way they had back in Krymmenos, as if they were outcasts who would bring chaos and destruction. Except that she and her sisters *had* wreaked havoc on Thebes.

No, Mel hadn't unleashed terror onto the city. At least not directly. That old man had handed her that jar. Calli had known something was not right about him. If she could go back in time, she would follow her first instincts and demand that Mel give him his jar right back.

It was too late now. Mnemosyne's daughters had made a name for themselves in Thebes, one they were not likely to live down. But Calli no longer cared what others thought about her or her family. Whether she was in Thebes or Krymmenos or even Corinth, the only thing that mattered was that her mother and sisters were safe.

Another loud bang rang out. The shrill cry of neighing horses told her yet another chariot had crashed to the ground. Calli closed her eyes tight and did her best to block out the horror happening around them.

Another deafening clamor resounded, shaking the buildings and the ground and sending people running into the streets and open square.

Suddenly, all fell silent, and everything went frighteningly still.

Thalia twisted around. "What . . . what's happening?"

"Is it over?" Mel asked.

Nearly a dozen blinding rays of sunlight shone down through the clouds. Moments later, the clouds parted, and ten larger-than-life beings descended from the sky and into the middle of the square.

Calli's body shivered—from fear or excitement, she could not be certain. Possibly both.

She, her sisters, and Sivas slowly stepped away from the library. Calli's eyes widened as she took in the gods she had only heard about in stories. They were all there, looking upon the masses with curiosity and a hint of derision.

The matronly goddess in green with flowers peppering her gown must be Demeter, the Goddess of the Harvest. And there was the goddess Athena, with her massive shield and lance. And the big, burly god with a wide beard was most certainly the God of the Forge, Hephaestus. In the stories her mother used to tell them, she claimed that Hephaestus could forge any weapon one could dream of, including Zeus's lightning bolts.

Zeus!

Calli's breath caught in her throat. There he stood in the center of the gods, along with his wife, Hera. Zeus was as massive and majestic as she had imagined. His royal purple chiton was held together by a gold medallion with a lightning bolt emblazoned on it, much like the one Apollo wore with the image of the sun.

Calli looked for him, but neither he nor Hermes seemed to be among the group of gods who had assembled.

"Well, who called us?" an aqua-colored god with a lacelike blue fin down his back asked.

"Is that—?" Calli asked.

"Poseidon," Clio answered, awe coloring her voice. "It's Poseidon!"

"*Some*one must have called us," another, who could only be Artemis, asked. The quiver filled with arrows was a dead giveaway. That and the fact she looked almost exactly like her twin brother, Apollo.

Then Apollo arrived in his chariot, pulling it to a stop directly in front of Calli and her sisters. With arms stretched out, he asked, "What happened to the concert?"

Calli hunched her shoulders, relieved to see a familiar face.

"We were still rehearsing when all of this happened," she answered. She didn't mention the donkey who had eaten that fruit, fallen in a dead faint, and then gone haywire.

Hermes flew in with his winged sandals, landing alongside Apollo's chariot.

"I don't know how you did it, but you ladies sure figured out a way to get the gods' attention," he said. "This whole fire-and-brimstone act you came up with worked better than anything I would have thought up. Where'd you get the idea to turn Thebes into a disaster zone?"

Calli's mouth fell open as understanding dawned.

"The jar," Mel said, taking the words out of Calli's mouth.

"That jar is cursed!" Ree said. "It caused this mayhem."

"Exactly," Mel said. "The jar was the call for help. It was a signal to the gods that they were needed down here in Thebes."

"Hmm . . . I think you may be right," Hermes said.

Apollo crossed his arms over his chest. "Well, I was promised a concert, and I still want to see one. I've been looking forward to it." He tightened his hold on the reins. "I will be in the amphitheater when you are ready. Do not take too long. We gods have things to do," he said. He turned to the others. "To the amphitheater. Entertainment awaits us."

He and his horses took off, but instead of joining Apollo, Zeus turned to his wife with a concerned frown.

"I cannot leave Thebes in such disarray while we attend a concert. Could you have Iris gather Kratos, Bia, and a few of the other gods to start addressing the needs of those in Thebes? I want them to make sure the destruction there is taken care of right away."

The girls stood frozen in awe as Hera summoned another goddess, whom Clio breathlessly identified as Hera's personal handmaiden, Iris. After issuing the orders Zeus had requested, Hera and Zeus departed for the amphitheater, along with Demeter and Dionysus, Artemis and Aphrodite, Athena and a scowling Ares, and all the others. Calli caught sight of the petite bird perched upon Athena's shoulder and frowned. Something about it pecked at the back of her mind.

"Let me get this straight," Ree said, turning to Mel. "Are you saying that we had the one thing we needed to get the attention of the gods all this time?"

Mel nodded. "It appears so. I knew there was something special about that jar. I just didn't know what."

Thalia tossed her hands up in the air. "We jumped through all those hoops for nothing? If you had just taken the lid off that jar when we first told you to, we could have skipped that maze and that trip to the lady with the pet lion?"

"Stop piling everything on Mel's head," Calli said. "She was following the instructions she was given."

"And listening to my heart," Mel said. "The old man who gave me the jar told me that I would know when it was time to open it, and something in my gut told me it was time."

"Your intuition is your gift," Calli reminded her. "You should always listen to it."

"That's what I did," Mel said. "And that's why I opened the jar when I did."

Thalia folded her arms across her chest. "Well, I still say you should have opened that jar when that old man gave it to you. You tortured us for nothing."

"No!" Calli said. "Girls, don't you see? It had to be this way. If Mel had summoned the gods by unleashing this fury on Thebes from the very beginning, we never would have learned about our special gifts. Clio would not have guided us through that maze. And Thalia, how would you have ever learned that your comedy is powerful enough to literally part the clouds in the sky? You gave the people of Thebes a reason to smile."

"I did, didn't I?" Thalia said, fluffing her hair.

"And Ree," Calli said. "The way you dance is so mesmerizing that you were able to subdue one of the greatest enchantresses this world has ever known. And you saved both yourself and Sivas."

Calli took Mel by the hand and gave it a reassuring squeeze.

"And you trusted your gut, the way you always do. You did exactly what you were supposed to do, and it has happened exactly the way it was meant to happen. This is what Mother wanted for us: to discover our power, the power that *she* gave to us. And now we have the attention of the gods of Olympus."

"But we didn't get any information about Mother from them," Clio said. "We didn't even get a chance to ask them about her."

"That's what this concert will do," said Calli. "We are going to tell them the story of how Mnemosyne's girls came to be and ensure they'll help us. And I think our performing should go far beyond just this concert for the gods. Gather around."

Calli looped her arms with Mel's and Clio's and gestured for the others to do the same. Once they were all joined, Calli continued.

"I know that we each have our own dreams we want to pursue, but what do you all think of forming a singing quintet?"

They all stared at her as if she had been hit in the head by fallen debris during the chaos that rained down on them earlier.

But then Clio grinned and said, "That actually sounds fun."

"Fun? It's a fantastic idea," Thalia said.

"I truly believe it is what we're called to do," Calli said. "If there is one thing we've learned on this journey, it's that we are stronger when we all are together. And when we sing? It's magical."

"Yes, it is! Magical and inspirational!" Mel said. "And living in Thebes sounds soooo exciting!"

"Live in Thebes?" Ree asked. "Why do we have to live in Thebes?"

"Because Thebes is where all the action is," Thalia said. "Now, what should we call ourselves?"

"Well, in the old language, *mousa* means a source of inspiration," Clio said. "Why don't we call ourselves the Muses?"

"Ooooh, I like that," Mel said with infectious excitement. "I never thought of us singing for anyone other than Mother, but when you consider the way the crowd reacted when we performed at Ree's studio—" She stopped, her face whipping around to Ree. "What about Ree's studio?"

Terpsichore's lips thinned in a pensive frown, and Calli immediately felt like a heel for not considering how her suggestion would affect Ree.

"I never meant to imply that you should give up on your studio," Calli told her. "I know how important is to you."

"But so are my sisters," Ree said, her frown deepening. The enthusiasm of a few moments before had dimmed.

“We don’t have to make the decision right now,” Calli said. “We should get to the amphitheater. We have a show to put on.” Straightening, she called to Sivas. “Are you sure you can play that aulos without missing a beat?”

“I’m certain of it,” he said, a huge grin on his face.

“Well, sisters, let us go inspire the gods of Olympus with song,” Calli said. “And, hopefully, convince them to help us find our mother.”

XXXIV

REE

The amphitheater just outside of Thebes's acropolis was large enough to hold twenty thousand, but they were performing before an audience of only a dozen or so. As the girls arrived, Ree tried her best to set aside the discussion that had taken place—Calliope's big idea.

She was torn and confused, and she had no idea what she wanted to do. On one hand, she adored the idea of forming a singing group with her sisters. Just thinking about the scores of people they would entertain sent excited chills down her spine. But what about all the work she'd put into opening her studio in Krymmenos? And what about her students? Sure, she would likely acquire many more students in a big city like Thebes, but was she to leave Cressida and Nephele without a teacher?

And what about Sivas? She liked him. She *really* liked him, and she was sure he liked her, too. But how could this fledgling courtship with Sivas ever compete with the love she had for her sisters?

Ree brought a hand to her chest to distract from the growing ache that had begun to build there. This was all happening too quickly.

"We're about to start," Clio said, knocking Ree out of her disconcerting ruminations. "Now, don't be nervous. We performed in front of more at your studio. This audience is small compared to that one."

"Right," Ree said. "It's only a dozen or so here."

Of course, they were the dozen or so most intimidating beings in the entire universe, but Ree tried not to let that fact get to her as they made their way to the semicircular stage in the center of the theater. Still, she could not fight the nerves that flittered in the pit of her stomach and caused her pulse to beat wildly in her neck.

This was the most important performance of her life. She was equal parts excited and terrified. She tried not to focus on the gods sitting patiently waiting for them to begin. Instead, she walked over to Sivas, who stood on the left side of the stage. Just the sight of his smile calmed her.

"Are you nervous?" Ree asked.

"Yes," he admitted without hesitation.

"Don't be," she said, taking his hands in hers.

"I am used to performing for the olive trees," Sivas said with a laugh. He gave her fingers a gentle squeeze. "But it helps knowing that their eyes will be focused on you and your sisters, and not me."

She laughed. "Well, that doesn't help my nerves."

He looked her in the eyes. "You have nothing to worry about, Terpsichore. You are mesmerizing when you dance."

Her heart melted then and there.

"Thank you," Ree said. She thought about leaning forward to kiss him, but before she could, she heard Calli say, "The gods are ready for us."

Ree quickly made it to the center of the stage, where her sisters stood. "Calli, aren't you going to tell us where to stand?"

"And what about our cue to start?" Thalia asked.

Calli shook her head, a proud smile breaking out across her face.

"You don't need me to guide you anymore," she said. "You all know what you have to do, so let's do it."

She stepped forward, lifted her hands, and said, "Greetings, gods of Olympus. We are the Muses, the daughters of the goddess Mnemosyne, and have we got a story for you! Hit it, Sivas!"

With a sharp nod, Sivas brought the ivory aulos to his lips and started playing the jaunty tune he and Ree had rehearsed.

Calliope lifted her hands with the kind of dramatic flair Ree was used to seeing from Thalia and began singing in her deep, resonant voice.

"In the beginning, there was Ouranos and Gaea!"

She and Clio proceeded to sing the story of the original Titans and their twelve children, of whom their mother was one, trading off the first few verses.

Flashes of recognition began to light up their audience's faces as Clio and Calli continued reciting what they had deciphered from their mother's journal as her history. Thalia added comic relief to the segments about the Titanomachy, playing up the strength of the Olympian gods and exaggerating the cowardliness of the Titans.

The gods' dispassionate expressions slowly morphed into displays of glee. Demeter's smile encompassed her whole face, and Hephaestus's belly laugh was so loud it nearly drowned out their singing.

When they arrived at the part when their mother approached Zeus with her offer, the leader of the gods of Olympus sat up straight. He stared in wonder at the five of them, as if he was seeing them in an entirely new light.

"And so our mother created us—her five daughters. She imbued us with incredible abilities. Let us show you."

Calliope then introduced her sisters one by one.

"The youngest, Thalia—the Muse of Comedy," she said. "It does not matter how badly your day is going; just a few moments with Thalia are sure to delight. I dare you not to laugh as my youngest sister entertains you."

In true Thalia fashion, her youngest sister won over their audience with wisecracks about the gods and their powers. Ree had questioned Calli's choice not to begin the performance by appealing to the gods for their help, but she now understood the reasoning behind her sister's approach. Winning the gods over with flattery would make them more persuadable. Having Thalia as their opening act was genius. Her humor was the perfect way to set the mood for the performance.

Raucous laughter erupted when Thalia exaggerated the size of the wings on Hermes's heels and dramatized how she imagined the fish of the ocean behaved whenever Poseidon was near them.

"Can you imagine a fish falling in a dead faint?" Thalia asked, leaning back and draping her arm over her head. "I know that's what I would do, and that's the gospel truth."

And then she did just that, dropping to the floor in a melodramatic display that was all Thalia.

The gods roared, their laughter practically shaking the stage.

"Next is Terpsichore, the Muse of Dance," said Calliope.

Ree followed Thalia's jokes about the sea with a captivating dance where she moved her body like water, leaping across the stage and ending in a pose that mimicked Zeus's stance when wielding one of his mighty lightning bolts. The ruler of Olympus broke out in zealous applause. He pointed to the stage, elbowing Ares, who had been expressionless throughout the performance. Ree was unsure if there was anything that could put a smile on the God of War's face. She continued, dancing to the dithyramb in honor of Dionysus, as she'd practiced earlier, before bringing her portion of the performance to a close.

"And now I present Clio, the Muse of History, and Melpomene, the Muse of Tragedy," said Calliope.

Clio and Mel then took center stage.

Clio sang a riveting recitation of the history of Thebes, with Mel chiming in with tidbits about how the gods had aided Thebans throughout time.

"Although King Cadmus had the guidance of the oracle, the founder of Thebes would have been lost without the help of the mighty Zeus and his brother Poseidon," Clio sang.

"And let us not forget Athena, whose assistance helped the young Cadmus conquer his fear and slay a dragon," Mel added. "Without her contribution, Thebes would never have come into existence."

Each god's face lit up when their name was mentioned. Even though some of the so-called generosities expounded on were not very generous at all, Mel had a way of making each action seem like the most magnanimous gesture ever performed.

"And now for our fearless leader," Clio said. "Tell the great writers of our time to make room, because there's a new voice in town. Calliope, Muse of Epic Poetry, the floor is yours."

With that, Calli belted out the opening lines of an epic tale that told the love story between a mortal sculptor, Pygmalion, and the woman he fashioned out of marble. Ree paid particular attention to Aphrodite, since it was well-known that Pygmalion had petitioned to the Goddess of Love and Beauty in hopes that she would make his statue real—a wish Aphrodite eventually granted him. The smile lighting up the goddess's face spoke to how charmed she was by Calli's performance.

Once Calli finished, the girls all gathered in the center of the stage. It was time to plead their case to the gods and solicit their help. For the first time since they arrived in Thebes, Mnemosyne's girls sang together in unison:

Gracious and compassionate is what our mother is.
The epitome of motherhood; when we call her, she appears.
Without her at our sides, we feel oh so lost.
To get her back we'll do anything, no matter what the cost.

The power of their collective voices rang through the air as they sang about all their mother had done to keep them safe and how, with the help of the gods, they could rescue her and reunite once again.

Suddenly, an ethereal haze formed above their heads, and images of the words they sang began to dance in the sky. The gods all tilted back in their seats, expressions of awe and delight illuminating their already glowing faces.

Ree nearly lost track of the lyrics when she glanced over and noticed that same glow radiating from Thalia. Then Mel. Then Calli. Then Clio. She looked down at her own body and marveled at the incandescent sheen covering her skin. She and her sisters all shone like the gods of Olympus.

How could this be?

Ree saw the same question reflected in her sisters' expressions. But they would have to wait until they were done with the show to find answers.

When the girls brought the concert to a close, the gods gave them a standing ovation. Ree reared back as their enthusiastic audience crowded around the stage, all speaking at once.

"That was sensational!" Aphrodite said.

Hermes applauded. "A true delight!"

"I knew you ladies would be a success," Apollo said, puffing out his chest like a proud papa. "I know talent when I see it."

"Remarkable storytelling!" Hera said. "Wasn't it remarkable, Zeus?"

"It was," Zeus answered. "Tell me, where is your mother? Why isn't she here to share in your triumph?"

"Yes, where is Mnemosyne?" Demeter asked. "It has been ages since I've seen her."

"You remember her?" Calli asked the Goddess of the Harvest, but it was Hermes who answered.

"Yes, I remember her now, too!" he said. "She came to live on Olympus after the Great War. She was the Goddess of Memory—she must have erased our memories when she left. But why would she do such a thing?"

"Yes, how odd," said Demeter. "I remember liking her a great deal."

Ree looked to her sisters, who appeared as shocked as she felt. Their mother was the Goddess of Memory, with friends among the Olympians?

"That would explain why none of the gods remembered her," Ree surmised. "But why would their recollection of mother suddenly return?"

"It was our singing," Calli said. "I think it restored their memory. That must be why Mother never wanted us to sing in public. She must have suspected that it had the power to affect her gift of memory."

"I think Calli's right," Clio said. "Our singing was so compelling that it broke through whatever prevented the gods from remembering Mother."

The five of you are never more powerful than when you lift your voices together.

How many times had her mother spoken those words? Ree now realized that they were not just words; they were a prophecy. There had always been something special about the connection she felt with her sisters when they sang together.

"Ah, yes! I remember Mnemosyne," Hephaestus said. He hooked his thumbs under the straps of his garment and extended them outward. "She showed great loyalty. Whatever happened to her?"

"They just told you, my love," Aphrodite said. "Were you not listening to the lyrics? She fled Olympus in the face of great peril."

"And she is in peril again," Ree said, her voice shaking as she spoke directly to the gods. "Our mother was kidnapped by two men who barged into our home in Krymmenos and snatched her away."

"We came to Thebes because we hoped the gods"—Thalia gestured to their audience—"*you*—would help us."

"Our mother left something with us," said Calli. She ran to where she'd stashed her satchel and produced the frayed journal. "It is where we found the story of our origin, but we are no closer to finding our mother."

Several of the gods inched closer to peruse it as she gently flipped through the pages.

"There is one clue that I have been unable to resolve," Calli continued. "But now that you all have gathered here, I believe I have finally figured it out." She turned to the goddess Athena, who stood quietly in the background with her blue helmet tucked underneath her arm and her owl perched on her shoulder. "It is you, isn't it? Your companion is the owl—a bird who flies in the night. You are the one my mother trusts the most."

A warm smile touched the goddess's lips.

"Yes," Athena answered. "Your mother was slow to trust anyone, and for good reason—her situation with her own family was a difficult one. But she came to trust me. She is the only person who could convince me to spend hour after hour picking flowers, but those were the times when she was most open to sharing stories of her upbringing. She was a dear, dear friend."

Athena studied Calli's face, then turned slowly, looking at each of them. "And you are Mnemosyne's girls. She told me she was working on something very special, but I never imagined she would create such magnificent beings."

"In her journal, it says she fashioned our sense of bravery from the one with the heart of a lion and the wisdom of the owl," Clio said.

Athena smiled again. She motioned to where the owl was perched.

"This is Ibid. Your mother was very fond of him, and he felt the same way about her." Athena shook her head, as if still trying to process what she had just learned. "For years, I have felt as if something was missing, and now I know what that something was. It was Mnemosyne."

"I remember her clearly now," Apollo said. He clamped a hand on Athena's shoulder. "The two of you were always together—and with my sister, Artemis, too."

"I recall working in the garden with her," Artemis said.

"Why didn't you say your mother and Athena were best friends in the first place?" Apollo asked the girls.

"Uh, we didn't know," Thalia said. "Calli just figured it out."

"Do any of you think you can help us find her?" Ree asked. "Too much time has passed already."

Zeus stepped up to them, a weary expression etched across his face. "I fear that I may have played a part in your mother's decision to leave Olympus all those years ago. I must help in bringing her home."

"Zeus, why don't you let me and Athena take care of this?" Apollo suggested. "Thebes is in rough shape. I think it would better for the people to see their leader setting the city to rights."

Zeus looked ready to object, but then Hera said, "There is merit to what Apollo says. I know you dispatched other gods to address the destruction in Thebes, but it would help if the mortals saw that you care."

"Fine," Zeus finally said, relenting. "I will leave the matter of finding Mnemosyne to Apollo and Athena. But I want a report the moment there is news."

Athena addressed Ree and her sisters. "What can you tell us about your mother's abduction?"

"It happened on her birthday—" began Ree.

"That was three days ago," Athena said.

"Yes, it was." Mel nodded. "As a family tradition, we host a concert on her birthday, much in the same way we just hosted this one for all of you. In years past, it has always been us five girls and Mother, but this year we invited others from our village."

"Mother was extremely upset," Ree said. "She feared that our performance that day would bring bad people to Krymmenos, and she was right. Those two men arrived that very evening and took her."

"You say there were two men?" Apollo asked.

"Yes, one short and stout, the other tall and slim," Thalia answered.

"And they were dressed in a peculiar fashion," Mel added.

"How so?" Athena asked.

"Well, instead of the standard white or gray tunic seen commonly around Thebes and the surrounding villages, one wore a crimson tunic and the other turquoise."

Athena and Apollo looked at each other. "Hades."

"Hades?" Calli asked, her voice filled with dismay. "The God of the Underworld?"

Clio's back went ramrod straight, her eyes growing wide with a sudden realization. "How did I miss this?" She snapped her fingers at Calli. "Give me the journal."

Calli handed it to her, frowning in curiosity as Clio thumbed through the pages.

"There," her sister said. " 'Beware the one whose flame burns hot and cold. He knows more than he should.' " She pointed at the page. "This is in reference to Hades. It has to be." She looked to Apollo. "Isn't it true that Hades's temperature changes with his moods?"

"Yes, and those men you describe sound similar to the two imps that Hades dispatches to do his dirty work," Athena said. "Transfiguration is their specialty. They can morph into any figure or person at any time."

The image of the old woman pushing a fruit cart suddenly popped into her head.

"The pomegranate merchant!" Ree said, the realization shaking her to her core. "She was wearing the same type of crimson-colored robe. She sold Sivas fruit that felled a donkey. The animal passed out after snatching one out of Sivas's bag, and when it awakened, it went mad."

"Yes, that sounds like something Hades would do," said Athena. "He probably tainted the fruit with some type of mind-altering potion so that he could gain control over your thoughts and actions."

"Like when someone in the agora put Sivas under that trance," Ree said, a chill racing down her spine.

"You all have likely encountered his minions many times since you arrived in Thebes without ever realizing it," Athena said.

Apollo slapped a palm to his forehead. "They are not the only ones who have encountered them. This is why you have been thwarted at every turn. Those imps have been feeding me and Hermes false information this entire time." He waved his hands. "It is like you have been chasing wild geese all around Thebes! I wish I had known."

"Well, we know now," Calli said. "The question is, what are we going to do about it?"

Clio stepped forward and said, "I know what to do, and I think I know where Mother is."

XXXV

CALLI

Calli regarded Clio with growing optimism as her sister paced back and forth, recounting a litany of facts she'd read about Hades over the years. This was the best lead they'd had since coming to Thebes.

"Are you sure about this?" Mel asked her.

"As sure as I can be," Clio said. "One of the entry points into the Underworld is a place called Taenarum. If what Athena says is true and Hades kidnapped Mother, then he would have taken her there. I am certain of it."

"But how can you be certain?" Ree asked.

"Several of the books I've read about the gods of Olympus state that Taenarum is Hades's favorite entry to the Underworld, because it is near the River of Woe."

"Yes, he gets a kick out of watching the souls enter the river," Apollo said, shaking his head. "That Hades is a dastardly one."

"Taenarum is also filled with caves and other places where one can stash something they do not want found," Clio said.

"Like Mother," Thalia whispered.

Clio nodded. "Like Mother."

"If this is the case, then we must go there," Calli said. "Why are we wasting time?"

"I agree. Let us be on our way," Apollo said.

Sivas started to follow, but before Calli could say anything, Ree stepped in. She put both palms on Sivas's shoulders and said, "I think it's best you remain here. I'm unsure of what the conditions will be like in Taenarum, and I do not want you to get hurt."

"What about you getting hurt?" Sivas asked. "I should be there to protect you, Terpsichore."

Ree's lips tilted up in a slight smile. "I will be traveling with two Olympian gods skilled in the art of war. Do not worry about me."

He cupped her cheek. "I will worry. There is nothing you can say that will prevent that."

It was clear to Calli how much Sivas cared for her sister. She now understood Ree's unenthusiastic reaction to her suggestion that they form a singing group.

"Did I not say that we should be on our way?" Apollo called.

"Come on, Ree," Calli said, urging her and Sivas to part. She and her sisters piled into Apollo's chariot, except for Mel, who begged to ride with Athena on her horse. They left the amphitheater and headed south, and within the hour arrived at Taenarum.

After their time in the big city, finding herself in this desolate terrain was jarring. Crumbling rocks of all sizes littered the dry landscape. It felt cold. Lonely. It hurt her to think that her mother was stashed away in a cave somewhere here.

Athena's horse landed next to them as they were climbing out of Apollo's chariot.

"You made it before we did," Athena said, snapping her fingers. "I would have beaten you here if not for the extra weight on my horse."

Mel grimaced. "Sorry."

"It is not a contest, Athena," Apollo told her. "If it were, though, I would still have won."

They did not have time for these two to get into a spat.

"Clio, you believe that Hades has most likely hidden Mother in a cave somewhere here?" Calli asked.

"Yes," Clio answered with a nod, her eyes roaming the stark landscape. "I suspect that he has chosen a cave that is deep enough that it would prevent Mother from using her memory-altering abilities." She pulled out the map she'd purchased from that merchant on their way to Thebes. "That is why I believe it is one in this region, probably near Ephyra. The caves are deep here, and it serves as the entry point that leads to the River of Woe—otherwise known as the River Acheron in the Underworld."

"Why would he not take her into the Underworld?" Mel asked. "Not that I would ever *want* Mother to go to the Underworld, but that is where Hades lives, isn't it? If he is the one who has kidnapped her, why would he not take her to the realm where he rules?"

"Because Hades is smart," Athena said. "He must understand her abilities, and how they can be a dangerous thing in the Underworld if she taps into the memories of the dead. It is safer for him to have stashed her just outside the entrance to the Underworld, but close enough so that he could easily pull her down there with him if necessary."

A shudder ran through Calli. The idea of the Underworld disturbed her so much that she never allowed herself to visualize it. Even though she knew the darkest parts of it—the ceaseless turmoil and unrelenting torment—were reserved for the worst of society, she could not imagine any of it was pleasant.

"But how would Hades know who Mother is if she wiped everyone's memory of her?" Mel asked. "We have never sung as a group in front of Hades."

"That is true," Clio said. "I believe I would have recognized him if he had attended the performance at Ree's studio."

"Were the two men who kidnapped Mother there?" Calli asked, trying to recall.

Thalia shook her head. "There were no strangers. It was only fellow villagers from Krymmenos, people we have known for nearly two years."

"Hades must have figured out Mnemosyne's true identity on his own," Athena said. "Maybe he found a way to subvert her powers."

"I would not be surprised if he guarded himself against it long before Mother wiped everyone's memories," Clio said. "Hades is purported to be very clever. Maybe he had a written account of Mother that he was able to refer to."

Apollo nodded, looking impressed. "You're a smart one, aren't you?"

"Keep up, Apollo. Everyone knows Clio is brilliant," Thalia said. "What I want to know is, why are we all standing here doing nothing if we know Hades is the one who kidnapped our mother? Let's find this cave and rescue her."

"Not yet," Athena declared. She stood before them like the warrior she was, completely in command. Calli did not even think of questioning her authority. "We must have a plan. Hades is too smart, too full of trickery. He will have thought of everything, especially if the reason behind this kidnapping has anything to do with his obsession with getting revenge on Zeus."

"Why else would he do it?" Apollo asked. "It's all he talks about."

"And Hades understands the power Mnemosyne wields," Athena said.

Mel's lips curved up in a grin. "But does he know the power that *we* wield?"

"No, he doesn't," Calli said, her smile matching Mel's. "I think it's time the God of the Underworld learns what Mnemosyne's girls can do."

XXXVI

HADES

"A donkey!" Hades slammed his fist against the armrest of this throne. "I cannot believe a donkey nearly ruined everything."

Despite the pomegranate disaster, though, his strategy remained on track—only thanks to his quick-wittedness. Just as he'd done by taking notes all those years ago to protect himself from falling victim to Mnemosyne's powers, Hades had put a contingency plan in place.

He'd constructed a jar of chaos just like the one Zeus had given to that mortal, Pandora, back when his brother had his little squabble with Prometheus. He then instructed Panic to give the jar to a wizened resident of Thebes, someone with a trusting face, and told him to order the old man to give it to one of Mnemosyne's daughters.

Hades thought she would open it immediately, unleashing pandemonium and giving him leverage to force Mnemosyne's hand. After all, what mother wouldn't want to save her children from such destruction and despair?

What he hadn't anticipated was her daughter waiting so long to uncap the jar.

But the moment he heard fire and brimstone raining down on Thebes, he knew the jar had been opened. And while his poisoned pomegranates had not worked, he would use the upheaval happening in Thebes to bargain with her for her freedom. If Mnemosyne thought it was the only way he would release her so that she could save her daughters, she would do as he commanded.

Just as he was heading to her dungeon, a noise stopped Hades in his tracks. He glanced to his right and spotted five shadows projected onto the wall of the cave.

Mnemosyne's girls! They'd finally found their way to him.

While he was still several yards back and out of their line of vision, Hades released a low rumble of a laugh. He heard the girls' collective gasp, and his grin grew wider. Tapping his fingertips, he stepped out of the shadows and greeted them with a smile.

"Well, well, well," Hades sang. "What do we have here? Interlopers?"

"Clio, is this him? Is this Hades?" the shortest one asked.

"Yes, it's him," her sister answered.

"So you've heard about me," Hades said. "All good things, I hope."

"Where is our mother?" the one with long, wavy hair asked. Hades could practically smell the fear rolling off her. Goodness, he loved that scent.

He tapped his finger against his temple. "Funny you should ask. I was just on my way to visit my friend Mnemosyne. Would you all care to join me?"

He pushed past them and burst through the door to Mnemosyne's chamber.

They released a collective gasp and together yelled, "Mother!"

Her girls rushed into the room and encircled Mnemosyne, pummeling her with hugs and kisses.

"Oh, what a joyful reunion," Hades drawled. "Too bad it cannot last."

"Yes, it *is* too bad."

He whipped around at the sound of a familiar voice. The goddess Athena and that dunderheaded Apollo stood just outside the door of the dungeon.

"You!" Hades said. "What are you doing here?"

"Helping to rescue my best friend," Athena answered.

No! This was not happening. He would not allow it.

Hades looked to Mnemosyne and her girls, then to Athena and Apollo. He had to do something. And fast.

He sucked in a deep breath, opened his palm, and blew across it, producing a massive blue cloud that filled the room. He ran to Mnemosyne and hooked an arm around her waist, hauling her to his side.

They were gone before the others ever knew what had happened.

XXXVII

REE

Ree waved her hands in front of her face, trying to disperse the blue smoke that had caused everyone to tumble into a fit of coughing. Once the air cleared, Ree looked around the chamber and then at the others.

There was a beat of silence before several of them spoke at once.

"Where did they go?" Mel screeched.

"What happened?" Clio asked.

"Where'd that blue-bellied, flaming-head rascal take my mama?" Thalia hollered, waving her fist in the air. "Where is he? Bring me to him!"

Ree was too startled to speak. Hades had swept out of the dingy cave under the cover of that blue cloud. He'd moved so quickly she'd had no time to react.

"Calm down," Calli said. "This carrying-on will get us nowhere."

They all quieted as Calli's reasoning broke through, but fear and tension still hummed in the air around them.

"Now, we've come this far, so there is no way we're giving up on Mother," Calli said.

"You're right," said Clio. She turned to Athena and Apollo. "From what I've read, very few mortals have taken a katabasis to Hades's domain and returned to the mortal world, but it can be done, right?"

"What is a katabasis?" Thalia asked.

"It's a trip to the Underworld," Clio said. "I have no doubt that's where Hades has taken Mother, because he knows it will be difficult for us to follow. But we *will* follow," she stressed. "Mother empowered us with everything we need to rescue her. We will use our gifts in the same way we used them when we rescued Ree and Sivas from Aeaea."

She retuned her attention to the two gods. "Do we have a chance of returning to this mortal world if we go to the Underworld?"

Athena nodded. "Yes, there is a chance, but know that there have been *very* few mortals who have completed the journey successfully."

"If it can be done, we will do it," Calli said, moving to stand next to Clio.

"You got that right!" Thalia said, flanking her other side.

"We cannot leave our mother to that . . . that monster," Mel said.

Witnessing this display of bravery in her sisters, Ree felt her fear dissipate, and in its place came sheer determination.

Something occurred to Ree. "It doesn't matter, because we're not ordinary mortals."

"You're right!" Clio said. "Mother is a goddess, and she is the one who created us. That has to account for something."

Apollo and Athena looked at each other and nodded.

"We are here to assist you in any way we can," Apollo said.

"Now, there are some things you should know about the Underworld before you venture down there," Athena said. "Cerberus will be standing guard."

"Hades's three-headed dog." Clio blew out an exasperated breath. "I'd forgotten about him."

"He is there to prevent souls from leaving," said Athena, "but Hades will undoubtedly have him standing watch, waiting for us to enter."

"I know what we can do," Calli said. "Terpsichore, remember how we lulled Circe into a trance? That is how we distract Cerberus."

"Yes!" Clio said, all vestiges of her previous frustration gone. "As for Hades . . . I have a plan for him, too."

She then laid out a strategy, but there was not time to second-guess or even rehearse Clio's plan. They needed to act, and quickly.

They filed out of the dungeon and swiftly made their way to another tunnel that Athena assured them was the entrance to the Underworld. Jagged, deadly-looking rocks poked out like spears on all sides of the entrance, a threat to any who dared enter. Just standing at the mouth of the tunnel sent a shudder of unease down Ree's spine. Something sinister lurked here.

Calli led the way as they descended what looked to be thousands of steps. The fact that none of her sisters complained proved the seriousness of the situation.

The air grew colder the farther down they went, and that malevolent feeling grew stronger with each step they took. When they arrived at the base of the stairs, they encountered a small plateau surrounded by murky water. Wails and moans rang throughout the cavernous space, and Ree wanted to cover her ears.

"What's floating in here?" Thalia asked, taking a step toward the edge. A gaunt arm shot out of the water. Thalia jumped back. "Sweet mother of the Underworld!"

"It's nothing to fear," Mel said. "They are just souls longing for someone to care about them."

She put a hand to her chest and closed her eyes, then began a hauntingly beautiful requiem to those floating in the waters below. The wailing eased and the waters calmed.

"Oh, Mel," Calli whispered. "Your ability to empathize truly is a gift."

Thalia leaned over and, in a hushed voice, asked, "Are we supposed to swim in this?"

"Coming through. Careful. Move to the side," Apollo called as he moved past them, carrying a flat wooden platform that was big enough for them all to stand on. Ree breathed a sigh of relief at the sight of it.

"Did you carry that all the way down here?" Thalia asked. "You really are a hero, aren't you?"

"No one wants to go into the River Acheron until it's their time," Apollo said.

"Thank you," Clio said. "It didn't occur to me that we would need a raft."

"We all remember our roles?" Calli chimed in. "I silently recited my poem the entire way down here."

Everyone nodded.

"Good," Clio said. "Then let's go get our mother."

"Wait," Mel said. "We don't have any pine cones. How do avoid being lulled to sleep by the lullaby?"

"We'll have to plug our ears with our fingers," Calli said. "Ree, you will have to concentrate hard not to fall asleep while dancing. Do you think you can do it?"

"I can," Ree answered.

She had to.

Athena used her spear to paddle the raft across the water. Just as the goddess had warned, they soon came upon the three-headed dog. Ree's entire body quaked, but then she shook off her fear and leaped from the raft onto the small island the monster inhabited.

The dog released a soul-shaking growl. Saliva dripped from

three mouths that bared the sharpest teeth Ree had ever seen in her life.

Her sisters began to sing the lullaby they'd used on Circe, and with shaky knees, Ree launched into her dance. Cerberus let out another awful growl, but then stopped. All three of its heads began to sway to the dulcet tones of her sisters' voices. Ree matched the languid rhythm of the song and in no time lulled the monster to sleep.

They all silently cheered when she returned to the raft, and then they waited several more minutes to ensure the beast was truly asleep. Each of its heads released matching loud snores.

"Good job," Clio mouthed.

Ree could barely contain her joy, but she would not claim a single victory until their mother was safe. Instead, she focused on the next phase of the plan Clio had devised.

They continued drifting along the river until they reached a creepy corridor with skeletons running up the sides of the walls. It was dark and cold and shadowy, and all so ghastly that it made Ree's skin crawl.

"Exactly how big is the Underworld?" Thalia said. "Because this river is never-ending."

"The Underworld is as vast as the land of the living, but we will not have to travel much farther," Apollo said. "We are nearing Hades's lair."

Only a few minutes had passed when they rounded a bend in

the river and came upon a colossal tower shaped like a skull. The menacing fortress was exactly what Ree had imagined for one as wretched as Hades.

They landed the raft at the base of the tower and quietly made their way up the staircase that wound around it. Once they reached the top, Calli moved toward the entrance, but Athena stopped her, holding her spear out like a barricade.

"Let me enter first," she whispered. "I am equipped to battle Hades if he attacks."

But no one attacked them when they filed into his lair, because there was no one there. A raised, circular platform stood in the center of the room with what appeared to be a map of some sort on top of it. Ree's eyes roamed around the macabre dwelling, her heart sinking at the thought that they'd come all this way only to discover that their mother had been taken elsewhere.

But then a disembodied voice rang out in warning. "Don't come any closer!"

Hades!

The God of the Underworld came out from behind the large platform, tugging their mother by the arm. She twisted and turned, fighting to break free.

"Pain! Panic! Restrain this one," Hades ordered.

Just then, two imps—one turquoise, the other crimson—scampered out from behind the huge throne that sat against the wall.

"Are those the miscreants who have been causing us all this trouble?" Thalia asked.

"Yes, you can tell by their coloring," Clio said.

The imps transformed into long straps and wrapped around their mother's body, constraining her.

"Let her go!" Mel called.

"Um, I don't think so," Hades said. He steepled his fingers and pressed them to his lips. "It didn't have to be this way, you know. Mnemosyne and I could have done so much good together."

"Good?" Calli asked. "You don't know the meaning of the word."

"Of course I do. It means *boring*," he said. "And I, for one, am never boring. I gave her so many opportunities—first . . ."

As Hades continued his diatribe about Mnemosyne messing up his plans, Calli called Thalia over and whispered, "It's your turn to shine. Keep him occupied."

Thalia nodded, then called out to Hades. "Hey, you! Hothead! Listen here."

She sauntered up to him and plopped her hands on her hips.

"Are you so weak that you need our delicate little mama to do your dirty work?" she said. "You want to know what I call someone like you? A zero! No, make that a zero with bad hair!"

"Why you little . . ." Hades's hair flared orange. "Let's get one thing straight, pipsqueak. My hair is magnificent. And I don't *need* Mnemosyne for anything."

"So why did you snatch her?" Thalia asked. "And why do you send those two rodents around to take care of all your no-good deeds? Something tells me the big scary God of the Underworld is nothing but a coward!"

"That's it," Ree whispered. "Keep going."

While Thalia kept Hades distracted with their spirited back-and-forth, Ree and Mel discreetly slipped to the side and rounded the dais behind their mother—just as Calli's sonorous voice began to belt out the words to the poem she'd composed.

"The fire you unleash to cause anguish will soon be extinguished," Calli sang. "You have an entire world to rule, yet your greed turned you into a fool."

"Stop that singing." Hades took a step forward, but then halted when the bright red flame burning atop his head suddenly went out. "What—what's happening?" He patted both hands on his bald, wrinkly head. "What! Is! Happening!"

His skin looked pallid without the luster of the fire he usually wielded.

Ree now understood what was going on. Just as had happened during the encounter her sisters had described with the Sirens, Calli's poem had turned Hades's own powers back on him.

"Stop that singing!" Hades bellowed, but Calli only sang louder.

The imps who had wrapped themselves around her mother suddenly released her. They slithered on the floor like snakes, careering toward Hades and then wrapping themselves around him. He was being made to suffer everything he'd unleashed on others.

Mel and Ree caught their mother in their arms as she fell back, her body limp from being confined for so long. But Mnemosyne quickly righted herself, and together they ran to where the others were, on the opposite side of the circular map.

"Oh, girls! My girls! Thank you so much," Mnemosyne said, gathering them all in a tearful embrace. "I knew you would come for me."

"We love you, Mother. We were always going to do whatever we could to save you," Calli said.

Mnemosyne went around in a circle, cupping each of their faces in her palms and placing a kiss on their foreheads.

Then she turned to Hades.

"I want to make myself clear. I *never* would have caved to your demands, no matter what," she said.

"Shut up!" Hades screamed. "I will make you pay for this! All of you!"

"Oh, and one last thing," Mnemosyne said.

She raised her hand in the air.

"Nooooo!" Hades screamed.

But it was too late.

XXXVIII

MNEMOSYNE

Mnemosyne swept her open palm in an arc, erasing all memories of herself from Hades's mind. He just stood there with his flames doused and a blank expression on his face.

"Mother, what did you just do?" Clio asked.

"What needed to be done," she answered.

"There's one more thing that needs to be done," Athena said. She walked up to Hades, reared back, and punched him right in the nose. He fell to the floor, his body writhing in pain before going limp. "I hope you remember that!"

Mnemosyne clutched her hands to her chest as gratitude flooded her being. "I can't believe you came for me."

"Of course we came for you," Athena said. She turned and wrapped Mnemosyne up in a hug. "I've missed you, my friend. Now let's get out of here."

"Not yet," Mnemosyne said. "Before we go, I need to find anything that Hades may have hidden here that references me or plans he had for us to partner together."

"So that *is* what he wanted of you?" Apollo asked.

She nodded. "He knew of my abilities and wanted to use them to exact revenge against Zeus."

"But how did he know?" Athena asked. "How was Hades able to subvert your efforts to erase his memories?"

"He made notations of my powers before I fled Olympus twenty years ago. I assume he has added to them this time," Mnemosyne said. "Please, help me find them."

With Hades still incapacitated from Athena's punch, they all spread out to search. Anxiety swept through Mnemosyne's bones as she followed Calli deeper into Hades's lair. It was cold and damp and triggered goosebumps along her arms, but having her girls near her made even this seem like no big deal.

"There are tiny holes and crevices all over this place," Calli said, pointing to skulls. "Hades could have stashed his journal anywhere."

"I found it," Clio called.

Mnemosyne scrambled back toward the entrance of the lair and came upon her daughter flipping through a sheepskin journal.

"I figured Hades would want to keep it close. It was hidden behind his throne."

"You really are the smart one," Apollo said, plucking the journal from Clio's fingers. He scanned the pages. "Such wretched penmanship, but what else would one expect from Hades?" He tucked the journal in the bag draped across his chest. "I'm sure Hephaestus won't mind if I toss this in his fire pit once we get back to Olympus."

"Thank goodness," Mnemosyne said.

She breathed her first easy breath in days, relief flooding through her. She was finally done with Hades and his threats.

The others returned to the entrance.

"Clio found the journal," Thalia announced before any of them could ask a question.

"If that is the case, I say we get out of this horrid place," Mel said.

"I agree," Mnemosyne said.

They made their way out of the Underworld and back into the land of the living.

"Did you know which cave he had imprisoned you in?" Athena asked.

Mnemosyne shook her head. "I suspected Hades had chosen Taenarum, but I was not sure of the exact spot." She examined their desolate, rocky surroundings. "The density of the rocks here makes it harder for my powers to function. That is why I couldn't reach you girls, but I could feel you. I felt you the entire time."

"We felt you, too," Melpomene said, wrapping her arms around Mnemosyne's shoulders.

Her most sensitive daughter could not seem to let go of her. She did not mind. She wanted to keep them as close to her as she could.

Before she was forced to let them go.

"Girls, I—"

"It's the one here," Athena interrupted, pointing to a jagged entrance.

"We must destroy this place," Mnemosyne said. "So that he can never do to another what he did to me."

"I agree." Athena nodded. She turned to Apollo. "Are you ready?"

Mnemosyne watched as her friend and the God of the Sun approached the mouth of the cave, reaching in unison for arrows from the quivers strapped across their backs. They aimed, and at Athena's command, released arrow after arrow after arrow, striking the rocks surrounding the cave until the ground underneath their feet began to rumble.

"What's happening?" Thalia asked.

In answer, the rocks at the mouth of the cave began to crumble, falling in rapid succession until the opening of the cave was nothing but a mass of rubble.

"That should put an end to Hades's games. For now," Apollo said.

"He will never stop," Mnemosyne said. "Not until he gets his revenge."

Apollo rolled his eyes. "Hades needs to find a hobby. Like singing." He gestured to her girls. "You have quite the quintet here. They brought all the gods to their feet at the concert they held at the amphitheater. In fact, if it were not for your daughters' restoring the memories of the gods with their beautiful singing, I doubt any of us would have ever remembered you."

Mnemosyne whipped around, staring at her girls in awe. "You held a concert for the gods of Olympus?"

"Yes!" the girls answered in unison.

"Remember what you always told us?" Calli asked. "That the five of us are never more powerful than when we lift our voices together? It's true."

"Yes, I know," Mnemosyne said. Hidden in her daughters' abilities was the talent to neutralize her own powers. "I designed your unique gifts to be potent on their own, but your power is at its purest when you are united."

Mnemosyne turned to Athena, but before she could say anything, Athena spoke.

"Why did you do it?" she asked. "We were the best of friends, Mnemosyne. Not only did you leave, but you took every part of yourself, even the memory of you."

"I know," she said. "I am sorry. You must know that I never meant to hurt you. I had no choice. I had to leave."

"And wipe away every memory of you?" Athena asked.

Mnemosyne held her hands out, pleading with her friend to understand. "I could not risk anyone discovering that my girls existed. Hades led me to believe that Zeus was no longer in favor of their creation. I was too in love with them at that point; all I could think to do was hide. Wiping your and everyone else's memory of me was the first step in my plan to disappear forever."

"But you could not hide forever," Calli said, walking up to her.

Mnemosyne took the hand she offered and squeezed it. "No, I could not."

She turned to her girls.

"I am sorry for the way I acted on my birthday. The truth is, your existence would have been discovered eventually, and honestly, I should not have hidden you from the world as long as I did. It was selfish. You were never meant to be enjoyed by one person alone. The wonderful gifts you have were meant to be shared with the world—and with one another."

"Do not apologize, Mother," said Ree. "We only have those gifts because you gave them to us."

Mnemosyne cupped her jaw in her palm. "That doesn't make it right, Terpsichore. But what is done is done. I will deal with the consequences." To Athena, she said, "I hope one of those consequences is not losing you as a friend forever."

Athena pretended to remain aloof, but only a moment later, a smile broke out across her face.

"Even if I could stay upset with you, this one here would never allow it," she said, pointing to Ibid.

Mnemosyne ran her fingers along the brow of the little owl. She had missed Athena's pet almost as much as she'd missed her friend.

She looked over at Apollo. "I suspect Zeus will want to have a word with me."

He laughed. "You may have been gone for some time, but you have not forgotten how things work around here."

"Well," Mnemosyne said. "Let's get this over with, shall we?" She turned to her girls. "It is time I show you Olympus."

XXXIX

CALLI

The world was filled with remarkably beautiful places, but Calli could not imagine any place in the universe could ever be as gorgeous as Mount Olympus. Even the clouds surrounding the mountain were perfect, all of them puffy and pillowy. She could make out the structures in the distance, of radiantly white marble trimmed in gold. She had not been able to close her mouth since they arrived. The moment she managed to do so, her eyes would land on yet another jaw-droppingly beautiful sight.

And they had not even passed through the gates yet.

Calli was unsure if they would be able to get inside. Only gods could enter through those elaborate golden gates, and she wasn't sure she was one.

As they approached them, she asked her mother, "Do you want us to wait here?"

"Why would I want you to do that?"

Calli looked at her sisters. "Well, because mortals cannot enter, can they?"

Mnemosyne looked to Athena, and they both laughed. "Oh, Calliope, my darling. You deciphered so many of the clues that were written in my journal. Did you not figure out the most obvious?"

The confusion on Calli's face must have still been apparent, because her mother looked to her, then to her sisters, and said, "You are goddesses."

"Me?" Thalia asked. "I'm a goddess?"

"Yes, you are," Mnemosyne confirmed. "I created you, and because I am a goddess, you all are too." Her face grew serious. "But just because you are goddesses, it does not mean that Zeus will go easy on any of us. And for that, I am sorry. Anything that happens in these next few minutes is my fault, and I take full responsibility for it. I also promise to eventually make it right."

Mel's expression darkened. "Do you think he will choose to send us back to Hades and the Underworld?"

Mnemosyne hesitated, but Athena stepped in and said, "It is difficult to predict what Zeus will do in situations such as these, but it is my hope that he is fair in the way he deals with the five of you. You did nothing wrong."

"So it is only our mother we must worry about," Clio said. "She may get sent back to the Underworld."

"I think we should just forget this whole thing and return to the mortal world," Ree said.

"Oh, really?" Thalia asked. "I wonder why that is?"

"Girls," Calli chastised. "Please, not now. This is serious."

She thought her days of having to mediate such tussles were behind her, but it looked as if some things would never change.

Calli looked to Athena. "Is there anything we can do to help our mother's case?"

She shook her head. "I am afraid not. Zeus will do what he will do."

Mnemosyne inhaled a deep breath. "No sense in waiting any longer to learn my fate."

The massive gates parted, and Calli and her sisters took their first steps inside Olympus. The beauty she'd encountered outside the gates was even more apparent on this side of them, but she was so nervous about what they were about to face that she could not appreciate it.

They approached a set of gleaming white stairs that rose from a bed of fluffy clouds.

"Not more steps," Thalia said with a groan, exchanging horrified looks with Mel.

"Thalia, not now," Calli said.

One by one, they began their ascent. When they reached the top, they found many of the gods who had been present for their concert milling about. Dionysus, who clenched a bottle of wine in one hand and a golden chalice in the other, was engaged in a spirited discussion with Hermes. Ares stood off to the side, sharpening the blade of his sword, while Apollo's twin sister, Artemis, held Aphrodite, Hephaestus, and Demeter captive with a story.

All the gods seemed to notice the new guests at the same time. They rushed over to Calli and her family, showering Mnemosyne with kind regards and welcoming her back to Olympus.

Calli knew better than to allow their warm greeting to lull her into thinking they would get the same from Zeus. Yet even before they reached his throne, she heard a loud voice call to them.

"There you are," Zeus said with a jovial smile. "What took you so long?"

Calli's eyes widened in shock. Her mother seemed just as stunned by Zeus's greeting.

"Hel—hello, Zeus," Mnemosyne said. "I have come to introduce you to my daughters and to apologize—"

He cut her off. "There is no need for introductions nor for an apology. In fact, I am the one who owes *you* an apology. Apollo already explained Hades's role in your disappearance all those years ago, and how he held you prisoner these last few days. However, I also imprisoned you. You did not take sides during the Great War, and you did not deserve to be confined to Olympus. I am sorry for not granting you the freedom to live as you wanted to live after the war."

Mnemosyne's mouth gaped open. After several moments passed, she said, "I . . . I don't know what to say."

Calli didn't, either. Never could she have imagined the mighty Zeus, leader of the Olympians, asking for her mother's forgiveness.

"You can say that you accept my apology," Zeus suggested.

"Yes. Yes, I do," Mnemosyne said.

He nodded. "Good. And as for my brother, you don't have to worry about him. I will deal with Hades." He waved that off. "But enough about him. What I want to know is, when do we get another concert from these songbirds?" He smiled at Mnemosyne. "You did an excellent job. They are even more spectacular than what I envisioned when you first approached me with the idea to create them."

"Thank you," she said. "They are more than just my greatest achievement. They are my . . . my everything."

Mnemosyne reached her hands out to them. Calli took one and Mel took the other, while Thalia, Ree, and Clio came to stand next to them.

"Well?" Zeus asked. "When is the next concert?"

"I guess they can put on another performance before we return to Krymmenos," Mnemosyne said.

"Krymmenos?" His voice turned thunderous.

"Zeus, calm yourself," Hera said.

"Why would you return to Krymmenos?" Zeus asked. "You are goddesses. You belong here on Olympus."

"Actually," her mother said, "if you can remember, they were originally supposed to reside in Thebes. After all, one of the reasons they were created was to bring joy to the people there."

Zeus nodded. "Yes, yes. Now I remember." He looked over Calli and her sisters. "I guess you can divide your time between the mortal world *and* Olympus."

He pulled a lightning bolt from a quiver near his throne and motioned for Calli and her sisters to stand in front of him. Then he stepped down from the throne and, one by one, touched each of their shoulders with the tip of the bolt.

"I hereby declare the five of you part-time residents of Olympus."

"Our group name is the Muses," Calli said.

Zeus smiled. "I like that. The Muses, Goddesses of the Arts and Proclaimers of Heroes."

XL

REE

They spent a bit more time seeing the sights on Olympus, but now that the threat to their mother was over, Ree and her sisters all agreed that they wanted to finally take a proper tour of Thebes. Clio seemed to be on the verge of bursting with anticipation as she talked about exploring the library and the theater.

They departed Olympus in their favorite mode of transportation, Apollo's golden chariot. When the quartet of horses deposited them at the base of the stairs that led to the temple, Ree was stunned at how clean and orderly things appeared to be around the agora. The last they'd seen of Thebes, structures were crumbling and general mayhem had taken over.

"This place cleans up pretty well, doesn't it?" Thalia said as she alighted from the chariot. "I guess living here wouldn't be all that bad."

Thalia's words brought to mind a subject that still needed to be discussed.

"Sisters," Ree called. "As eager as we all are to explore Thebes, there is something we need to talk about first."

"You want to discuss us remaining in Thebes instead of returning to Krymmenos, don't you?" Mel asked, putting her hand on Ree's shoulder.

"Perceptive as always," Ree answered. She blew out a sigh and said, "There's not much to discuss. I want to be with my sisters; it's as simple as that."

"Really?" Mel asked, her eyes growing wide.

"Yes, really?" Clio asked. "Aren't you the same Ree who pitched a fit when Mother asked us to leave home?"

"I know," Ree said. "But things are different now. I cannot imagine living back in Krymmenos while the four of you and Mother are somewhere else, whether it's Thebes or Olympus or a combination of the two." She shook her head. "I do not want to be separated from all of you."

"But what about your studio?" Calli asked.

"I'll miss Cressida and Nephele so much, but hopefully, I can visit them every once in a while, depending on our duties as the Muses!" said Ree. "Plus, I can teach young children dance in Thebes, too. There are even more possible students here!"

"Forget the studio," Thalia said. "What about your man?"

She nodded, indicating a place just over Ree's shoulder. Ree turned to find Sivas running toward her.

"Terpsichore, you're back," Sivas said, enveloping her in a tight hug. He pressed a kiss to her forehead and placed his palms on either side of her face. "I was so worried about you." He lifted his head to look at her sisters. “But then I realized that I had nothing to worry about, because you were with your sisters, and they would never allow anything bad to happen to you.”

“Of course we wouldn’t,” Thalia said. She gave Ree a pointed look. “I think you and Sivas have some things to discuss.”

Sivas looked at her with a curious smile as her sisters all dispersed. “Terpsichore, what is going on?”

“Oh, Sivas.” She released a humorless laugh. “Where do I even start?”

She decided to start with Zeus’s decree and how discovering the power of her sisters’ collective voices had changed everything.

“As much as I love Krymmenos and my students, I belong here with my sisters,” she finished.

“Ree,” he said, “you have no idea how happy this makes me.”

She reared her head back. “Happy? You’re happy that you and I will no longer live in the same village?”

“No, no, you don’t understand,” Sivas said with a laugh. “I made plans to leave Krymmenos months ago. It was never my dream to be an olive grower like my father. I’ve always wanted to move to the big city and study music.”

“Why didn’t you?” she asked.

His cheeks instantly reddened. “Because one day my father sent me to fetch Cressida from her dance class, and I fell in love with her teacher at the first sight of her.”

Ree gasped, her heart flooding with warmth at his words. She threw her arms around Sivas and kissed him square on the mouth.

The sound of someone loudly clearing their throat caused them both to pull apart. Ree whipped around, finding her mother standing only feet away, her arms crossed over her chest and her right brow arched in inquiry.

"Mother!" Ree said. She quickly let go of Sivas's hand but then just as quickly grabbed hold of it again. She would no longer hide her affection for him. "I don't think you have met Sivas."

"Not formally," Mnemosyne said. She held her hand out to him.

"It's a pleasure to meet you," Sivas said, grasping her mother's hand and pumping enthusiastically.

"That's enough," Ree whispered to him. In a louder voice, she asked, "Was there something you needed, Mother?"

"Yes." Mnemosyne nodded. "I need to speak to you and your sisters. It's important."

The hairs at the back of Ree's neck immediately stood on end, but she reminded herself that her sisters and her mother were all safe, so nothing her mother shared could be *too* bad.

She turned to Sivas and said, "Give me just a moment." Then she followed her mother.

Once they'd all gathered on the steps of the library, Mnemosyne began.

"I know I said this before, but I want to apologize to all of you again," she said.

"Mother, you do not have to apologize to us," Clio said. "We would brave Hades's wrath a dozen times to rescue you."

"I know you would, and my gratitude for what you did is as vast as the ocean," she said. "But I owe you an apology for concealing the truth about your origin from you for so long. And for not giving you girls the space to explore the beautiful talent I bestowed upon each of you. I kept you all hidden when I should have encouraged you to pursue your dreams." She clasped her hands in front of her. "That being said, I want you to know that you do not have to do as Zeus has ordered."

"You want us to defy *the* Zeus?" Thalia asked. "Did you bump your head while you were down in the Underworld?"

"I refuse to allow Zeus to dictate your lives in the same way I have dictated them," she said. "I will deal with the ramifications if you choose not to heed Zeus's demands."

"Mother, we *want* to be the Muses," Calli said. "But there is something else that we should discuss. I've held on to this for too long, and now that you're apologizing for what you perceive as your wrongs, I think it is time you acknowledge it."

Ree's eyes widened as she looked from Calli to her mother and back to Calli. It was difficult to read her sister's expression, but the way she pressed her lips together told Ree she was having a difficult time with this.

After sucking in a deep breath, Calli said, "Mother, I resent having to do your job all these years. I love my sisters dearly, and I would do anything for them, but it still is not fair that you made me feel as if I *had* to raise them."

"Calli . . . I—" Mnemosyne started, but Calli cut her off.

"There were so many times when I wanted to find a quiet place and work on my stories, but I could not because you had drifted off into one of your sitting spells. Even when you were right there, I couldn't trust you to *be* there for the girls, and it was not fair."

Mnemosyne dropped her chin to her chest. When she looked up again, tears glistened in her eyes.

"You're right," she said. "I am sorry, Calliope. Add this to the list of things I am so very sorry to have done over the years."

Calli's bottom lip trembled, but then a smile lifted the corner of her mouth. "Thank you for that. I just wanted you to acknowledge the extra responsibilities I've been forced to carry."

"I do," her mother said, reaching for Calli's hands. "I appreciate all that you've sacrificed. And know that I want you to pursue your own dreams. I want that for all of you."

"Can we hug?" Thalia asked. "I think we all need a big hug right now."

Calli and their mother both laughed before opening their arms and inviting them all in for a hug.

With her arms still linked with her mother's and Mel's, Calli said, "As for being the Muses, we agreed that we belong together even before Zeus's edict. You designed us so that our power is fully realized when we sing with one voice, and that is what we want to do."

"But it isn't the *only* thing we want to do," Clio said. "I plan to visit Corinth and Ephesus and maybe even Rhodes."

"And I'm thinking of entering the university here," Thalia said. "Don't get me wrong, I like telling a good joke, but I can argue with the best of them. I want to study debate, and maybe theater, too."

"And I want to study philosophy," Mel said. "We can go to the university together, Thalia!"

Ree thought of the children she'd encountered in the agora when she was practicing for their performance. "And I still want my own dance studio. I already know of a few students."

"What about you, Calliope?" Mnemosyne asked.

A cunning smile tilted up the corners of Calli's mouth. "Clio said it best during our concert for the gods. Those other writers had better move to the side, because there's a new voice in town, and I plan to write the most epic tales this world has ever seen. And after I write them, the Muses will sing them in our own unique style."

Thalia lifted her hands in the air and sang, "And that's the gospel truth!"

Epilogue

CALLI

The sun shone brightly on Thebes as the residents prepared themselves for an event unlike any other. The line to enter the amphitheater snaked all the way back to the Elektrai Gate and seemed to be never-ending.

In the months since she and her sisters had been revealed as goddesses, so much had changed, yet so much remained the same. Mel and Ree were still griping, despite both now having bedrooms of their own in their new homes in both Thebes and Olympus.

Clio had taken a short trip to Athens to study the architecture there but had returned in time for the concert. She would be journeying to Corinth next; however, their family home remained her base.

Thalia held comedy shows each week at the theater in Thebes. There was a waiting list for those wanting to see the performance.

Their mother was still getting reacquainted with the gods, but Calli could tell how much she was enjoying herself, especially when she spent time with her best friend. She and Athena often joined

Artemis on hunts, or they hung around with the other gods. She checked in on her daughters often, showing interest in each of their individual pursuits and embracing their new role as goddesses of the arts. Mnemosyne had even helped them during their rehearsals, adding a soulful element that had become the hallmark of their routine.

As for herself, Calli had never felt more at peace. She carried her journal around the city, using the sights and sounds she saw every day as inspiration for her epic tales.

People continued to pour into the amphitheater. The concert starring the goddess Mnemosyne's sensational creations was sure to be the most magnificent spectacle the world had ever seen.

Calli sat at the looking glass that had been set up in the skene. The area behind the stage was filled with peploses in various colors, ties and other baubles for their hair, and an array of instruments Mel had spent the past weeks learning to play. In the end, she had decided to stick with her trusty lyre.

Calli knew that it didn't matter what instrument her sister had settled on. This concert would be well received, because the people of Thebes had been thirsting for something to believe in.

And they believed in the Muses. Just yesterday, a satyr had approached them, asking if they could write a song for a hero he was in the process of training.

"Are we ready, ladies?" Thalia asked. "Because it's showtime."

The smallest tingling of nervousness teased Calli's stomach, but nerves had no place here. She was with her sisters, and together they could do anything.

"Let's do this," she said.

They made their way onto the stage and were greeted by such raucous applause that, for a moment, Calli was afraid the entire amphitheater would crumble to the ground.

Her mother, Athena, Apollo, Hermes, and many of the other gods sat in the very front row.

Calli saw Ree wink at Sivas and his little sister, Cressida, who'd made the journey from Krymmenos with their parents.

Taking a deep breath, she stepped forth, held her hands up high and proclaimed, "We are the Muses!"

Acknowledgments

I am a wordsmith by trade, but I cannot come up with the words to adequately express what an honor it has been to bring this story to life. It has been the most amazing journey, and I would be remiss if I didn't take a moment to acknowledge those who helped to make it so. A huge thanks to my editor Hali Baumstein for the tremendous amount of work she poured into this book. To my agent, Evan Marshall, for always lending an understanding ear and giving the best career advice. And for not saying "I told you so" on the occasions when I go against that advice and live to regret it. To my family: these last five years have been the most difficult any of us have had to endure, but we've done it together. You all continue to be an inspiration to me. Lastly, to all the people out there who unabashedly share their love of all things Disney. I get my joy from watching you share your joy. Don't ever stop.